End of the Road

Also by LS Hawker

Body and Bone
The Drowning Game

End of the Road

A Novel

LS HAWKER

WITNESS
IMPULSE

An Imprint of HarperCollins*Publishers*

Excerpt from *The Drowning Game* copyright © 2015 by LS Hawker.

END OF THE ROAD. Copyright © 2017 by LS Hawker. All rights reserved. Printed in the United States of America. No part of this book may be used or reproduced in any manner whatsoever without written permission except in the case of brief quotations embodied in critical articles and reviews. For information, address HarperCollins Publishers, 195 Broadway, New York, NY 10007.

Digital Edition JANUARY 2017 ISBN: 978-0-06-243523-1

Print Edition ISBN: 978-0-06-243524-8

WITNESS logo and WITNESS IMPULSE are trademarks of HarperCollins Publishers in the United States of America.

HarperCollins is a registered trademark of HarperCollins Publishers in the United States of America and other countries.

FIRST EDITION

17 18 19 20 21 LSC 10 9 8 7 6 5 4 3 2 1

To the Marks family: Michael, Kyle, and Megan,
but most of all to Kim.

Chapter 1

September 7

JADE VEVERKA UNWRAPPED the frozen Bomb Pop she'd bought from the gas station on the corner of Main and 3rd and took a bite. She sat gazing at the pile of magazines on the barbershop coffee table while a rhythmic alarm-clock buzz went off in her head. Not an urgent warning, just *buzz buzz buzz.*

Her friend and coworker, Elias Palomo, sat in the barber chair, getting his customary fade crew cut, the same one he'd presumably sported since his plebe days at the Naval Academy. So the background to her mental alarm clock was an actual buzzing from the electric razor punctuated now by a sharp yip of pain from Elias.

"Sorry about that," the barber said.

Elias rubbed his ear, and Jade attempted to keep her face neutral, looking at his scowl in the mirror.

Buzz buzz buzz.

She leaned forward and fanned the magazines—*Popular Mechanics, Sports Illustrated, ESPN*—all this month's issues. Jade took another bite of Bomb Pop and grinned.

"What are you smiling at?" Elias grumbled, rubbing his nicked ear.

"I don't know how to tell you this," Jade said, "but you are not the center of my universe. I do occasionally react to things outside of you. I know it comes as a shock."

"Shut up," he said, his dark eyes flashing.

Jade stared now in fascination as the razor tracked upward on Elias's skull, his glossy black hair—or what was left of it—uneven, his scalp an angry pink. This guy was the worst hairdresser Jade had ever seen. And the least talkative. In her experience, growing up in rural Ephesus, Kansas, barbers had always fit the stereotype—gregarious and gossipy.

Elias was the shop's lone customer, and only a few folks walked by outside the window, through which Jade could see the hardware store and the occasional slow, passing car.

Buzz buzz buzz.

It struck Jade now that this was less a barbershop than what amounted to a barbershop museum, complete with an actor playing the part of the barber. She wanted to point this out to Elias, but it would mean nothing to him. He'd grown up in Reno, Nevada, a vast metropolis compared to Jade's 1200-population hometown an hour southeast of this one, which was called Miranda, Kansas.

Not only was this man not a barber, he wasn't a Kansan either, Jade would have bet money.

"Hey," she said to him. "What's your name?"

The man went on butchering as if she hadn't spoken. Elias's

eyes met Jade's in the mirror, and his dark thick brows met on either side of a vertical crease, his *WTF?* wrinkle. He leaned his head away from the razor, finally making the barber pay attention.

"The lady asked you a question," Elias said.

Jade had to hold in a guffaw. This never failed to tickle her, him referring to her as a lady. No one other than him had ever done that before. Plus she loved the authoritative rumble of his voice, a trait he'd probably developed at Annapolis.

The barber froze, his eyes locked with Elias's. Weird.

"Need a prompt?" Elias said. "Your name."

The man cleared his throat.

"Is it classified?"

Jade did guffaw this time, and she watched the barber's jaw muscles compress as she clapped a hand over her mouth.

"My name's Richard."

"Hello, Richard, I'm Elias. This is Jade. We work out at SiPraTech."

Jade could see from Richard's face he knew very well where they worked. He nodded and got back to destroying the remains of Elias's hair.

"Whereabouts you from, Richard?" Jade said.

He pulled the razor away from Elias's head and blinked at her. What in the world was this guy's problem?

Buzz buzz buzz.

Elias emitted a loud sigh, clearly exasperated by the guy's reticence, and waved a hand as if to say, "Carry on, barber-not-barber."

Jade laughed again.

"Here," Richard mumbled. "I'm from here."

Like hell. What was he, in the witness protection program or something?

And then it hit her. The magazines, every last one of them, was a current issue. In a barbershop. The place where back issues of magazines go to die.

She'd worked for SiPraTech just over three months now, and Miranda, the closest town, had always given her an itch. Something about it was slightly off, but she couldn't say what. She'd brought it up to her team members—Elias, Berko Deloatch, and Olivia Harman, and each of them had looked at her as if she was schitzy. They all came from big cities, so Miranda struck them as weird in general.

Buzz buzz buzz buzz buzz buzz.

As if drawn by static electricity, her eyes tracked to the window where a man in mirrored shades peered into the barbershop. The man had a dark mustache and wore a blue baseball cap pulled low over the sunglasses.

What was he staring at? She glanced behind her, but there was nothing to see but a white wall. When she turned back, the man mouthed something at her, his exaggerated soundless enunciation wringing a sharp intake of breath from her.

"What?" Elias said in response to her gasp.

Was it her imagination, or did this man she'd never seen before say her name?

Jade Veverka.

She looked at Elias, and said, "There's a man out there—"

Elias swiveled the barber chair toward the window, causing another near miss with the razor.

But when she looked back at the window, the man was gone.

"Where?" Elias said.

Jade hesitated, because Richard had turned off the razor and stared hard at her.

"Um," she said.

Richard's scrutiny unnerved her.

"What was he doing?" Elias said.

"Nothing," Jade said. "I . . . I guess I thought I recognized him, but I was mistaken. Sorry."

Richard gazed for a moment longer, then went back to work.

Elias rolled his eyes. "I've never known anyone with a more pronounced startle response. I wonder what you'd do if something truly startle-worthy happened?"

Jade's phone vibrated suddenly, making her jump.

Elias laughed, watching her in the mirror. "Case in point," he said.

Jade pulled the phone from her pocket and her mother's image appeared on the screen. All thoughts of the strange man evaporated and were replaced by the usual anxiety that accompanied calls from Mom. Jade's compulsion to answer and her fervent desire not to made her heart race, the question that circled her mind anytime Pauline Veverka called barging to the forefront.

Would today be the day? The day she would no longer be able to understand her mother's speech?

Jade thought about stepping outside, but it was too hot even in the shade, and she absurdly feared the man was out there waiting for her. Ridiculous. Jade had never been the kind of girl men waited for, with her frizzy burnt-orange hair that would never grow past her shoulders, her too-close-together brown eyes.

She clicked the answer button and said, "Hey, Ma."

"Hi, honey. How's it going?" Pauline Veverka's voice was slow and thick, but still understandable.

Relief untangled the knots in Jade's gut and head. She remembered her Bomb Pop and caught the dribbles of red, white, and blue sugar water that threatened to jump ship.

"I think we're getting close," she said.

"Really?"

Before her ALS diagnosis, Pauline could have fit four or five words into the time it now took her to say the one. And it wouldn't be long before she couldn't say any at all. But today was not that day.

"Yeah," Jade said. "We're running tests right now. Once Berko wrote the linguistics program—that was quite the time suck, let me tell you—we were able to start with some small tests, and seriously, Mom. Chills. What this program can—" Jade turned her head and lowered her voice, although she was sure the barber wouldn't know what she was talking about or even care. "It's beyond what we originally thought. You should see the brain simulation Olivia ran, the parallels were incredible. The program might as well be an actual brain."

"Tell her hi," Elias said.

Jade ignored him. "I don't know how long they'll let us keep testing—"

"Jade. Tell her hi for me."

Elias had never met Pauline.

"Before they pull the funding plug—"

Jade's words withered in her mouth. Since the diagnosis, she'd found certain expressions offensive, expressions she used to toss off carelessly. *Pull the plug.* Beautiful.

Elias raised his voice, as if she hadn't heard him instead of ignored him. "Jade."

She covered the phone and said, "Will you shut up? I'm talking on the phone, right? You're like somebody's grandma."

Elias gave her an elfish smile that never failed to crack Jade up. She relented in the interest of expediency. "Mom. Elias says hi."

"Tell him hi for me too."

"Mom says hi," Jade said, and Elias nodded, satisfied.

"Anyway. Enough about me. What's going on there? How's Clem?"

"She's okay," Pauline said. "She had a pretty epic tantrum at the center yesterday because I couldn't bend over and pick up a dime."

Cuz I coon ben ovr n pig ub a dime.

This new super-slo-mo-slur voice haunted Jade's dreams. No, that wasn't quite right. Mom's *old* voice haunted them. In the dreams, Pauline would say, *"I was shining you on! Pretty funny, huh?"*

And in the dreams, Jade was always furious at her mother for doing this to her.

Pauline's illness had sent Jade's sister reeling backward in development. And Jade didn't know what Clem would do once their mom finally . . .

Jade always cut herself off before she could complete thoughts like these. They were the minor chord that constantly thrummed in the basement of her consciousness, like a bleating smoke detector with a failing battery you could never seem to find.

Forcing herself back to the present, she said, "Has Dad started planting the wheat yet?"

"Not 'til the fifteenth," Pauline said. "That's what the *Almanac* said. Maybe you can come home and see all of us this weekend."

"Yeah," Jade said. "Maybe so."

Pauline hesitated, and Jade intuited her mother had something important to tell her.

"So the reason I called," Pauline said, "was to let you know we've decided to go ahead with the feeding tube."

Jade seized up, as if her throat and heart and lungs had been stoppered. And then she launched herself from the chair and out the door. She glanced up and down the street, her mind casting about for a diversion, a distraction, anything to halt the assimilation of this new information. The door to the Laundromat across the street swung open and a woman backed out with a heaping basket full of clean clothes, and Jade inhaled the warm, nostalgic scent of dry-cleaning chemicals.

So. Mom was one step closer to giving up. By putting in the feeding tube, Pauline was acknowledging that her tongue and throat muscles could no longer allow her to swallow medication. It was one more step toward being unable to eat food at all. One more step toward . . .

Two women in their twenties left the market, arms full of bagged groceries. Jade glanced the other direction and watched a man gas up his car.

She had known the time would come. But she'd made herself believe it was a long way off.

A huge, drowsy weeping willow swayed next to the gas station and, in her mind's eye, Jade saw herself as a kid playing on willow branches. Her mom would swing with her, then fall onto her butt with a thud and laugh so hard she couldn't breathe. The same raucous, startling laugh Jade had. Her bright, shining mother.

Jade would not cry. She had to be strong for her mom. For Dad and Clementine too.

A hand touched her arm and she whirled around to see Elias standing there, his forehead furrowed. *"Everything okay?"* he mouthed.

Jade nodded and turned away from him, the concern on his face—damn him!—adding to her despair, somehow giving her tear ducts permission to start up production. Added to this was a completely inappropriate shame response, as if crying reflected badly on her somehow.

"I know what you're thinking," Pauline said.

I no wad yer thinging.

"And I just want you to know—"

"Can you reverse the flow?" Jade said.

"What?" Pauline said.

"I mean, let's say you eat too many Twinkies," Jade said, trying to keep the hitch out of her voice. "Can you just vacuum that crap out?"

Her mother's laugh, playing at half-speed, resonated in Jade's ear, bringing more unwelcome tears to her eyes.

"I'll ask Dr. Trask," Pauline said.

Lass dogger trass.

"I love you, Mom," Jade said.

"Look at your arm."

This is what she said nowadays when Jade said *I love you.*

Right after Pauline was diagnosed with ALS, Jade had asked her to write "I love you" on a piece of paper. She did, and Jade had it tattooed on her left forearm. This was a huge about-face on her part. She had vowed never to get a tattoo, even though Pauline had three of them. This was the exception. In times of stress, Jade would rub her arm, as if the tattoo were a talisman, as if it could summon the mother of her youth, bring her back, give the comfort she was no longer able to give.

And now, less than a year later, her mother could no longer hold a pen.

Jade said goodbye and clicked off the call then inhaled and turned toward Elias.

"You okay?" he said.

"Yeah," she said, wiping her eyes. "I need toothpaste." She walked toward the grocery store.

"That *is* tragic," Elias said, following her. But he didn't say anything more, because over the past twelve weeks he'd learned exactly how far he could push her—and he always ran right up to the wall, but never scaled it. Until now, because then he said, "So how's your mom doing?"

Too many thoughts in her brain grappled for her attention—who was that guy outside the barbershop window? How did he know her name? How long did Mom have? What were they going to do with Clementine? What was it with this town?—that if she opened her mouth, they would twist and snarl together and she'd never be able to make sense of any of them.

"Okay," Jade said.

"She's worse, isn't she?" Elias said.

"Of course she's worse," Jade snapped. "ALS is a progressive, degenerative disease."

Elias didn't react, which made her immediately remorseful. If he'd acted hurt or huffy, she could have maintained her righteously angry posture. This was the thanks he got for being concerned, for being a friend.

"I'm sorry," she said, and sniffled.

Elias clicked his tongue and said, *"Ay, que lastima."* He gathered her to himself and she let him. *"Pobre tomate,"* he said, which made her give a weepy laugh, and she playfully shoved him away. He'd called her "poor tomato," a reference to a children's cartoon series from the nineties called *VeggieTales.*

Jade wiped her eyes again and stepped inside the cool, bright grocery store. A few shoppers wheeled their buggies through the aisles. A clerk stocked shelves near the cash registers up front. Jade was struck by how fit and buff the woman was. In her late twenties or early thirties, Jade guessed, her muscles flexing noticeably beneath her skin.

The woman was stacking the shelf with disposable diapers, right next to the Depends adult undergarments. Elias headed toward the rack of magazines by the cash register, pulled out a *bon appétit*, and flipped it open. Jade walked past the clerk toward the toiletries aisle, and followed it to the far end, where the dental care items were.

She bent over, hands on her knees, and struggled to get her breathing under control, thankfully out of sight of Elias and the other shoppers.

And then she felt a hand on her back, and peered behind her, expecting to see Elias standing there. It wasn't him.

It was the man from outside the barbershop.

She snapped upright.

Quietly, he said, "I need you to come with me."

Jade stood blinking at him, and immediately thought he was a store detective, under the mistaken impression she was shoplifting.

"I'm just getting some toothpaste," she said.

"Out the back door," he murmured, his hand still on her back, pushing her forward. She dug in her heels.

"What are you—"

"Jade. Now. Out the back door."

Her legs went watery at the sound of her name. She hadn't been imagining it back at the barbershop. He took hold of her wrist and yanked her toward the exit.

As he looked back at her, her warped reflection in his mirror sunglasses displayed the terror on her face. The man was shorter than she but burly and ungodly strong, his grip like a coyote trap, and she couldn't shake free. Her tennis shoes slid along the tile floor as if she were roller-skating. She reached out to grab a shelf and only succeeded in knocking boxes of denture cleaner to the floor.

"Elias!" she yelled, and the man grimaced at her and yanked harder.

Elias appeared at the head of the aisle. "Hey!" he shouted, and the man spun Jade around, as if he were going to shield himself from Elias with her body. She felt his hand on her ass, and thought, *oh, great. One quick feel before he escapes. Gross.*

Elias sprinted toward them.

But the man shoved Jade toward him and ran out the back door.

Chapter 2

ELIAS LOCKED EYES with Jade then turned and pursued the man out the door.

Jade took a step to follow but her legs turned tottery and she collapsed onto the hard floor, belatedly hit with adrenaline that made her shake all over and breathe in shredding gasps.

What had just happened?

Oscillating spots appeared in her vision and she was glad to be so close to the ground now because she felt light-headed. She leaned back against the shelves and rubbed her wrist, which felt raw and sore, the bones loose and brittle.

Had the guy been following her? For how long? Had he seen her before in town?

If he wanted to kidnap a girl, why had he chosen her, six feet tall and a hundred and eighty pounds? It didn't make any sense.

Her thoughts bounced around chaotically, now lighting on a memory from college. She'd been in a bathroom stall when she overheard two girls she didn't know well talking about her. They called her the Clydesdale. An accurate assessment, but it still hurt.

So she couldn't imagine this guy had seen her galumphing down the streets of Miranda and said to himself, *I gotta get me some of that.*

She also couldn't prevent her imagination from following the logical path of what might have happened had he dragged her out of the store and into a minivan. One thing was for sure—she would have put up a hell of a fight.

Elias burst in through the back door, gleaming with sweat but only slightly out of breath. The guy was in incredible shape.

"Where did you go?" she asked.

He gave her a perplexed look. "Where did I—I thought I heard the ice cream man. Where do you think I went? I went to catch that guy. But he drove away in a white crossover. I lost him. What the hell happened? Are you hurt?"

"Not exactly," Jade said, and an inappropriate urge to laugh suddenly seized her.

He squatted down next to her and examined her bright red wrist.

"Grabbed my ass, is all," Jade said.

Elias wrinkled his face in disgust.

"At first I thought he was an undercover cop who thought I was shoplifting, but then he tried to pull me out the back door there."

"We need to call the cops."

"We don't have time," Jade said. "We're going to be late getting back."

Why on earth didn't she want to go to the cops? She turned it all over in her mind. It wasn't logical. It wasn't right.

"Screw that," Elias said. "They can damn well wait."

"Investors are coming. That's why you got the freakin' haircut, remember? The presentation? Money waits for no man."

She worried less about holding up the presentation than describing to policemen how some guy had tried to kidnap her, because she could just imagine the skeptical looks on their faces.

Really? Someone tried to kidnap a heifer like you?

She couldn't explain this to Elias. It was ridiculous, a childish reason for avoiding the cops.

A better reason occurred to her, however: What if her folks found out about this? It would be one more in an endless, agonizing list of things to worry about, to stress out about.

She was mentally and emotionally exhausted and had to reserve the little energy and brainpower she had left for the presentation.

She endeavored to focus on the upcoming dog and pony show, but her mind kept wandering back to the grocery store.

The guy knew her name. Somehow, he knew her name.

"We could reschedule the presentation," Elias said.

"No we can't," Jade said. "They had to charter a plane, remember? We have to do it today. I'm fine. And let's not tell Martin. I don't want to give him another excuse to treat us like thirdgraders. Okay? Promise me."

Elias said, "But what if—"

"Listen," she said. "This would be one more reason to regret hiring a woman, right? Kicks up a huge fuss just because some guy grabs her butt, gets the cops involved because she needs to make a point. If it had happened to you, you would have shaken it off and gone on with your day."

Elias searched her face.

"Are you hiding something from me, Jade? Like a police record or something? Is that what this is?"

"No," she said, which wasn't exactly lying.

She didn't want to tell Elias the guy knew her name. But why? Because now that she thought about it, maybe he hadn't mouthed her name standing outside the barbershop. Maybe he hadn't said "Jade" in the grocery store. Now that she thought about it, it sounded crazy. Maybe Elias would think she was some paranoid nutcase.

"Let's forget it, okay?"

"Okay," he said, reluctant. "But I reserve the right to force you back here to file a police report later."

"You could *try* to force me," she said, attempting to inject her voice with menace.

He smiled. "Did you get your toothpaste?"

Jade had completely forgotten why she came here in the first place. "Oh, right," she said, and held up her hand. Elias pulled her to standing and she grabbed the first tube she saw. He looped his arm around her waist without her asking—she was listing a little. She put her purchase on the counter and pulled out her wallet.

The clerk picked up the toothpaste and inspected each end of the box, looking for a price tag, Jade guessed. Once she found it, she turned to the electronic cash register and stared at it.

Jade glanced at Elias, but still the clerk stared. She stretched out a hand toward the keyboard, as if it were electrified and pressed number buttons. Then she stared some more.

"Do you . . . need help?" Jade asked.

Flustered, the clerk said, "This is my first day on the job. I'm not quite sure how to . . ."

As Jade reached forward, she saw the look on Elias's face, his eyebrows drawn together. But Jade showed the clerk how to work the cash register then handed her a five-dollar bill.

The clerk stuffed it in the drawer and then puzzled over how much change to give.

"A dollar eighty-four," Jade said.

The clerk gave an embarrassed half smile, dug the cash out of the register, and handed it to Jade, who put it in her wallet and returned the wallet to her pocket. She stuck the toothpaste in her front shirt pocket.

Elias and Jade walked outside into the September heat.

"That girl was lying," Elias said.

"What do you mean?" Jade said.

"I've seen her in there before. This is definitely not her first day on the job."

Jade turned back toward the store. *Buzz buzz buzz.* "Why would you lie about something like that?"

"There's a lot of screwy stuff going on here today," Elias said.

"Is it a full moon or something?"

Elias shrugged then headed toward one of the company cars they'd used to drive the three miles to town, the blue Chevy Volt. "Want me to drive?"

She tossed him the keys and he got in the driver's seat and pressed the blue start button as she got in the passenger side.

"I'll never get used to this," Elias said. "It's more like a golf cart than a car."

"The environment thanks you," Jade said.

She turned up the car stereo, blasting Beyoncé. Elias sang along, not well, but with gusto.

He drove out of town, taking the dirt roads to the Compound that had been built specifically for SiPraTech's inaugural project, which would kick off the new start-up. She remembered the first time she'd seen it, rumbling down this dirt road. The only difference between this dirt road and those near her hometown was that the first time she'd come to the Compound, she'd been riding in the back of a Cadillac Escalade, driven from the Salina airport by a silent man.

Right after SiPraTech had officially hired her the last week of May, she'd made the move out here, and on that day, the prairie was green and full of wildflowers, dotted with oil wells, tractors, grain silos, and barns. The sky was a large, hazy blue, with massive puffy clouds on the horizon.

She'd boxed up her life at the University of Kansas and called for a UPS pickup, using the account number emailed to her by Martin Felix, the project supervisor. He assured her all her things would be waiting for her at her destination.

The company people called it the Compound, which of course made her think of *The Godfather* and the gated, guarded enclave of Corleone family houses. But what met her gaze was different altogether. At the top of the short rise in the prairie at the end of the road, nestled between two wheat fields nearly ready for harvest, was a cluster of three brand-new structures. The largest was an office building, surrounded by lush sculpted landscaping. To the north, across a greenbelt sat a sprawling, ranch-style house, similarly landscaped with a waterfall, pond, and rocky river extending from it. At the eastern edge of the greenbelt was another building marked FITNESS CENTER/CLUBHOUSE.

She started getting excited. It was so pretty. Next to the fitness center was a large swimming pool surrounded by palm tree sculptures, cabanas, and a bar. The setup reminded her of one of the major tech company campuses, Facebook, Google, Pixar. It appeared SiPraTech had spared no expense.

A ten-foot-high chain-link fence surrounded the entire Compound, and her driver drove up to the gate, rolled down his window, and waved a keycard in front of a reader on a stand to the left. The gate swung open and they drove through. The gate shut automatically behind them.

The driver parked in the office building parking lot and opened her door for her.

"You can wander the Compound if you'd like, see what's here before your first meeting," he told her.

"Thanks," she said, and put her purse over her shoulder. She walked the perimeter of the pool, the cool deep blue of the water and the evocative smell of chlorine making her think of coconut-scented sunscreen and hamburgers frying at her hometown pool. Inside the clubhouse were several enormous flat-screen televisions, air hockey, foosball, and Ping-Pong tables, even an old-fashioned pinball machine. There was an Xbox One, a PS4, and a Wii U. One wall sported a floor-to-ceiling bookcase, stuffed with books. There were smartphone docks everywhere.

Jade's heart swelled. All her favorite things were right here.

Once she'd thoroughly investigated the workout rooms, she walked to the house and knocked on the front door.

When she'd accepted her position with the company, she'd been given the choice of either renting a house in Miranda, or living rent-free on the property itself. She'd chosen the rent-free option. For now anyway.

A gardener looked up at her and said, "You don't need to knock. It's open."

Jade tentatively opened the door and surveyed the spacious living room and, beyond that, the vast kitchen. She went upstairs and counted five bedrooms, and found the one with her name on it. She turned the doorknob, but it was locked.

"Hi, Jade," said a voice from the end of the hall, startling her out of her happy reverie.

She whirled around. "Hi," she said to the woman standing there, a blonde in her thirties, dressed in jeans and a red top.

"I'm Greta. Welcome to your new home!"

"Thanks," Jade said.

"It's my job to make sure you have what you need to feel at home here. If you're missing anything, just let me know. But you won't see me unless you need me." She handed Jade a business card. "This is my cell number, and you can call it anytime of the day or night. If you get sick or injured, you call me and I'll get you medical help. If we don't have food you like, let me know." She smiled. She pulled a lanyard out of her pocket with a badge attached and handed it to Jade. "This is your ID as well as electronic keycard that will open your bedroom door and any other door you have access to, including the front door of the house, your work area, and so forth."

She turned to go but then said, "Oh, by the way—there's no Internet here."

"You mean it's down?" Jade said.

"No. The program you're working with must be contained. It has to be secure, and if any of the computers or your devices are networked, the program could leak out and do who knows what. You'll notice you can't use your smartphone to access the Internet either, or make or receive calls." Before Jade could object, Greta said, "Don't worry. We have landlines you can use for phone calls. We're not trying to cut you off from the outside world, of course." She smiled at Jade, who smiled back. Funny they hadn't mentioned any of this when she signed her employment contract. She lived more than half of her life online. It would be inconvenient, but not intolerable. She hoped.

"Thanks, Greta," she said, accepting the lanyard and waving the keycard in front of the electronic lock. A green light illuminated, and she turned the knob and pushed open the heavy door then stood against it.

She draped the lanyard around her neck. "When do the other . . . my coworkers get here?"

"A couple are already here," she said, glancing at her watch. "You've got your first meeting at four p.m. in the office. That's the big building across the garden square from us."

Jade peered out the window and saw the "garden square" was indeed a square with grass, park benches, water features, landscaping—a miniature version of Central Park.

"You can go in that front door and someone will be there to guide you to the conference room."

"Thanks," Jade said.

Greta disappeared.

Jade's things were indeed already there, and she sighed with relief. The walls were painted sky blue, her favorite color. Country modern furnishings occupied the room with an overstuffed chair next to a table and sturdy blue ceramic lamp, a window seat decorated with colorful pillows and a bookshelf beneath it.

A Jack and Jill bathroom connected her bedroom to another. The smartphone dock in the wall linked to speakers hidden in the ceilings, so she connected her phone and put her music library on shuffle while she went about unpacking her suitcases and boxes. She put T-shirts, shorts, underwear, and socks away in the chest of drawers and the closet and the shelves. She found a hammer and nails in the closet and hung up posters of her heroes—Hermione Granger, Scarlett Johansson as Black Widow, and Imperator Furiosa.

As soon as she got them up, she had second thoughts. She was twenty-four years old. Wasn't she too old for posters? But she needed the company of these fictional badasses to face her new coworkers, who, she'd been given to understand, were all accomplished, brilliant, and most likely good-looking too.

Finally Jade hung up framed photos of her family.

She undocked her phone and noticed it was quarter to four, so she stowed her suitcases in the top of the closet and then took the boxes out into the hall and closed her door behind her. It locked automatically.

Striding across the Compound, she tried to quell her nervousness about meeting her teammates. Even though she'd bombarded the driver with questions, he'd had no answers for her. She wanted to know who her teammates were and where they'd come from. But she'd have to wait.

She made her way to the office building and used her keycard to open the door. Inside, she found another woman, dressed in a skirted suit. Jade contemplated her own outfit. "Should I go change?" she said. "I think I'm a little underdressed."

"Oh, no," the woman said. "We're very informal here. We want you all to wear whatever makes you comfortable. Follow me."

Jade did, and her stomach churned. Her limbs felt stiff and uncomfortable. What was she walking into? What if no one liked her? She followed the woman onto the elevator and she took them to the top floor, three. Jade breathed deeply, trying to clear her mind, trying to relax, but it was impossible. She had to believe everyone else was nervous too.

On the third floor, she followed the woman down the hall, where Martin Felix, her new supervisor, stood outside a door.

"Hello, Jade," he said, holding out his hand for her to shake. "You can call me Martin." He wore a collared golf shirt and khaki slacks, his approximation of casual.

"Am I the last one here?"

"Yes. Come on in."

He held open the door to a large, generic-looking conference room. Jade inhaled to the count of three and then plunged in.

Sitting with looks of anticipation on their faces were an Asian woman with peacock blue hair and a pierced nose, who smiled at Jade. Next to her sat a serious, ramrod straight-postured Latino man, likely older than Jade, but she couldn't be sure. And across from them, an African-American man with glasses and large arms.

"Jade," Martin said, "This is Olivia Harman."

"Hi," said Olivia brightly. "I'm so glad you're a woman."

Jade smiled at this, and something loosened in her gut. "Me too," she said.

Olivia then regarded everyone. "We've got a regular United Nations here, don't we?" She pointed at Jade. "Plus the token white girl, of course. The EEOC would *love* this crowd. The cultural diversity special interest money is going to come pouring in. Anyone gay? Do we have any disabilities represented? No? Too bad."

Jade didn't know how to take her at first, and the other team members recoiled at her politically incorrect remarks. But Jade later learned Olivia was a force to be reckoned with.

That day, she could have never guessed how close she would become with all three of her teammates. Maybe it was living in the same house working on this complex project, eating together—

everything together. She imagined it was not all that dissimilar to the intense relationships formed in a combat situation.

Now as Jade and Elias returned to the Compound from their haircut outing in Miranda, Elias parked the company car in the garage and Jade's stomach started to burble with tension. They walked silently toward the office building. The lab was in the basement—easier to cool all the hundreds of thousands of dollars of computer equipment—and Jade and Elias played their usual game of racing to see who could get out their keycard first—pushing each other, shoving in front of each other—that always left Jade helpless with laughter. Elias got there first today and he opened the lab door for her. The room was always cool, cool enough that both Jade and Olivia wore cardigans most of the day, despite the oven-like heat outside.

Olivia swiveled in her chair when Jade and Elias entered and theatrically eyed her watch. "Where have you two been? Did you forget?" Olivia shook her head, her blue hair fluttering around her face, her expression tense. "We have visitors."

Elias and Jade both dropped into their desk chairs. Elias began typing furiously and within seconds their phony command prompt screen appeared on Jade's monitor.

OH SHIT, it said. *THEY'RE ALREADY HERE.*

When the computer system designer, a stoic military type with thick glasses named Mark, had first introduced them to the lab's computer system, Elias and Jade had been surprised by the clunky interface they were supposed to use to access the system. The two of them found their way into the back end and made some modifications to streamline access. They installed a back door that could circumvent the interface, although they didn't tell Berko and

Olivia, who weren't quite as computer literate as they. For what those two needed to do on the system, the interface worked just fine.

In addition to the back door, Elias had installed a basic chat function disguised as a command prompt so the two of them could in effect pass notes to each other.

Jade's stomach immediately went into acid overload as she turned toward the glassed-in conference room and saw the three men, straight-backed and suited, standing around the refreshments Martin had no doubt laid out.

"Oh, crap," Jade said.

"Jade! There you are!" Dan's voice boomed out across the room. No matter how anxious and upset she was, the sound of that voice always cheered her. Colonel Dan Stevenson, USAF retired, was her mentor. The man who'd recommended her for this job so close to home.

He strode toward her as she turned back to Olivia and muttered, "You're not going to believe what happened to me today."

Olivia raised her eyebrows and stood, smoothing her skirt and putting on her best ingratiating institutional welcome smile. "Colonel Stevenson," she said. "It's so great to see you."

Dan smothered Jade in a bear hug, his large arms engulfing her, even though he was an inch shorter than she at five foot eleven. Over her shoulder he said, "Hello, Olivia. How's it going?"

In full faucet mode, Jade's usual flop sweat made her self-conscious, so she disengaged from Dan as soon as socially acceptable.

He looked her over, and his expression became sympathetic. In a lowered voice, he said, "You ready? Did you do what I told you?"

Jade aspired to keep her expression neutral. He knew public speaking was her *bête noire*. But he believed in not just facing your fears, but kicking the crap out of them.

Jade just didn't need this today. Not with the feeding tube. Not with the weirdness in town. Not with the attempted kidnapping . . .

"Yes, sir," she said. "I'm ready."

"Great," Dan said.

"We're running tests as we speak," she said.

He looked delighted, his deep brown eyes crinkling. "You think you've got it? Does it work?"

Such a simplistic question for such a complex subject. "It's a little more complicated than does it or does it not work. But I believe we're coming close to what we talked about."

She tried to sound self-assured, as if she only added that last part to convey a sense of humility instead of abject fear that the program wouldn't work at all.

Damn her intellectual overconfidence. How many times in her life had she boasted about the things she could do, having no idea how to actually do them? Her outrageous claims about the Clementine Program might be just that—claims and bravado. If it didn't create its own culture as she'd predicted it would, she'd be exposed for the fraud she was. She'd have to go back to KU in disgrace, and face that bastard Professor Sauer, the Computer Science Department head who'd nearly ruined this opportunity for her. Sauer, who ridiculed her program in front of her fellow students, called it science fiction. "You need to concentrate on practical applications, not theoretical, nonfunctional programs. We're not a beard-stroking intellectual group here. We're the pragmatists. If you want to keep playing around with games, go back to Carnegie Mellon."

No, she wouldn't go back there. Maybe she could go ahead and start her company anyway, but where would she get the money if she didn't earn the substantial, almost embarrassingly large bonus from completing this project? She had to finish, and it had to be successful.

"Wonderful," Dan said, spinning her 180 degrees, putting his arm around her shoulders and steering her toward the conference room. "My friends would love to hear all about it."

"Can I go freshen up first?" she asked.

"Quick, quick," Dan said, and released her. Olivia threw a worried look over her shoulder at Jade, then followed Dan to the conference room.

Chapter 3

JADE RAN TO the restroom, where she splashed water on her face and cursed her lack of a hairbrush. Her red, blotchy face looked like it did after every football practice in high school, and she resembled anything but a team leader. Oh, well.

She scanned the gleaming bathroom and remembered that every time she'd come in here, she'd thought they should stock the place with deodorant, toothbrushes, and other grooming items. And then she remembered the toothpaste sticking out of her shirt pocket. She cracked it open and rubbed it on her teeth and gums with her finger and then rinsed her mouth.

And the toothpaste made her think of the grocery store, and the man. And that her mom was going to die.

Crap. Maybe Professor Sauer was right. Maybe women were too emotional, scattered, and distractible to be relied upon in high-pressure situations, or to even get their code right.

But she'd come through. She'd never cried in front of Sauer, never pitched a foot-stomping tantrum at him, unlike some of her diva classmates like Nishant Sharma. And neither Sauer nor

Nishant had ever in their lives devised as potentially powerful a program as she had.

Screw Sauer. He was jealous, a cynical, disappointed old man at forty-five. *Those who can't do, teach.*

She left the toothpaste on the counter and strode out of the restroom, feeling a little better.

Back in the conference room, she took her seat, the only one left, next to Olivia, across from Elias and Berko, who scowled at her from behind his horn-rimmed glasses. She shrugged at him.

Then she glanced around, and all eyes were on her.

"The floor is yours," Dan said.

She stood and walked to the head of the table in front of the 48-inch monitor mounted to the back wall. What she wanted to say was *get the hell out of my lab*, but she'd learned. She smiled around at the suits and cleared her throat.

Olivia sat with her laptop open in front of her, ready to run the slides.

The conference room door flew open and Martin Felix stumbled in, running into a chair. "Sorry I'm late," he said. "I thought you said the presentation would be at three." He shot Dan an accusing look.

"We bumped it up," Dan said. "This is the project supervisor, everybody. Martin Felix."

Martin waved, sat in the chair he'd run into, and pulled himself toward the table, knocking what sounded like his knee into the table base with a loud *thwack*.

"You all right?" Dan said. Without waiting for an answer, he turned to Jade, and said in his loud clear voice, "Why don't you explain the genesis of your program." She could imagine him barking orders that compelled people to obey.

"I'd like to introduce my team first," Jade said, even more rattled now by Martin's scattered presence.

Dan gave her an approving nod.

She gestured. "Berko Deloatch, our linguistics and cryptology expert, comes to us from the PhD program at Stanford. He grew up in Atlanta and earned his BS from Purdue, where he competed on the fencing team."

Berko pushed up his glasses and nodded around the table at the expectant faces.

Without looking, Jade knew the slide behind her portrayed Berko in his cap and gown at college graduation, flanked by his beaming mother and sister.

"Next to him is Elias Palomo, who's from Reno, Nevada, and graduated with a double BS in Information Warfare and IT from the US Naval Academy. Elias played fullback for the Midshipmen."

As always, Elias sat ramrod straight with his hands folded in front of him on the table and continued looking in her direction. His slide was the photo of him in his dress whites, his cap square on his square forehead, his dark eyes flinty, his expression proud and stern.

"And Olivia Harman, from New York, who received her MD and is pursuing a PhD in clinical research from Johns Hopkins University." Jade turned slightly to see what photo Olivia had used of herself this time. Once it had been of her face Photoshopped onto the iconic still from *Aliens* where Ripley is wearing the giant mechanical suit, about to take on the monster. Another time it was Olivia at graduation, a bottle of tequila in one hand and her middle finger extended from the other. This time, to Jade's relief, it was a straight shot of her shaking hands with Ruth Bader Ginsburg. Jade conjectured that if any of Dan's guests were of the conservative persuasion, they would sour at the liberal justice's image. But even they would have to admit it was an impressive one.

"Hi, everybody," Olivia said, making eye contact around the table. She'd seen, as always, the looks of befuddlement on the faces surrounding her when they'd heard her surname. "I know what you're thinking—the last name doesn't quite fit, right? So I'll answer your unasked question: yes, I am a Jew."

Jade laughed every single time Olivia did this, her embarrassing, booming laugh that was off-putting to so many people. Berko and Elias smirked too.

Uncomfortable laughter rumbled around the table, and Jade had to smile at her newest and fastest female friend.

"Actually," Olivia said, "my parents adopted me from China when I was eighteen months old."

This always brought on a round of "Ahs" and head nods from visitors.

Then all eyes fixed on the screen behind Jade, where her homecoming photo blazed, Jade riding on the back of a '62 Cadillac convertible in her muddy football uniform, a tiara on her head, sash across her chest and an armful of roses.

"And my name is Jade Veverka, and I'm from Ephesus, Kansas. I got an academic scholarship to Carnegie Mellon University in Pittsburgh because of the program I'm about to explain to you. I thought I might earn a football scholarship since I was an all-state punter/kicker in high school. Imagine my shock when I found out they don't hand those out to girls."

Appreciative laughter.

She and her four teammates had worked on an easy shtick just to liven up these repetitive proceedings early on.

"I began working on computers when I was six years old, around the time my sister Clementine was born. But it wasn't until she was diagnosed with autism when I was ten that I became interested in using computers to communicate in unconventional ways."

The photo of Clem in her fox-ear headband sitting behind her music keyboard setup loomed behind her now.

"Although Clementine started talking at an early age—which is unusual for autistic people—she didn't use language in the same way other people do, and so no one could understand her. We went through all kinds of drama with doctors who thought she had infantile schizophrenia, a brain tumor . . . I'm not going to go into the details of this, because it'll bore you, but the upshot is I discovered Clementine used a tonal mode of communication, similar to the tonality of the Chinese language."

As usually happened, everyone glanced in Olivia's direction, and Jade nearly laughed again. Olivia waved at everyone, enduring their veiled stereotyping with long-suffering humor the way she normally did.

"I swear I had nothing to do with it," Olivia said. "I can't even speak Chinese."

"I can, though," Berko said, adding his bit to the comedy routine.

"My parents bought her a keyboard," Jade went on, "and the two of us worked out a system via music to communicate. Clementine has since learned to speak English, but her musical virtuosity has led her to compose several symphonies, cantatas, and operas. We hope one day she'll be able to attend a music school like Juilliard."

Jade always said this, but she knew ▸
pendent enough to fulfill that drear.

Now came the tricky part of the pres▸
most people think they're a lot smarter than ▸
it was important not to talk down to them. But s▸
head off the predictable and endless questions that ▸
clarity or understanding to a complex subject.

"I programmed her tonal language into computer langua▸
Python, specifically—and, as is usually the case, happened upor.
something by accident. The computer used the data I put into it to
begin to form its own language."

And here came the questions. "Computer language? Like FOR-
TRAN or BASIC?" one suit asked, obvious pride at knowing these
technological terms.

"No," Jade said. "The closest analog is . . . human language."

"But don't programs that generate new languages already
exist?" one of the suits said.

"Yes," Jade said. "But the difference is that we didn't code our
program to do that. It generated the language spontaneously. And
now that SiPraTech's supercomputer—"

"Did you design the system?" one of the potential investors
asked Martin. All heads swiveled toward him.

Naturally they thought this, since Martin was the "adult"
member of the team.

"No," Martin said. "Mark Bowen did."

"Can we talk to him?"

"He's not on-site," Martin said. "I oversee the team."

"Our supercomputer is one of the fastest and most powerful
in the world," Jade continued, "almost equal to the record-holder,

.vay TaihuLight in mainland China, with a LINPACK

.ark of eighty PFLOPS—"

FLOPS?" another suit said.

It's a measure of a computer's processing speed. Peta floating-

.int operations per second. It equals one quadrillion floating-

point operations per second, or one thousand teraflops. In other words, it can do a lot with thirty-thousand 64-bit RISC processors."

Dan enjoyed the audience's confused mutterings. He loved this part of the presentation as much as Jade hated it.

"The exact specs are in the prospectuses in front of you," he said. "How much power it uses, et cetera. But we're getting off track. We're not trying to sell you a computer system. We're talking about the Clementine Program. Jade was explaining the spontaneous generation of language."

"What does this mean?" another man in a suit asked.

"Berko?" Jade said.

The heads now turned Berko's way.

"Linguistically, it's significant," he told them. "Tracking how and why the computer interprets the information and synthesizes its own language tells us a lot about the origins of language itself, back to the dawn of Homo sapiens."

"I'm sure you're aware," Jade said, "that computer programs in general can only do what the coder tells them to do. This one has begun to act independently."

The confusion on the investors' faces was typical.

"And what are the applications of such a program?" a suit asked. "In other words, why should we invest in something like this? I understand the money sunk into the massive computer system you have here is significant. How can the program be monetized?"

"We're just beginning to scratch the surface of what Clementine can do," Elias said. "We're interested in investing the time and money in research and development."

He couldn't help being deliberately vague, teasing them, even though he knew what the applications were, and how it could revolutionize the way corporations, governments, and other groups organized data, even without access to a massive supercomputer.

Elias was not their strongest fund-raising asset, and Dan had actually requested that he not attend presentations. Jade said absolutely not. He was part of the team.

"Our goal is to advance our understanding of this planet, this universe," Elias said, "and in fact plenty of moneymaking opportunities have arisen out of pure research. As you are no doubt aware."

"We don't have the luxury of funding 'pure research' anymore, son," one of the men said.

Jade, Olivia, and Berko all traded glances that said, *Oh, no. They called him son.*

As she knew it would, this made Elias's face glow red. "All right," he said. "Then let's shut down the universities, although you might as well anyway, the way they've been dumbed down to the lowest common denominator since—"

"Thank you, Elias," Jade said.

Dan laughed. "This is not the crew you want to debate academic pursuits with," he told the men. "Jade, please explain some of the medical benefits."

"If we can use the program to trace how language develops not only in social usage but at the cerebral level, we may be able to unlock the mysteries of brain trauma and neurological disorders."

Disorders like autism, Jade always thought here. Always. But it was implied, and she didn't need to say it. Clementine's angelic visage always left an impression.

"How can you do that?"

"The program analyzes and compares the tissue of a damaged or disordered brain to a healthy one, and identifies and analyzes the specific problem areas," Olivia said. "Then it works backward to map how the brain reroutes the neural pathways away from or around the damage or disorder. So far we've input more than three thousand case studies, which has allowed the program to familiarize itself with brain physiology and various damage scenarios. It's quite fascinating to watch it work."

"I assume," one of the suits asked Elias directly, "that your role on the team, as a military man, is to develop military applications for the program."

"Actually," Jade said, "Elias was selected for this project because of his . . . idiosyncratic coding acumen."

"We're not pursuing military applications at this time," Elias said, almost primly. "We're more interested in communication, in unlocking the secrets of the human brain. In testing the limits of computer data organization."

The suits deflated with obvious disappointment. They always did. Jade guessed a lifetime of watching action movies in which villains used computers to rob casinos or take over the world colored their thinking.

Berko slid his hand forward on the table toward the questioner and said in his quiet, measured voice, "I know you and all the people around this table understand the benefit of diplomacy and how the tiniest nuances in language can ease international relations, can help break down the cultural barriers between one nation and another. Clementine is allowing us to study these nuances. I know you're as interested as we are in peace. That's why Colonel Stevenson and Ensign Palomo joined the military. To make the world, this country, a safer place. What better way than by improving communication?"

Berko didn't say a lot—which seemed weird to Jade since language was his thing—but when he did, it was always worth listening to.

"But most important," Martin piped up, "by mapping how the program works, which we're right in the middle of, we're seeing it functions like a human brain, adapting to changing conditions. The program thinks for itself and integrates all systems as a brain does, rerouting or killing off inefficient protocols. We've got some kinks to work out, of course, but we think Clementine has the potential to streamline computer infrastructures by eliminating software conflicts within them. Rather than developing and running different programs for different applications, it's an all-in-one framework. This is the by-product of a program that creates its own language."

"What you're talking about," one of the suits said excitedly, "is AI, correct? Artificial intelligence?"

Reluctantly, Jade said, "Yes. But unfortunately the term has negative connotations. People envision robots that take over the world. That's the old way of looking at AI. In the past, scientists coded a program explicitly to develop its own basic language, then set up a physical environment in which mechanical robots carrying the program could 'live' and develop their own culture from primitive beginnings. But the problem with robots, as you all know, is that having to move through space presents all sorts of obstacles, both figurative and literal. If they fall over, break one

of their own parts, they're essentially done without outside inter-
vention. Scientists have spent a lot of time trying to improve the
design of robots so they can learn as they go, but the limitations
of the physical universe make it a slow and ultimately useless process. With the Clementine Program we've cut out the 'robot' portion of the equation, and Clementine has begun to create its own
culture within the theoretical environment, and with that freedom, it's able to manipulate exponentially more elements than it
could in physical space. We're currently testing Clementine's ability to create work-arounds spontaneously as we change variables
from instant to instant."

"That's why our processors only have one connection," Elias
said, "and that's to the mainframe in Mr. Felix's office, because
we're not quite sure what would happen if this program went out
over the Internet."

Before the investor group could grab on to this information
and fall down a rabbit hole of pointless questions, Jade continued.
"My initial Clementine program was fairly rudimentary. Once the
four of us teamed up, we began to put all these pieces together—
Berko with his language development, Elias's unconventional
coding, and Olivia with her medical background. Together, we've
been able to do extraordinary things."

Olivia said, "We know you all can see the potential of this technology. Once our testing is complete, we'll have a better idea of
what the program can and can't do. Investing always carries risk,
but the potential of this program represents the very definition of
a buzzword phrase that's been overused to the point of cliché, and
that's paradigm shift."

The suits asked some more technical questions, the answers to which doubtless did nothing to increase their understanding. As usual, the interest defaulted to robots. So Jade cut them off.

"Any more questions?" she asked. "About Clementine. Not robots."

Before anyone could speak, Dan slapped his palms on the glossy table and stood. "Thank you, team. I know all these gentlemen are very grateful you took valuable time away from your project, and we'll let you get back to it."

After the visitors filed out of the conference room, Elias shook his head. "Why does everybody assume that all I want to do is blow shit up?"

Jade and Olivia laughed and Berko smiled.

"Think it's the crew cut, homes," Jade said, reaching out to fluff it, but he batted her hand away. She laughed.

Jade hoped Dan would leave, and she felt guilty for it. He didn't, of course, because he'd want to do a postmortem on her presentation. She was appreciative, but she was also impatient. She wanted to talk to Olivia alone.

"It's one thirty now," he said. "I'm going back to the motel to make some phone calls, and then how about I take the team out to dinner at the Hungry Harrier about six?"

"We'll meet you there," Jade said. It was an unspoken rule that following a presentation, work was suspended until the following day. Which was great news for Jade, because it would give her just enough time to run home to see her mom.

Chapter 4

"Berko and I are going to play drone disc golf," Elias said. "You guys want in?"

Jade loved playing with the drones, loved watching them soar over the Compound. She'd been ridiculously impressed by how Berko how tricked his out with a tiny but deafening Harman Infinity One speaker, but today she had other plans. "I'm going to go for a drive."

"Olivia?" Berko said.

"I'm going with Jade," Olivia said. "I need to get out of the Compound."

"You just don't want a repeat of the last time we played," Berko said. "Coward."

Olivia shrugged, but Jade knew how competitive Olivia was—how competitive they all were.

"See you at dinner," Elias said.

Berko waved as they left the conference room.

Jade didn't want to tell Olivia her plans while they were still in the office building, so she pretended she didn't mind Olivia tagging along. Martin wouldn't approve, but Olivia wouldn't rat her out.

Jade led the way to the house and once inside, turned to her friend. "I'm doing more than going for a ride," she said. "I'm running home to visit my family right quick."

"Oooh," Olivia said. "Scandalous. Playing hooky. Leaving campus. For shame!"

Jade rolled her eyes and mounted the stairs. Olivia followed her up. "Don't worry, I won't snitch. And I'm still going with you."

Jade tensed. She didn't want the stress of having to prepare Olivia to meet her sister—or to see her mom's condition in person. "Oh, you don't have to," she said. "I'll be back before dinner." She pulled her purse out the closet.

"No, really," Olivia said. "I want to go."

No, really, you don't.

One of the shames of her life was the unconquerable anxiety she experienced when people met Clementine for the first time. It had lessened over the years but never completely went away. Clem's odd behavior repulsed people.

"You want to come to Ephesus?" Jade said. "What for?"

They went downstairs and out to the attached garage.

"To meet your family," Olivia said. "Especially the girl your program is named for, of course. I know Berko and Elias want to meet her too, but all four of us trooping out of here would get you busted for sure."

"Okay," Jade said slowly. "But you need to understand—"

"Yeah, yeah, I know. Clementine is strange. I get it."

Both company cars, the Chevy Volts, were parked inside, and Jade and Olivia got in the blue one.

"Here's the thing," Jade said. "People always say, oh, yeah. She's autistic. Of course she's different. But then people meet her and they freak. Her weird grunting and hooting and hand flapping embarrasses people. It wasn't until I was twelve and able to babysit that my parents could go out alone together."

"I can't even imagine what that must have been like," Olivia said.

Jade pressed the Volt's start button, then backed out of the garage. She stopped at the gate, rolled down her window, and waved her keycard in front of the keypad. The gate retracted and Jade drove through. She turned south on the dirt road, lost in her thoughts.

"So Clementine was four when she was diagnosed?" Olivia said.

"Yeah," Jade said. Olivia already knew this, but it was her attempt at keeping Jade engaged, an invitation to keep talking. She loved this about Olivia, this trait so unlike the other East Coasters she'd known. "I was the only one who understood her. I'd translate what she said for my parents. We were at the Sunset Zoo in Manhattan one time, and there was a peacock wandering around, and Clementine chased after it. Over her shoulder, she said to my mom, *'Cam I soft that kind?'*"

Olivia gave her a quizzical look. "What did she mean?"

"'Can I pet him?'" Jade said. "After that, anytime Clementine spit out gibberish, Mom would ask for a translation. I was kind of the Anne Sullivan to my sister's Helen Keller—working as an interpreter of the world to Clementine and an interpreter of Clementine to the world. Only a couple of times did I pull something like, 'She wants you to let me go to the dime store and buy us some candy' or 'She thinks I should stay up past my bedtime to watch *Saved by the Bell.*'"

Olivia laughed. "I would have done that all the time."

"I know you would," Jade said. "But my superego is much more sophisticated than yours."

"You can say that again."

"My superego—"

Olivia swatted at Jade's arm. "Knowing you, I'm surprised you went so far away for undergrad."

"Yeah, well, Mom and Dad told me I needed to find my own life and not define myself in terms of my sister. They encouraged me to do all the stuff a high schooler does—4-H, football, band, dances. They never made me feel guilty for wanting to have a normal social life."

"If I were going to have kids—which I'm not, of course," Olivia said, "I'd want to be like that."

They drove past tillers planting in the wheat fields, the sky a cloudless blue.

Olivia gawked out the windows. "Wow. You can see horizon to horizon. Nothing between us and the edge of the world but corn and dust."

"This is God's country," Jade said.

"You mean the god of straight white Republicans," Olivia said.

"No, I mean God with a capital G."

Olivia grinned. "Oh, hey," she said. "You were going to tell me about what happened in town."

"Oh, right," Jade said, glad for the change of topic. She recounted the afternoon's events.

"Are you shitting me?" Olivia said, her eyes wide in disbelief. "You didn't file a police report?"

"We had the presentation," Jade said, defensive.

"If there's a guy in Miranda who's going around grabbing

women's asses, you need to report it. Other people are at risk." Olivia looked out the window then back at Jade. "When we get back to town, we're going straight to the police station."

Jade didn't say anything. Arguing was pointless. Once Olivia issued a decree, that was it. But now, hours later, the attack seemed unreal, dreamlike, as if it she'd only imagined it.

They hit Ephesus fifteen minutes later and drove up to Jade's family home.

"Listen," Jade said as she turned off the car. "Don't say anything about the . . . incident in Miranda to my folks. Okay? They've got enough on their plate."

"Okay," Olivia said. She got out of the Volt and gazed up at the house, at its turrets and wraparound porch. "This is beautiful," she said, with a complete lack of sarcasm that surprised Jade.

"It's home," Jade said.

"I guess I was picturing tar-paper shacks or something."

"Of course you were. That's *Ar*kansas, not Kansas."

"My bad."

Jade parked on the street in front then stepped out into the pressure-cooker heat, breaking into a run to get to Clem, as if propelled by rocket fuel. She opened the door and called, "Clementine." Olivia followed her inside and she closed the door behind them.

Clementine came galloping out, wearing a silky nightgown, ballet shoes, and her fox-ear headband. She stopped short when she caught sight of Olivia, mesmerized by her royal-blue hair. She stood frozen, staring, trying to make sense of what she saw.

"This is Olivia, Clementine," Jade said. "She's our friend. Can you say hello?"

Clementine didn't move, just stared.

"Hi," Olivia said.

Once they were away from campus and its cell jammers, Jade had called and warned Pauline that she was bringing a friend, hoping she'd persuade Clementine to bathe. This was always an ordeal, because Clementine couldn't take showers. The jets of water felt like hot needles to her, so luring her into a tub of water was tricky. It had to be the perfect temperature, or she wouldn't get in. Sometimes it was easier to let her go grimy. The family had resorted to makeup-remover cloths and baby wipes stored in a warmer to keep her somewhat clean.

Apparently there hadn't been time for a bath, so Clementine's hair was greasy, but Pauline had cleaned up her hands and face.

"Do you like my hair?" Olivia said to Clementine, her hand going up to it.

Clementine slowly raised her hand toward it, as if it were a magnet.

"You can touch it if you want," Olivia said.

Clementine had not made eye contact.

"Olivia," Jade said quietly. "Let her come to you, okay?"

"Sure," Olivia said.

As if pulled by an invisible line, Clementine drew nearer, staring, her hand out. Olivia stayed perfectly still. It took a good forty seconds for Clementine to make it all the way to Olivia. Then she lightly smoothed her hand down the left side of Olivia's head.

"Hi," Clem said, eyes on the hair.

"Hi," Olivia said. "Do you want your hair to be this color?"

Clementine gaped at Jade, her eyes alight in wonder.

"That would be cool," Jade said, "except she probably couldn't stand the bleach." Jade spoke to Clementine. "Your hair's so dark, we'd have to use chemicals on it, and the bleach can feel like burning on your scalp, so we might not be able to do it on you." Jade needed to nip this idea in the bud before it took root in Clem's mind. Because once an idea germinated there, it turned to bindweed and would not be uprooted no matter how hard or how many times you yanked. Jade turned again to Olivia. "Clementine feels things more intensely than we do. Right, Clem?"

"I do," Clementine said, the high-decibel level of her speech making Olivia jump. Clem smiled at this and said, "I also am learning to modulate the volume of my speech. I used to be a lot louder."

"You did," Jade said. She held her arms out. Sometimes Clementine would hug her and sometimes she wouldn't. Today was a would day, so Clementine disengaged from Olivia's hair and wrapped her arms around Jade's waist and closed her eyes. "Sissy," she said.

Jade rubbed her back and breathed in the fusty scent of her hair.

Pauline walked into the room with the aid of her cane.

"Look, Mom," Clementine said. "Sissy's here."

"I know," Pauline said, then turned her attention to Olivia. "Hello! We've heard so much about you, Olivia."

"Hi, Mrs. Veverka," Olivia said, shaking Pauline's limp right hand. Clementine's eyes fastened on to their shaking hands and finally traveled up to Olivia's actual eyes before quickly looking away, and she squeezed Jade's waist tighter. She let go and leaped to her mother's side, draping Pauline's arm over her shoulders. Apparently, she'd learned to help steady Pauline. Jade kissed her mother's cheek as her dad came in the room.

"Hi," he said to Olivia.

"This is my dad, Robert," Jade said, hugging him. "What are you doing home in the middle of the day, slacker?"

"Mom told me you were stopping by, so I wasn't going to miss it." His eyes welled up. Robert had turned into a crier. Jade wasn't sure if he'd always been this way, or if the birth of their special-needs daughter had done it, or the ALS.

Since the diagnosis, she and her dad had a hard time looking each other in the eye, because whenever they did, their shared guilt over being the only healthy members of the family was almost too painful to bear for either of them.

Olivia shook Robert's hand. Clementine went to hang on Robert's back, hopping as if she wanted a piggyback ride, but she'd been told countless times she was too big now. That didn't stop her from trying. He let her jump on, but he didn't catch her legs so she finally gave up. She turned back to Olivia and said, "Do you want to see my studio?"

"Sure," Olivia said.

Clementine headed for the stairs. As always, Clementine's head wagged side to side as she climbed the stairs. Jade and Olivia followed. Clementine opened the door at the top of the stairs and flipped on the lights. Olivia and Jade joined Clem inside.

Clementine's setup included a Mac desktop computer loaded with the latest digital audio software with two large monitors. Three different keyboards were arranged in an L shape, with two of them stacked in a riser configuration. Robert had retrofitted the third, their grandmother's old Lowrey Genie organ, with MIDI to turn it into a synthesizer. A long soundboard completed the horseshoe shape of the workstation. Four studio monitors stood sentry at the corners.

Cables snaked away from the equipment into three different wall sockets with surge protectors. Microphones, music stands, and three sets of headphones were scattered about as well as stacks of songbooks and sheet music. The walls were design free to minimize distraction for Clementine. A handmade sign that said NOT ABOVE 5 NOT ALL AT ONCE hung on one wall.

Olivia pointed at it. "What's that mean?"

"Our house is almost a hundred years old," Jade said. "So the electrical is a little iffy, even though Dad's upgraded it. If Clem turns the volume up above five with everything on at once, it'll blow a breaker and maybe even take out the whole neighborhood with it."

Olivia lifted her eyebrows as she took in the impressive array of studio equipment.

"Play something for her, Clem," Jade said as Clementine seated herself on the stool they referred to as her throne. She moved her fingers over the bottommost keyboard and began playing.

Olivia's mouth dropped open at the sweet, ethereal sounds that emanated from the speakers. Jade swelled with pride for her sister's talents.

The music came to an abrupt halt as Clementine straightened, her expression unfocused and faraway.

"Uh-oh," Jade said. "Autisma's getting an idea for a song."

Clementine's hand began floating through the air, counting time, then her expression turned serious.

"You have to go now," she said, putting on her headphones and turning away from them. But she turned back, uncovered her ears, and rose to give Jade a quick squeeze. To Olivia, she said, "Nice to meet you. Bye!" and plopped back down onto her stool, replacing the headphones.

They left the room and Jade closed the door behind them. "Did you see that?" she said as they descended the stairs.

"What?" Olivia said.

"She stopped herself and remembered to say goodbye. That's a huge improvement over past behavior."

At the bottom of the stairs, Olivia fixed Jade with a horrified stare. "*Autisma*? What's wrong with you?"

"Dude," Jade said, leading the way into the living room where Robert and Pauline sat. "She knows she's autistic. We've told her. It's not a secret."

Her parents laughed, but Olivia was clearly not amused. Jade got a kick out of the random list of things Olivia found offensive. All of Olivia's UN talk at their first meeting had given Jade the impression nothing was off-limits, but she'd learned Olivia could be very touchy about certain things. Clementine made jokes about her own autism all the time, and Olivia no doubt wouldn't approve of that either. Jade didn't care. Olivia wasn't on the inside of this, so she didn't get a say.

As Jade and Olivia sat on the couch opposite Robert's and Pauline's favorite chairs, Pauline said to Olivia, "Jade tells me you're getting close."

Jay dells me ur geng glows.

Jade hoped Olivia had understood.

"Yeah," Olivia said. "We're pretty excited. I just hope it works."

"It'll work," Pauline said.

"So I'll be here for a whole weekend as soon as I can," Jade told her parents.

"Great," Robert said. "In fact, I wonder if you could get a little more time than that off."

Robert looked at Pauline who smiled encouragingly at him.

"Your mom wants for the four of us to go on a Caribbean cruise. There's one that's just for autism families, with therapy and activities especially for the kids." He turned to Olivia and said, "Trying to take Clementine on a trip surrounded by regular folks would be too stressful—for everyone."

Jade's heart clenched like a fist. It would be the farewell tour.

"I should be able to get some time off," she said, trying to sound excited.

"Jade says Clementine is making all kinds of progress with this new therapist," Olivia said.

"She is," Pauline said.

"I remember the first time she let me hold her hand for more than a few seconds," Jade said. "I sat there not moving, as if a butterfly had landed on me and I didn't want to scare it away."

"Physical contact is very difficult for her," Robert told Olivia. "When Jade was in junior high she set up a demonstration to simulate Clem's physical reactions to ordinary stimuli for the science fair. It was a big hit, and a reporter from the *Kansas City Star* came and interviewed her." He beamed proudly at his eldest child.

Jade tolerated her parents' bragging about her, because she owed it all to them, of course. Olivia's expression indicated her familiarity with this sort of parental behavior as well.

"Did Jade ever tell you about the time she got in a fight to defend her sister?"

Jade rolled her eyes. "It wasn't exactly a fight, Dad." She could never stop him telling this story. It was one of his favorites.

"When Jade was almost nine and Clementine was three, Pauline took them to the playground. Clem hadn't been diagnosed yet, but we all knew something was wrong. Anyway, Pauline saw a friend of hers on the other side—"

Pauline held up her hand and said, "I had to go to the restroom."

"Well, whatever. At any rate, she left the two of them alone for a second. So Jade followed Clementine around while she did her hooting and flapping routine, and these three teenagers, a girl and two guys, wandered onto the playground smoking cigarettes, laughing too loud, and the noise and smell made Clementine slap her hands over her ears and scream. The teenagers freaked out and started calling Clem retard and feeb—a three-year-old, can you imagine? And Jade got pissed. So she motions to the girl. 'Come here,' she says. 'I want to tell you something.'"

Overcome with laughter, Robert couldn't go on for a moment.

"So one of the boys said, 'What do you want, kid?' and Jade says to the girl, 'Come here and I'll tell you. I want to whisper it to you.' So the girl comes over and bends down to Jade, who hooks her thumb into the girl's open mouth and closes her fist.'"

All three Veverkas were laughing now, to Olivia's obvious bemusement.

"So Pauline sees what's going on from across the park, and Jade is hanging from the girl's mouth, while she's punching Jade, who's dangling about two inches off the ground. Jade's thumbnail had gouged the inside of that girl's cheek, and blood's running down the girl's face and shirt, but Jade wouldn't let go no matter what the girl did. Pauline finally had to pry Jade's hand off the girl's face, and then the three teenagers ran away, yelling over their shoulders that they were going to call the cops on the retard and her bruiser sister. Jade was beat up pretty good, bruised and battered, fingernail scratches all over her, but just as calm and cool as could be."

Olivia's horrified expression made them all laugh even harder.

"Don't mess with Autisma, man, that's all I'm going to say," Jade said. "Don't mess with my family."

Chapter 5

THE DRIVE BACK to the Compound always seemed shorter than the drive home. As they neared SiPraTech, Olivia studied the fields and the intersecting dirt roads in front of them. "How do you know where to turn? I always miss the damn turn."

"You city people," Jade said. "Look to the north over there."

"Which way is north?"

Jade pointed. "See that stand of trees? It's the first turn after you pass that."

"I never noticed that," Olivia said.

"That's because everything out here looks the same to you. When you grow up in the country, every landmark is significant. I drove over there a couple of weeks ago. It's a horse ranch."

"You just drove up to it?"

"Yeah," Jade said. "I talked to the owner—real nice lady. She rents out the horses for rides."

"Who knew there were actually things to do around here?"

"There're always things to do."

When they returned, Berko sat in the living room reading Marc Graham's *Of Ashes and Dust*.

"Watch this," Olivia whispered to Jade. Olivia now raised her voice. "What, Jade? You think Nikola Tesla's death ray caused the Tunguska event?"

Berko raised his eyes from his book and pushed his glasses up. "You don't really think that, do you?" he asked, his tone accusing.

"Well, I—"

"I can't believe you believe that," Berko said. "It was a superbolide, of course it was. Just because Admiral Peary said Tesla had told him to look for a 'sign' while he was up near the pole does not mean that—"

"Jade also loves the new *Star Trek* movies," Olivia said, and Jade groaned. Why had she told Olivia she liked them? She knew Berko despised "JJTrek" (so named for the reviled director JJ Abrams) and reviled the movies as canonical heresy.

"I have four words for you, Jade," Berko said. "Big hands and lens flares. That's all there is to the first one. Oh, and it's so rebellious to steal your stepdad's car to a hundreds-of-years-old Beastie Boys song—"

"I like 'Sabotage,'" Jade murmured. She couldn't help it. She did.

"That would be like me stealing my stepdad's Conestoga wagon while blasting out Haydn's Symphony no. 8. And rather than going for story, they blow up Chris Pine's hands, because that's 'hilarious'!"

"Thanks, Olivia," Jade said.

"Where's Elias?" Olivia asked Berko, who paused midrant.

He deflated. "He's working out."

"Why didn't you go?"

"I already ran this morning."

"I'm going to change and then we're going to head to the restaurant," Olivia said to him. "You want to come with or you waiting for Mr. Universe?"

"I'll wait. See you over there."

Jade decided she had time for a quick shower and a change of clothes before they were due at the restaurant. She'd done a lot of sweating that day, so she wanted to be fresh. She took off her blouse and then peeled off her jeans. She shook them out before putting them in the hamper, and a folded piece of paper fell out of her back pocket. She bent to pick it up. Was it the toothpaste receipt? But she didn't think she'd gotten one.

She unfolded the piece of paper. Handwritten on the paper was 785-017-3021.

A phone number. Where had it come from?

But then in a flash, she remembered her would-be kidnapper's hand on her butt. He wasn't playing grab-ass. He'd slipped this into her pocket.

This was the most bizarrely original pickup tactic she'd ever seen, and she snorted in disgust. She couldn't wait to tell Olivia. Jade crumpled the piece of paper, three-pointed it into the trash basket, and went into the bathroom for her shower.

Thirty minutes later, Jade and Olivia drove into Miranda on mostly deserted streets, except for a lone pickup truck that cruised Main Street slowly.

"Okay," Olivia said. "Where do you suppose the police station is? We need to report this afternoon's grope-fest."

Jade glanced at the clock. "In a little town like this, they close up shop at five," she said. "No point in going until tomorrow."

Olivia reluctantly agreed, as if Jade had somehow planned it that way, then pulled up to the brand-new restaurant that had opened just prior to their arrival in May. There were only a few cars parked diagonally on the street in front of the eatery, and two of them had out-of-county plates.

Jade had been surprised when she moved to Pennsylvania that not all states required license plate stickers with the county in which they were registered. Wherever she went in Kansas, though, she could tell where the cars were from, and Robert had made a game of it when they went on road trips. Jade had learned the two-letter designation for every county in Kansas. This was not a skill, however, that she shared with people.

The Hungry Harrier Restaurant served family chicken dinners. Decorated in a country antique style, it reminded Jade of a Cracker Barrel, one of her favorite restaurants. A little old-fashioned general store was attached, with bright, pretty clothing, knickknacks, books, music, movies, candy, pastries, as well as electronics of all kinds.

Jade and Olivia went into the dining area where they waited for their colleagues. Berko and Elias appeared fifteen minutes later. Elias's face shone red after his workout, fresh from the shower, his hair still wet.

Berko fixed Jade with a concerned stare. "Elias told me about the guy in the grocery store," he said. "Are you okay?"

Jade scowled at Elias who shrugged. "Yeah, I'm fine," she said. She pointed at them one by one. "Do not tell Dan about this."

Everyone grumbled but agreed.

Dan entered the dining room wearing a sport shirt and shorts. Jade had only ever seen him in business clothes, and the fitness and size of his legs surprised her.

Two families, one with an infant and toddler, and one with three boisterous children between five and ten years old, were seated in the dining room. Jade watched them as the others perused the menu and ordered drinks. Something about these families struck her as odd, but she couldn't figure out what.

Of course, Jade's anxiety about Pauline and Clementine, her ever-present impostor syndrome, and the near-assault this afternoon made it impossible to concentrate. She needed to climb out of her head and join the living, so she turned her attention to Dan, who was showing photos of his wife and two kids to Jade's coworkers.

"That's Cecily," Dan said, pointing at his phone, "and next to her is Dan Junior. He's going to the Air Force Academy in the fall, just like his old man. Cecily is a junior at the University of Michigan." He swiped at the phone screen and held it up, an image of him and a dark-haired, dimpled beauty of a middle-aged woman glowing there. "And that's my honey, Melissa."

"Where do you live?" Olivia said.

"We've been in Virginia for five years," he said. "We both work in D.C."

"What exactly do you do for the Crane Group?" Berko said.

"I do recruiting tours of universities and conduct seminars and generally travel around and meet people and schmooze. It's a great gig, especially since I'm not actually qualified to do anything."

Jade snorted. "Right," she said. "He's got an MBA from Wharton. He served in the Air Force for twenty years, made colonel, as you know, and has been involved in all sorts of amazing stuff."

Dan held up his glass of iced tea. "But compared with you four, I'm a yahoo." Everyone else held up their glasses and clinked them together.

After their food arrived, Dan went into storytelling mode, which Jade always loved. "I was in Chicago for a conference in the late nineties, and I bumped into this extremely well-dressed middle-aged lady trying to make sense of a map—this was before smartphones and Google Maps, of course—and so I offered to help her. I've spent a lot of time there, so I know how to find my way around. What I didn't know when I offered to help was she's the wife of The Rolling Stones's drummer, Charlie Watts, and she thanked me by giving me two front-row tickets to that night's Stones show. That may not mean much to people your age, but it dazzles the hell out of my generational peers."

Jade could see from her friends' expressions that they were suitably impressed.

Dan did seem to know everyone. He was one of those people who somehow became friends with the rich and famous the way normal people find pennies on the sidewalk. He was tight with a former US Attorney General and hung out with PJ O'Rourke. One of his good friends was George Clooney, because of course he was.

Jade's awestruck team members listened raptly, and Elias barraged Dan with questions he patiently answered, details about being in Berlin in 1989 the day the wall came down.

Dan leaned forward and gestured for everyone around the table to lean in too. "I've got a piece of the wall at home," he said. "I smuggled it out of there. Don't tell anyone. If you come to D.C., I'll show it to you."

Jade felt proud he'd chosen her as mentee. And felt stupid for feeling so proud.

"But enough about me," Dan said, turning to Berko. "Tell me about your name."

Berko startled, took an uneasy drink of his soda, and said, "It means 'firstborn' in the Akan language, which originates in—"

"Ghana, isn't it?" Dan said.

Berko looked even more surprised. "Yes."

"See?" Jade said. "I told you. He knows everyone and everything."

"I have approximate knowledge of many things," Dan said, and Jade laughed.

"*Adventure Time*," Olivia said. "Nice." She lifted her glass once more to Dan.

"Absolutely my favorite animated show," Dan said, then turned back to Berko. "Did your ancestors come from Ghana, or did your folks just like the name?"

"It *is* a great name," Olivia said, her chin in her palm. "Very cool."

Both pleased and embarrassed, Berko said, "We don't know what our ancestry is exactly. My mom thought it was a good strong name, even though I'm not the firstborn."

"So how did you meet Jade?" Elias said. Being around Dan had made Elias unusually talkative. Dan routinely had that effect on people.

Dan threw a proud-father look Jade's way and said, "I was visiting KU on a recruiting trip and happened into one of the auditoriums where Jade was giving a presentation."

Jade's face flamed red. The worst day, the worst presentation ever.

"I was standing in the back, and I happened to notice these three guys there completely and loudly ignoring Jade's PowerPoint—which was about the Clementine Program, by the way—and watching a video on one of the guys' tablets."

"My personal Draco Malfoy," Jade said, trying to keep her tone light. "Flanked by his Crabbe and Goyle."

That was the day Jade nearly threw in the towel and quit the CS program. They'd almost won. But then Dan came into her life.

Chapter 6

JADE HATED TO think about that day. KU's Hoch Auditorium had smelled like Axe body spray and onions, which only added to her angst, those insidious worms eating away at her stomach lining. That's how she pictured what happened to her body when her anxiety crawled into the driver's seat. She was self-confident—overly so—inside her own brain, but her body had never gotten the message. Stammering, the pitch of her voice climbing ever higher the more she talked, sweat taking over her clothing, the humiliation of letting her weakness show.

Her archenemy's name was Nishant Sharma, the guy who was watching videos with his henchmen at the back of the auditorium. He competed with her for everything in the Computer Science Department. He did anything he could to undermine her, with the blessing if not the encouragement of the department head, Professor Sauer. Her own personal Snape, to continue the Harry Potter metaphor, only he wasn't secretly a good guy. He aggressively campaigned against the idea of women in computer science.

Nishant and his buddies huddled together at the back of the

auditorium, their heads bent, their faces aglow from the tiny screen they were all scrutinizing. They wore that YouTube look of anticipation, of gearing up to laugh uproariously whether they found it funny or not.

Seeing this from the stage, Jade put her hands on her hips—a power pose that allegedly made the poser feel ten feet tall and bulletproof. All it did was expose her soaking armpits to the air conditioner and send a chill through her body. She attempted to continue even without the attention of the three jerks in the back. She tried to raise her voice, but her constricted throat emitted only raspy noises.

And that's when they started laughing—at first trying to cover it up, but the video apparently was too hilarious to hold in their hysteria. They tittered in that self-aware "you all need to know what a great time we're having" kind of laughter. It seemed these days everyone behaved as if they were always being filmed, always being watched. Everyone was the star of their very own YouTube show while simultaneously watching YouTube, on and on, spiraling into infinity.

She remembered the list she'd made that morning detailing everything that could possibly go wrong, and somehow she'd missed this one. She wished she'd worn all black—another power thing—but it didn't fit her. Bright colors were more her style.

Her ankles wobbled. She shouldn't have worn heels this high, but she needed them for confidence. The flip side of that coin was physical peril. Her size eleven four-inch heels grew her to a towering six foot four, which still wasn't imposing enough.

Remember what the book said. Project your power. Power through the sweat and shaking.

But her knees locked up then, and her imagination transported her back to the gymnasium at Ephesus High, where she'd crouched, paralyzed, after mounting the balance beam. Her hands became claws that would not release their grip and let her stand. Ultimately, her coach had to physically pluck her from the beam in front of an audience of a hundred. The most humiliating moment of her life. Her mind should be able to take control. But her body had proved the victor time and again. She'd tried hypnosis, counseling, beta-blockers—nothing could overcome her nervous system's boundless power.

Jade glanced at her instructor, who sat in the front row smiling at her, but nothing could overcome the derision filling the room.

As the laughter in the back of Hoch Auditorium amplified, Jade lost her place in the presentation, and she'd seen the burly man walk over to her saboteur and pluck the tablet from his hands. "Learn some manners, kid," he'd said in his big thunderous voice. "Your colleague is speaking."

Jade locked eyes with the man she now knew as Dan, and he nodded encouragingly at her.

Jade cut the presentation short, and ended by saying, "You can read about the rest of it on my website," she said. *At fuckoff.com*. She grabbed her iPad and clomped ungracefully out of Hoch, and Dan had followed her and asked her to have coffee with him at the KU student union. Within an hour, it seemed as if she'd always known him.

"I hope this isn't presumptuous of me," Dan said. "But why didn't you stay at Carnegie Mellon for grad school?"

Jade explained about her sister and her recently diagnosed mom and how she needed to be close to home.

"That's some heavy self-sacrifice for a person your age," Dan said, stirring his coffee.

Jade shrugged.

"Or did you dislike CMU?"

"No, I didn't dislike it," she said. "It was a shock though. Here I am a big Kansas farm girl, and I had no idea what I was walking into. Other than the CS school and the drama school, the rest of the students are Ivy League rejects, and they're all from the East Coast. I'd never met anyone from the East Coast before, so I felt like this giant, carefree toddler who bumbled into a room with my arms and heart wide open, ready for everyone to love her, and then a two-by-four of New England aloofness and scorn knocked me out."

"Sounds rough," Dan said. "You could write a book for people like you—sort of an instruction manual."

"I should," Jade said. "It would have helped tremendously to know what I was walking into. The only real friends I made in town went to the University of Pittsburgh, kids I met at Cornerstone, the student ministry at Bellefield Presbyterian Church. Even so, I love Pittsburgh and Carnegie Mellon with a fierce loyalty. Stupid, huh?"

"Not at all. I think that's fairly common."

"I roomed with three Pitt girls, all nursing students, in Oakland, near a strip club, sophomore year through graduation. When CMU people found out I played high school football, they were *amused. How quaint. How provincial. How adorable!*"

"Are you kidding?" Dan nearly shouted. "It's just one of the many ways you're a badass."

"At Carnegie Mellon, I literally had to retrain myself in so many ways. I tried to relearn how to laugh." Her high school friends always had made a big deal about how funny her laugh was, how it made them laugh harder. But at CMU, her laugh brought on silence, along with almost concerned looks. She learned to check herself and be aware of how she appeared at all times. She'd learned to slouch then, to draw in on herself, when her dad had always told her to stand up straight and take up as much space as she needed to. She was a loud, outgoing person trapped in social situations she didn't quite understand, and trying to be a dainty girl exhausted her.

Going to Carnegie Mellon had given her a deeper understanding of Clementine's autism—the social cues there were different, the way social cues were always mysterious to her sister, coupled with the constant fear of acting foolishly.

And she'd carried this on to KU, apparently, because their CS department didn't want her either. The women in the department were treated like second-class citizens.

"How am I supposed to survive in this industry if I can't stand up to misogyny like that?" she asked Dan.

"All it takes," Dan said, "is some confidence, surrounding yourself with supportive people who believe in you, and time. You'll look back on this stage of your life and laugh. You might even feel sorry for your hecklers."

She was about to say that would never happen, but then she remembered the incident with the teenagers in the park, when she made the teenage girl bleed for taunting Clementine. She did feel sorry for them, because they were probably underemployed, smoking weed every day, just drifting through life.

"Colonel Stevenson," she said.

"Call me Dan."

"Dan—did you wander into my presentation by accident?"

He leaned in close, conspiratorial, and whispered, "No. I've heard about the Clementine Program."

Jade was more than surprised. "Who—"

Dan waved his hand. "It's not important. But your program is. If it's half of what I've been told, you have a stellar future ahead of you." He sat back. "I'm a loud advocate for women in the sciences. My mother was a brilliant physicist who was stymied in the field just because of her gender. I've spent my career mentoring women, and I think you just need a little help to make it to where you're destined to be."

Jade couldn't respond to this lavish praise.

"Since you didn't get to finish your presentation," Dan said, "why don't you take me through the process of developing the Clementine Program."

This was a rare opportunity. Most people glazed over when she talked about her work. "I started to hear patterns in my sister, Clementine's, vocalizations, and I picked them out on our old upright piano in the living room," Jade said. "The first time I matched the tones she vocalized, she made prolonged eye contact with me, which is very rare in autistic people."

To this day, that had been the most exciting, gratifying moment Jade had ever experienced. It was then she realized the possibilities of computers. Those days of figuring things out, of building and designing, were so sweet.

"Clementine's usually always moving," Jade continued, "but this froze her, and she repeated the musical line and pointed at a bag of chocolate kisses on top of the piano. I pointed at it also and repeated the line, and she just kind of dissolved. I'd discovered the tonal 'word' for chocolate. So I would point at an object, and she'd vocalize, and I'd repeat it on the piano until we had a rudimentary vocabulary of nouns worked out in music. I wrote an algorithm based on it. That's how it all started."

"How old were you?"

"Twelve."

"What was the significance of the chocolate?" Dan asked.

"It's the only thing that motivated her," Jade said. "Not time-outs, not taking things away. It's still the best way to motivate her. Chocolate is to Clementine what money is to most people."

"Interesting."

"So then I was able to teach Clem to talk once I understood her language," Jade said. "I designed several phone apps to help her understand the world around her. An app that explains facial expressions, that helps her express emotions she has no words for, stuff like that. I designed one for her we could use to communicate secretly through her tonal language. I still send her texts that way. It's how I keep in touch with her because she can't talk on the phone. If she can't see a person's face and see their mouth moving, it's as if the person is speaking in a foreign language."

Dan stared in awe. "That is fascinating."

"She also experiences music in pictures, which is part of her neurology. The first time I understood this was after she heard the song 'Just a Girl' by No Doubt. Do you know it?"

Dan shook his head.

"It's a song about how women are treated like children. So when Clementine hears a song, she ignores the words and just sees the image the music itself—the melody, the notes, the chord progressions—describes to her. What she sees when 'Just a Girl' plays is a female angel with massive glowing white wings flying in specific patterns over a large stage."

Dan shook his head.

"So this was another component I used in my algorithm," Jade said. "By combining sound and image in the way Clementine sees them, the program began to make unique connections. Began to create patterns independently I couldn't predict. It grew from there, until it acted completely autonomously."

"Then you've been working on this for—what, almost fifteen years?"

"That's right." She sighed. "If I had access to a supercomputer, there's no telling how far I could take it."

Dan scrubbed his hand over his face. "I think I might be able to land you access to that kind of computing power," he said. "I've just learned about an opportunity that's starting very soon."

He fished a business card out of his wallet and handed it to her. MARTIN FELIX, it said. SiPraTech. "They're holding an on-campus interview three days from now. Give him a call, and I'm sure he'll squeeze you in."

"How can you be sure?"

"Because I'll tell him to."

She didn't know at the time how much pull Dan had in all sorts of places.

In the days before the interview, she spoke to Dan on the phone several times.

"Will you be there?" she asked him the day before.

"No," he said. "It's a start-up I didn't have anything to do with. I'm just making the introductions. You'll do the rest. Just be yourself. This is a once-in-a-lifetime opportunity."

"Give me a pep talk," she said.

"You're smart enough, you're good-looking enough, and darn it, people like you."

"Not quite what I had in mind."

"I need to tell you," Dan said. "My buddy Martin requested a recommendation for the position from the computer science department head. Professor Sauer?"

She knew what Dan was going to say.

"You didn't make the list. No surprise there. No women at all on the list, but I told Martin they needed you. So do me proud, lady."

"I'll do my best," she said. "Did you tell me about Sauer just to rile me up?"

"Of course," he said. "Rage is a great motivator. I'll tell you what I know that Sauer doesn't. I know you're going to kick the world's ass. I just hope the world's ready."

"Thank you, Dan," she said.

"Go get 'em."

Jade drove to the Oread Hotel at the east end of the KU campus and parked. The cement sidewalk threatened to trip her at every opportunity as she approached the hotel entrance, but she strove to stand in the light of Dan's belief in her. She wasn't just a great big farm girl. She had control. She had this.

In the lobby stood a man in a suit, looking very secret service, holding a printed SiPraTech Interview sign.

"Hi," she said, shaky already. "I'm Jade Veverka. I'm here for the interview."

"Follow me, please," he said.

She did, stepping carefully inside the elevator. As the doors slid closed, she strained to think of something, anything, to say to this taciturn man, but he stared intently at the ascending numbers, so she did too. *This isn't important*, she kept telling herself. *What's the worst-case scenario? They don't hire me. My life goes on as before. Being overlooked and unappreciated in the CS department.*

As she said this to herself, she remembered Dan's phrase—life-changing. Did she want her life to change? She wanted to be taken seriously and to stop being so fearful. She wanted people to listen to her and not think of her as an ungainly, horsey, nervous wimp but a confident, take-charge woman. She'd heard fake it 'til you make it, but she'd been faking it for years and hadn't made it yet.

When they got to an upper floor, the man walked on silent shoes down a hallway and Jade followed. He stopped in front of a door and said, "Can I have your NDA, please?"

"My—what?" she stammered, hating herself for it. She'd heard him. She just didn't have what he wanted.

"You should have received an NDA via email. You were supposed to read it over and sign it before coming today."

"Oh," she said, her face heating. "I didn't get it."

His skeptical expression made her want to shout, *I'm the most organized person I know. If I'd gotten it, you'd have it in your hand. I'm not an absentminded nitwit.*

"I'll need to get one for you now," he said. "Your appointment is in five minutes, but it has to be signed before you go in."

Before she could say anything, he put a card key into the slot and opened the door, disappearing inside.

She stood staring at the door, as if he were on the other side and she could see him. She had the horrifying thought that he'd leave her out here, laughing about it with whoever else was in there about how he'd tricked her, made her look foolish.

But the man reappeared moments later and handed her a stack of paper, possibly fifty pages thick, and a pen.

"I don't have enough time to read this," she said.

"It's a standard NDA," he said. "We really just require your signature."

The man removed the last sheet of paper and pointed. Then he held the rest of the paper like a tray. She obeyed and signed. For the first time, he smiled at her.

"Thank you," he said. "Please come in."

He opened the door for her and held it while she wobbled on in.

The room was more like a very expensive hotel suite, the likes of which Jade had only seen pictures of but never stayed in. When she rounded the corner, the first thing she saw was a dining area with a long table, on which sat four gleaming new ASUS laptops, probably K501UXs with Core i7. And the second was Nishant Sharma, flanked by his YouTube-watching cronies, his great big teeth biting into an appetizer. He froze midbite when he recognized her, then his eyebrows rose in surprise. "Hello, Jade," he said, using her first name for maybe the first time ever. "Great to see you."

Really? He'd never spoken a kind word to her, but he was clearly putting on his awkwardly friendly interview personality.

She froze. Dan hadn't told her this was a group interview. Maybe he didn't know.

"Hi," she said.

He held a chair for her as if he were a maître d', and she had the sneaking suspicion he would pull it out from under her, but she forced herself to sit in it and say, "Thank you, Nishant."

"I see you two know each other," a man in a linty brown suit said, standing up and smoothing his cobalt blue tie as he did so. "You must be Jade Veverka. My name is Martin Felix." He stretched out a hand to shake hers, but he overshot and stabbed her in the chest with it. He drew it back and his face reddened. "Sorry. Please, have a seat."

She fully expected him to say what people always said, which was "How tall are you? Did you play basketball? How's the weather up there?" But he didn't. He didn't register surprise at her appearance at all. Dan must have told him about her freakish height so he wouldn't be shocked when he saw her.

Jade acknowledged Nishant's friends, who smirked at her. She wished she could disappear. As usual, it was three against one. They would speak as the hive mind. They would support each other and prop each other up and talk each other up. They'd be chosen. Not her. Of course. Because Nishant got the fellowship she'd coveted. Because Sauer had the final say, and Nishant was his golden boy.

Martin sat on the cream sofa in front of a window with a spectacular view of the beautiful KU campus. "You four were listed as the top four KU CS candidates."

What a load of crap. Crabbe and Goyle weren't even in the top half. Jade knew Haruko Suzuki and Yeong Rhee, two of the other top CS students, weren't here because Sauer wouldn't have identified any of the women as the top students. She was only here because of Dan.

"Before I explain the position to you," Martin said, "may I offer you something to drink?"

"Water, please," she croaked out, crossing her legs.

"Sparkling?"

"Just—wet," she said lamely, and Nishant tried and failed to keep from laughing. Her face flushed. How many times could this happen in a day before the capillaries in her cheeks burst?

She counted to five as she inhaled through her nose. She held it then blew out through her mouth slowly. Jade ground her teeth, thinking of light to try to keep the darkness of anxiety at bay. The darkness circled the edges of her consciousness, always ready and waiting to take over, like a fog surrounding a lake. Sometimes it won, but in the past few years, endless self-help positive thinking books and blogs and lists and mindfulness meditation had helped.

When she needed to conjure light, she thought of waking up as a kid in her childhood bedroom that first day of vacation, the early summer cast of light from the eastern horizon, the echoing birdsong, the green smells of the growing wheat, the turned dark brown earth—all the clean country smells she missed when she was away from them.

She tried to picture her happy place in the morning prairie light, but all she could see were angry hornets' nests and knots of worms and decaying roadkill. She blinked.

Martin handed her a glass of ice water, but he seemed to have some sort of spatial-awareness deficit, because he nearly missed her hand, and it was so sweaty anyway the glass almost slipped right through. She caught the bottom with her left hand then took a big gulp before holding it in her lap.

Martin scanned the group. "We're interviewing CS grad students all over the country, so just being here says a lot about how highly esteemed you all are."

Nishant grimaced, and Jade could guess what he was thinking. They were up against the guys from MIT, and Cornell, and of course, the number one CS school, Carnegie Mellon. Maybe the fact that her BS was from CMU would work in her favor, but it wasn't a fair fight. If American universities had been ranked by weight, the East Coast would sink beneath the ocean, flipping the entire country over, capsizing it. Jade's heart dropped further.

Nishant and his friends looked at each other, as if it had just occurred to them that they wouldn't all be going together, that they were competing against one another. She watched as they subtly shifted away from each other. This gave her a tiny bit more confidence.

Nishant raised his hand tentatively, his elbow stuck to his side as if unwilling to fully commit.

"You don't need to raise your hand," Martin said. "Just speak up. This is an informal interview."

Sure it is.

"Why are you even bothering to interview *here*?"

"I assume you've heard the phrase 'Silicon Prairie,'" he said. "The company is based in Kansas, and we'd like to hire at least one team member locally. If we can."

If we can. There was no way. This was just a token gesture.

"But we're getting ahead of ourselves," Martin said.

"So what does the position entail?" asked Nishant's bestie, the guy Jade thought of as Crabbe, even though his radiant green eyes and the squarest jaw she'd ever seen made it hard for her to look at him, he was so beautiful.

Martin rubbed his hands together and crossed his legs. "The project will be getting underway by the end of May," he said.

"And what's the actual project we'll be working on?"

Martin adjusted his security badge. "That's the second layer of the NDA. We can't tell you until you're hired."

Goyle straightened his tie and said, "I've never interviewed for a mystery position like this."

"Here's what I can tell you," Martin said. "You'll be part of a four-member cross-discipline team, working on a project that involves research, testing, coding, problem solving with shifting variables—but I can't be more specific than that. I can also tell you if you're hired, you will receive a signing bonus of thirty thousand dollars."

Goyle sank back down into his chair, his eyes fixed on Martin Felix.

Thirty K? Up front? Jade was stunned. This was the amount her parents had been trying to raise for the wheelchair-accessible van to accommodate the electric wheelchair Pauline would soon need.

"Our benefits package includes the repayment of all your college and grad school debt. We will also reimburse you for any expenses you've already paid, including books, living expenses, rent, tuition, travel, et cetera."

Nishant's eyebrows shot up.

Jade experienced a sweeping chill. She'd racked up $56,000 in undergrad debt, and $22,000 in grad school so far.

"You had to pick one of the most expensive schools in the country, didn't you?" her dad had said when he learned what CMU tuition cost. He'd sighed and signed the mortgage paperwork. Their Kansas farmland was leveraged to the hilt, and it was all riding on her shoulders. Pay her parents' mortgages off. Pay off her student debt. Freedom.

"But that's not all," Martin said, and Jade pictured him as a TV pitchman for ShamWow! or the Miracle Mop. "If you complete the project, you will receive a one-hundred-thousand-dollar bonus plus stock options worth another five hundred thousand."

"To split among the team?" Nishant asked, his voice dry and cracked.

Martin let the question lie there before them, as each of the students held their breaths. Then a slow smile spread over his face. "Each," he said.

Crabbe whistled.

Instead of elated, Jade felt bereft. This was so far out of her league, even a telescope couldn't help her see it.

"And finally," Martin said, "if at the end of the project you'd like to move on, you'll be given a research grant at the institution of your choice. Or we will guarantee you a lucrative, prestigious position in the industry. We've already talked to Google, Facebook, the Department of Defense, et cetera."

Who the hell were these guys?

"You can't guarantee something like that," Goyle said, skeptical.

"Oh, trust me," Martin said, dropping into a lower vocal register. "We *can* guarantee it. In writing. We have connections."

"Universities?" Nishant said. "Associate professor-type positions?"

"Absolutely," Martin assured him. "Tenure track."

This time the boys didn't look at each other, but seemed to be doing the same kinds of calculations in their heads that Jade was.

She finally spoke up, her curiosity getting the better of her. She had to restrain herself from holding up a hand. "Mr. Felix? I wondered if you could tell us about the company itself."

He chuckled again. "I can tell you we are very well funded. Let's say it's a tech company and leave it at that." He stood and rubbed his hands together. "Now, if you'll leave all your things here and move on over to the table, we've got some laptops on which we'd like to test your algorithmic thinking."

Everyone rose, and Goyle said, "And then you'll interview us?"

"The coding challenges *are* the interview."

Jade seated herself at the head of the table, facing away from the window, and opened the laptop. A page of coding problems appeared, some she recognized from the practice interview questions she'd Googled earlier, several of which she'd already completed. Her shoulders relaxed, and she smiled, realizing this would be much easier than she'd expected.

"You've got thirty minutes to complete five of the problems." Martin said. He marked his watch. "Everyone ready? Begin."

Jade read the text at the top of the screen.

1. Compute the nth Fibonacci number. Careful—the recursion can quickly spin out of control!

Everything else faded away as she sank into the questions. There was no death here, no fear about the future, no autistic sister, no dying mother. Coding was poetry, poetry she understood and could manipulate to make things happen, unlike in the real world.

"Time," Martin said.

Jade emerged from the virtual world and regarded those around the table, having forgotten other people were present in the room for the timed thirty minutes. Martin walked around the table, making notes on a clipboard on each of their screens, while Jade and her competitors flexed their wrists and fingers, rolled their necks and shoulders.

"We've already been talking to your professors about your work," Martin said, tucking the clipboard against his chest, "so you won't need to give us recommendations."

Jade caught Nishant watching her, a smirk on his face. His expression transmitted his unflagging belief he would be chosen. He had the fellowships, scholarships, awards. He was the guy with an assured future, with moneyed parents. She was just here to add some estrogen to the proceedings for at least the appearance of political correctness. Since it was a private company, they weren't bound to affirmative action or EEOC. They could do what they wanted.

"Well," Martin said. He set down his clipboard, smoothed his tie, and rebuttoned his coat. This seemed to be the signal for them all to stand and prepare to exit the room. He shook each of their hands in turn. "I don't need to tell you not to talk about this to friends or family. We take the NDA very seriously, and as you can imagine, we have some of the best lawyers in the country." He used the lower register again on that last part so they all knew he meant business.

Jade stood and drew herself to her full height, allowing herself to tower over Nishant. What the hell. He glowered up at her, and she smiled down at him.

"It was so nice meeting all of you," Martin said.

Nishant turned away from Jade. "May I have your business card?" he asked Martin obsequiously.

"No," Martin said with a smile to soften the blow.

Nishant tried to smile back but it more closely approximated a sneer, and Jade took comfort in this.

"You will only be contacted in the event you are hired," Martin said. "If you don't hear from us by the thirteenth, you can assume you weren't chosen." And he ushered them out the door.

Chapter 7

"I'LL BET YOU'D have liked to see Nishant's face when he found out you were hired," Berko said, his eyes gleaming. He'd been the target of far worse discrimination than she. He sat on Jade's right at the Hungry Harrier, Dan to her left.

"And Professor Sauer's," she said. "But I made it a point to be magnanimous, even though neither of them would have been." Jade would love to see Sauer's face once they finished testing and the Clementine Program successfully and completely created its own culture. She'd love to gloat and sneer at him like a schoolyard bully.

"I'm glad I didn't have to do a group interview," Elias said.

"You didn't?" Jade said. "How did it work at Annapolis?"

"Martin interviewed me over the phone. One of my mentors put my name out there, he said."

"We had a group interview at Hopkins," Olivia said. "But there was none of that he-man woman-haters' club bullshit there. Lucky me."

She had no idea.

Dan turned to Berko. "What do your folks do, Berko?"

"Mom works for a rental car company at Hartsfield-Jackson. I never knew my dad." He said it matter-of-factly, but Jade ventured to imagine her own life without her father and couldn't. She felt sympathy mixed with admiration for Berko.

"And your sister," Dan said. "What's she up to?"

"She's a senior at Emory."

Dan nodded. "Nice," he said. "What's her major?"

"Behavioral neuroscience," Berko said.

Jade turned to him. "I didn't know that," she said. "She could be working on this project with us—that's right up our alley. Hey, Olivia, you should talk to her!"

"Yeah," Olivia said vaguely.

An awkward silence followed and Jade sought to fill it. "I'd love to meet her, Berko. And your mom."

"You should come down to Atlanta," Berko said. "You ever been there?"

"No," Jade said. "I've only ever been to Pittsburgh, and Lawrence, and Ephesus, and now Miranda, Kansas."

"You've never done any traveling?"

"My dad's a farmer, so we couldn't go on vacation during the summer when we were harvesting, and my folks have never had a whole lot of money."

"Mine either," Berko said. "But when we're done here, I'm going to buy my mom a house, and I'm going to pay off my sister's student debt."

"What are you going to do with your share, Elias?" Jade said.

"I'm going to pay my parents' debts off first thing," he said. "And then I'm going to buy a Dodge Challenger Hellcat."

"Oooh," Jade said. "I wouldn't mind having one of those."

Dan looked like he was enjoying this conversation immensely, his kind eyes crinkling at the corners, smiling between bites of fried chicken.

"How about you, Olivia?" Jade said.

"I want to travel," she said. "Take some time and see the world. Maybe you'll come with me, huh, Jade?"

Jade held her smile, but she would not be going anywhere. She had responsibilities. Taking an autistic young adult on a world tour didn't seem likely. She stretched her arms over her head and Dan's eyes lit on her tattoo.

"New ink?" he said, and held out his hand.

She held out her forearm for him to examine. He considered her quizzically, and she explained.

"I told her she should have got her mom's face on there instead," Elias said.

"Ah, but this is much more personal," Dan said. "It's her heart instead of her face."

Jade breathed deeply to keep the ever-threatening tears at bay. Pauline had to take medication because of what the doctor termed "ALS-caused emotional incontinence." Jade didn't have ALS, but her emotional incontinence was nearly as bad, and it was undeniably caused by ALS.

"Plus most face tattoos look like bad cartoons," Olivia said, buttering a roll.

"She has beautiful handwriting," Dan said.

Had beautiful handwriting.

"How's she doing, Jade?" Dan asked.

"Pretty good," Jade said. All eyes turned toward her and her face reddened.

"And speaking of which," Olivia said, shooting Jade a "better to ask forgiveness than permission" look. "Dan, have you heard of the experimental stem cell treatment they're using with some pretty great success for ALS?"

He nodded. "I have." He addressed Jade. "I read about the man in Alabama who's lived nine years past his diagnosis thanks to the treatment."

Jade nodded, trying not to look too hopeful and desperate. Although what did it matter? She *was* hopeful and desperate.

"You seem to know everyone," Olivia went on, "and I wondered if you have any connections, any strings you could pull to place Jade's mom in one of the research studies. We all know it's impossible to get into one of those things if you don't know someone."

"What's the word on the street at Hopkins?"

"I'm just a student," Olivia said. "I don't have any pull. But I know you do."

Dan winked at Jade. "I know some people working on it at Harvard and a couple at Emory." He pointed at Berko with his fork, emphasizing he remembered Berko's sister was a student there. "Let me see what I can find out."

Jade clamped her teeth together to prevent her chin from quivering. "Thanks, Dan."

Dan paid for dinner then led the team out of the restaurant and onto the sidewalk.

"Does it ever cool down here?" Dan asked, tugging at the neck of his shirt.

"Nope," Jade said. She hugged him and promised to call the second they made a breakthrough. Then he got in his rental and drove toward the Salina airport to catch a flight back to Virginia.

Jade scouted up and down Main Street. While it shouldn't have been teeming with crowds, it shouldn't have been this empty either. Again with the alarm buzz in her head, and she had a sudden urge to walk to the baseball diamond and see if everyone was congregating there. Or in the city park. Or anywhere.

"You guys want to go for a walk?" Jade asked everyone. "Take in the sights?"

"The 'sights'?" Elias said. "Maybe another time. Let's go back to the house and watch some Bruce Campbell."

"*Evil Dead* again?" Olivia said.

"*Army of Darkness*," Berko said.

"I'd really like to go walking," Jade said. "Olivia, you want to walk the town?"

"You think we're going to let you two girls go walking alone after what happened today?" Elias said.

Olivia bristled. "First of all, we're women. And second of all, you don't 'let' us do anything. And third, I've got my pepper spray with me."

Jade was cheered by this. "And I can't imagine that the guy is hanging around here. You said yourself he drove away."

"He did have out-of-state plates," Elias said.

"Which state?" Jade said. This was new information.

"I don't know," Elias said. "I just know they weren't Kansas plates."

"What make of vehicle?" Berko said.

"A white Japanese crossover," Elias said.

"What's a crossover?" Olivia asked.

"It's a cross between an SUV and a minivan," Berko said. "Big with soccer moms and small-town abductors."

"Not funny," Olivia said.

But Jade laughed.

"Not that you need our permission," Elias said, "but I'd feel better if you didn't walk the town until after you report it to the police. Just my opinion."

"I'm with Elias," Berko said apologetically. "Although I'm baffled something like that happened in a little town like this."

"You callin' me a liar?" Jade said, putting on her Western cowboy voice.

"Naw," Berko said, intoning John Wayne, making his hands into pistols and putting them on his hips as if ready to draw. "I'm sayin' yer yella."

This surprised Jade so much she let out a loud belly laugh, and Elias joined in. Olivia smiled indulgently.

Embarrassed, Berko shook out his pretend pistols and pushed his glasses up, grinning self-consciously.

Jade socked him in the shoulder. He'd always been polite and friendly, but this was the first time he'd actually joked around with her, and she felt like a dam between them had broken.

"Thanks, guys," she said. "So if we shouldn't walk, Olivia, would you mind if we drove around the town for a little while? I'm not ready to go back to the Compound yet. If you don't want to, you can ride home with the guys and I'll meet you all back at the house."

"Oh, no you don't, not by yourself, Miss Deathwish," Olivia said. "All right. We can drive around for a little while, although why you want to is beyond me." She turned to Berko and Elias. "See you at home."

The guys got in their car and drove away.

"Thanks, O," Jade said as she got in the driver's seat of the blue Volt.

"You're welcome."

As she pulled out of the parking space, Jade noted only three cars parked on the street. In Ephesus, you always met lots of walkers on a fine evening like this one. But as she drove west down Main Street, the sidewalks were empty, the sun setting before them.

Olivia Bluetoothed her smartphone to the car's computer system and put her music on shuffle, lots of Adele and Lady Gaga and the occasional rap song.

Jade and Olivia drove toward the cemetery in companionable silence, Jade thinking about her sister and her mother, Dan, and the families in the restaurant. One of the little girls reminded her of a younger Clementine. A by-product of having a special-needs sister was Jade constantly assessed other people's placement on the autism spectrum, and this girl appeared to be on the high-functioning end. She was adorable, of course, reddish hair and freckles, and her father had to keep moving her different foods apart, making sure they didn't touch.

Jade hadn't had the opportunity to be around kids for a long time—college, then grad school, and now SiPraTech. She relished their giggles and high-pitched voices and inability to stay seated at a table for more than a few minutes at a time.

She pointed the car toward the city park next to the public swimming pool at the west end of town, where surely some teenagers would be hanging out or people walking their dogs.

Jade turned in to the park, driving past the playground, with teeter-totters, swings, a merry-go-round. No kids, no dog-walkers. She was disappointed. Of course, it was after seven o'clock on a school night. But Jade had driven through here a half dozen times at varying times of day, and it was always deserted.

She drove slowly toward the municipal swimming pool, stopped in the empty parking lot, and killed the engine. Tinny radio music—"Wide Open Spaces" by the Dixie Chicks—echoed over the cracked asphalt.

"What are we doing?" Olivia said.

"Just want to take a look," Jade said, and exited the car.

"At what?" Olivia said, following her.

Jade kept an eye out for a white Japanese crossover, but no one was around. They walked to the white-painted cinder block locker room entrance, where a hand-written sign hung. CLOSED, which seemed weirdly ironic in contrast with the song.

They strolled around to the pool itself, enclosed behind a chain-link fence, and gazed out over the deep blue of the water. Jade hooked her fingers into the chain links. "When I was a teen-ager during wheat harvest, we wouldn't finish cutting wheat until late at night, and it would be hot and dusty, and we'd be desperate to cool off. So a lot of times we'd hop the fence at my hometown pool and go skinny-dipping. Good times."

"Just girls?" Olivia said. "Or guys and girls?"

"Guys and girls," Jade said. "But when you're that overheated and worn-out and covered in wheat dust, sex is the last thing on your mind."

"On yours, maybe," Olivia said. "But I guarantee you it wasn't the last thing on those boys' minds."

That pool didn't close until nine p.m. from the first of May through the end of September.

Jade checked her phone. It was eight-fifteen, and the sun's light still lingered just beyond the horizon.

"You want to hop the fence after it gets dark?" Jade said. "Go swimming?"

"We've got a pool back at the Compound," Olivia said.

"What's the fun of that?"

"I see your point. But I think to really make it fun we need to include the guys."

Jade's face got hot, thinking about skinny-dipping with Berko and Elias. "Never mind," she said.

"What?" Olivia said, all innocence. "Don't tell me you haven't thought about one or both of them in that way."

Jade had, in fact. Both of them. You couldn't help it, being in such close proximity, with hormones flying through the air. With reasonable certainty, however, she figured neither of them had given her a second thought, especially Elias, since they talked to each other like guys.

"I overheard this girl at Carnegie Mellon once tell someone I wasn't the type of girl guys go for. I'm too big and loud and not that attractive."

Olivia whirled on her. "Bullshit. You're a beauty. You're an Amazon princess warrior."

Jade flashed on the fact that she wished Olivia had been there to say exactly those things to that nasty girl from Philadelphia.

They got back in the car and drove the residential streets, by house after house, with neat, manicured lawns, trimmed hedge-rows, tall elms, sycamores, and oaks surrounding them, shading them from the relentless late-summer heat.

Jade liked driving these streets, imagining what it would be like to have one of these houses to herself instead of living on the SiPraTech grounds. But she paid no rent to live in the brand-new Compound house with all the latest comforts and amenities.

Jade drove down a street that led to a sprawling one-story building with its own playground. She parked at the curb.

"Now what are we doing?" Olivia said. "More nostalgia?"

"Just want to take a look," Jade said.

"Come on," Olivia said, impatient. "Let's go home."

"I'll be right back," Jade said.

She walked toward the school, remembering her enduring excitement about the first day of school every year. The elementary school building would be clean and shiny, new collages up on the bulletin boards, cardboard cutouts of apples and pencils and stacks of books.

When she got to a window, she peered into one of the classrooms. It was empty. Not just empty of people, but of signs of people. No stick-figure drawings, tempera paintings, lumpy clay ashtrays.

No desks. No chairs. This classroom must not be in use. She moved on to the next one.

Same thing. No bulletin boards. No artwork. No chairs. No desks.

In each room, it was the same. No signs this building had been used in years.

Miranda must have been swept into a consolidated school district as it and other nearby farm towns shrunk.

She walked back to the car, thinking, her buzzing alarm going off again, and she combed the environs for a glimpse of the baseball-capped stranger who'd grabbed her. But there was no one.

Jade got back in the Volt. "The school's empty," she said as she started it up and drove.

"Dude," Olivia said, "It's nighttime. Of course no one's there."

"No," Jade said. "It's empty. It's not being used."

"Oh," Olivia said. "That's weird."

"I know," Jade said. "The kids must be bused to another town to go to school. Except that . . ."

"Except that what?"

"I've never seen a school bus in town."

Olivia looked back out the windshield. "Have you been in town when buses would be running?"

Jade thought. "Guess not," she said. But still, it bothered her. Something tickled the edge of her brain, but she couldn't grab hold of it. *Buzz buzz buzz buzz buzz buzz . . .*

She thought of the families in the restaurant, and she realized that both vehicles out front had out-of-county plates. The families didn't live in Miranda.

Jade remembered the people she'd seen in town today, the women at the dry cleaners, the men at the gas station, and realized something strange. They were all the same age—between twenty and thirty.

In the grocery store. Women were food shopping, but no kids with them. No babies or toddlers. No children.

That was it. What was weird about this pristine, adorable little Kansas town.

She'd never seen a baby, child, or teenager.

There were no children.

No children anywhere.

Chapter 8

THIS STUNNING SUDDEN realization narrowed her vision for a moment as her blood pressure rose. She was conscious of every move she made, worried she'd blurt out her nonsensical thoughts.

This couldn't be true. It just couldn't. As it usually did, her brain went into list-making mode. Possible reasons for a town without children.

But she couldn't let her mind go there. She couldn't. It was science fiction stuff.

Jade remembered the stacks of diapers in the grocery store, next to the Depends and sank to another level of unreality: she realized she'd never seen an elderly person in town either, which was even weirder. These little farm towns always were top-heavy with elderly populations, because the young people tended to move away to where the jobs were.

Jade needed a drink. And come to think of it, that was a great idea. If she could impel Olivia to have a couple of cocktails, what Jade had to say might not sound quite so crazy.

"Hey," she said as she pointed the car toward downtown again. "Why don't we go to the bar and get a beer?"

Olivia's lips curled. "I don't think it's exactly my type of establishment."

"It's got booze," Jade said. "That's your type of establishment, right? And anyway, these little dives are the best kinds of bars. Really. You ought to try it."

"Let's just go home and drink there," Olivia said, cajoling.

But Jade didn't want to talk about this in front of Elias and Berko. She felt weird enough about it already. "After the day I've had," she said, "the feeding tube news, and the assault, I'd like to sit in the bar and have a couple of drinks."

"Oh, honey," Olivia said, putting her hand on Jade's arm. "I'm sorry. Sure. We can go have a couple of drinks. No worries."

Jade felt only slightly guilty for pulling the mom card. Because she needed to sort this out. She had to know if she was losing her mind.

They'd talked many times about dropping by the town beer hall, but Jade realized each time, Olivia had talked her out of it. Now as they got out of the car, Olivia looped her arm through Jade's solicitously, and Jade expected that once they'd consumed some booze, she could make her observation sound less demented.

Jade and Olivia entered the dim coolness of the tiny tavern. Olivia wrinkled her nose looking around, and Jade stifled a laugh. Some of Jade's high school friends had been desperate to shed their small-town roots and begin a life of genteel urban living. But not Jade. She yearned for small-town life. She felt at home here, and she'd come to grips with the fact she always would.

Hank Williams yodeled on the jukebox and a couple of guys

played pool against the back wall at one of the two pool tables. A lone man sat at the bar on a stool. A TV mounted high up behind the bar played the Royals game.

"What can I get you?" the bartender asked as they slid onto barstools, a few down from the seated man. The bartender was a clean-shaven, short-haired mountain with dark brown eyes, over six feet with impressive biceps stretching the sleeves of his plain white T-shirt.

"Bud Light," Jade said.

"You got any Stella?" Olivia said.

The bartender stared at her and then opened the cooler. "We've got—Bud Light, Bud, Michelob, Coors, Coors Light, Miller, Miller Lite."

Olivia wrinkled her nose again. "Give me a Michelob," she said, but she wasn't happy about it.

The bartender pulled two bottles out of the cooler and opened them before setting them on the bar.

"Could we get some napkins?" Olivia said.

"Oh," he said. "Right." He pulled two square Budweiser napkins out of a holder, set them down, and replaced the beer bottles on top of them.

Jade spun on her barstool, and the other patron side-eyed her before sliding off his stool and relocating to a table.

"Didn't mean to chase you away," Jade said, hoping to strike up a conversation.

He waved and took a drink of his beer, fixing his eyes on the television.

Jade turned back toward the bartender and waited for him to ring them up, but he didn't. He just stared at the TV.

Jade glanced at Olivia. "How much?" she said to the bartender.

"How much what?" he said. "Oh. You mean—sorry. That's—that'll be . . ."

Jade glanced up at the chalkboard behind the taps and said, "Nine bucks, right? Four for the Bud and five for the Michelob?"

He followed her gaze and turned back to her. "Right."

She pulled a ten out of her pocket and slid it toward him. He looked as if he didn't know what to do with it and finally wandered over to the cash register, which he stared at for a minute before punching some buttons.

He reminded Jade of the clerk in the grocery today. Did *anyone* know how to run a cash register in this town?

"I've bartended before," Jade said. "You want me to do that for you?"

"I don't usually work here," the guy said. "I'm filling in for a friend."

Again, déjà vu from the grocery. First day on the job, filling in for a friend . . .

Jade turned. Both pool players and the guy they'd chased off were watching her and Olivia.

"Filling in for a friend," Jade said. "Right. You want me to ring us up for you?"

"I don't know," Olivia said. "What if you're accused of robbing the register or something?"

Jade turned back to the bartender who scowled at Olivia.

"You won't do that, will you?" Jade said to the bartender. She hopped off her barstool and went around the counter, where she rang up their beers, put the ten in the drawer and pulled out a one, and handed it to the bartender. "There you go," she said.

He stared at the one in his hand.

"That's a tip," Jade said.

Jade sat back down and Olivia leaned toward her and muttered, "Here's a tip for him—get another line of work."

Jade laughed and took a long swallow of her Bud Light. Just what the doctor ordered on a hot, weird night.

"What's your name?" Jade said.

"Don't bother the poor guy," Olivia said.

"I'm just asking his name," Jade said. She smiled at him.

He didn't smile back. "Steve," he said.

"What do you normally do, Steve?" Jade said.

"I'm a—farmer," he said.

"You got someone else planting your wheat, or you done already?"

"Yeah," he said, turning back to the TV.

Jade cocked an eyebrow at Olivia who shrugged at her.

"Not the talkative type, I guess," Olivia said. "Cute though."

Through the closed door, Jade heard a car rumble by outside, no muffler, "Achilles Last Stand" by Led Zeppelin blasting at ear-splitting levels. Then both sounds abruptly ceased, and the bartender focused on the door as if awaiting a battering ram. Jade laughed.

The door banged open and in walked three visibly intoxicated farmer types, in wheat-dusty jeans and boots, bringing in the scent of whiskey and man sweat with them.

"Hey!" one of them shouted, a blond with a matching mustache, his arms outstretched as if he were entering a surprise party just for him. He looked all around, ceiling to floor. "Will you look at this place! What the hell!"

The other two bellied up to the bar, both with dark hair, one with a beard and the other with a Jack Daniel's cap.

Steve the bartender regarded them skeptically.

"Hey," the blond shouted to Steve as he ambled around the room, squinting at the shiny new beer advertisements on the walls. "When did you all open back up?"

Steve inexplicably flicked a glance at Jade and Olivia. "What are you talking about?"

"This place was, like, boarded up. The whole freakin' town was, practically, like just nine months ago."

The guy turned to his friends, his elbows behind him on the bar. "Hey, back me up here," he shouted.

"Are you going to order something?" Steve said, with an odd warning note in his voice. But Jade couldn't help feeling excited. These were her people, and she hadn't seen many of them in a while. All the cares of the day faded to the background for the moment.

The blond took his place next to his friends at the bar and leaned around them, eyeing Jade and Olivia. "Hello, ladies!" He turned to Steve and said, "We'd like to buy these two a couple of beers." He leaned again and raised his eyebrows at them.

Jade laughed and then got a look at Olivia's face, which advertised her obvious distaste. What was her problem? The guy reminded Jade of her best friend from high school, Kenyon. He was a goofball too, but a great linebacker. She held up her beer bottle in his direction and said, "Hey. How you guys doing tonight?"

Olivia leaned into her line of vision, giving her a "what the hell are you doing" look, as if Jade were teasing a pack of dogs suffering from distemper. Olivia didn't understand that these guys were harmless. They were good ol' boys. Nothing to be alarmed about, but like so many girls of her generation, she'd been taught to fear guys who were just wanting to chat, to believe that unless the guy approached with a notarized negotiation about appropriate actions, he was a creepy, dangerous dude. It made her sad, but also cemented her belief that she didn't belong anywhere but here.

The blond guy's friends turned from the TV to look at her and nodded then turned back to the TV. Olivia watched it all without expression.

"Fine, fine," said the blond, winking at Jade. "Bartender! Three Buds and two of whatever they're having." He pointed theatrically at Jade and Olivia.

"No thanks," Olivia said, and Jade turned to give her a look of consternation.

"Since when do you turn down free drinks?" she said.

Olivia's expression turned frightened, which irritated Jade, then she immediately felt regretful. Olivia couldn't help it if she felt threatened, even if she had no reason to.

"I'll drink hers," Jade said. She turned back to Olivia and said quietly, "These guys are harmless. Trust me. I've been around guys like this my whole life. They're not going to drag you out into the alley by the Dumpster and assault you. They just want to have a little fun."

"I can just imagine what their idea of fun is."

Jade labored to suppress her impatience.

"We need to be getting back anyway." She gave Jade a meaningful look.

Jade now leaned toward the blond and whispered, "My friend is a little nervous. She thinks you guys might be dangerous. But I know you're all gentlemen, aren't you?"

"Of course," the blond said. "I'm Rodney, and this is Dave, and that's Fireball."

"Fireball?" Jade said, and Rodney and Dave collapsed against each other laughing. Obviously, there was a story there.

"Shut up," Fireball said, his red face getting redder and scowling.

"We need to go," Olivia said to Jade, her voice almost pleading.

Jade leaned toward her and said, "These guys are innocuous."

"I'm not used to being harassed by drunk hillbillies, I guess," Olivia said.

"Do you see any hills around here? I realize these guys aren't exactly Rhodes scholars, but that doesn't mean they're out to take advantage."

"You don't know that."

"Yes," Jade said. "I do. Like I said, I've been around guys like this my whole life."

Olivia remained freaked out and unconvinced. Jade couldn't help but feel not only disappointed but suddenly judged to be a small-town inbred rube as well as an innocent who had to be protected from imaginary threats.

Olivia's expression was inscrutable. "I'm sorry," she whispered. "Drunk guys are kind of a trigger thing for me."

Jade hated that word with every fiber of her being. But she wanted to respect her friend's fears and anxieties. "I'm sorry. But if you feel uncomfortable, why don't you just go on back to the house, and I'll hitch a ride with one of these nice gentlemen or the bartender."

Alarmed, Olivia said, "Like hell. Have you already forgotten what happened today? A guy tried to kidnap you!"

"But that guy was older, and he wasn't a townie, I'm sure of that."

This gave Jade pause. He was the oldest man she'd ever seen in town, probably in his forties. He unmistakably wasn't from Miranda. But no one in this town seemed like they were from Kansas at all—except the three guys who'd just entered the bar.

"I'm not leaving you here alone," Olivia said, "the only woman in a bar surrounded by horny drunks. Just one more beer, okay? And then we leave?"

Jade was still ruminating. "Okay," she said.

Then Olivia did this amazing one-eighty. She waved at the guys as Steve the "bartender" opened two more beers for them. "Hi," she said. "I'm Olivia, and this is Jade."

Rodney lifted his Coors bottle off the bar and walked over to them, and they both swiveled their stools to face him. "Ladies," he said, and kissed each of their hands, Olivia's first, then Jade's. His mustache tickled. As he looked up from Jade's hand, a wave of recognition swept over his face. "Hey," he said, letting go of her and pointing at her. "I know you. Where do I know you from?"

"Where'd you grow up?" Jade asked, taking a drink.

"Medicine Lodge. How about you?"

"Ephesus."

"Well, God dog," he said, the dawn breaking. "You're that girl kicker, aren't you? Holy shit. Hey, you guys, this is that girl kicker from Ephesus!"

They leaned back on their stools to scrutinize her face and nodded.

"I knew that was you! Holy smokes!" Rodney said, taking a drink. "What are you doing here?"

"Well—"

"Of course, what is *anyone* doing *here*, huh?" He studied the barroom as he had when he first arrived.

Did he mean it in an existential sense, or . . .

"Right," she said. "You planting?"

"Yup," he said. "Just got done. That's why we're celebrating." He leaned toward his friends and said, "Right?" And the three of them whooped in unison.

Then Rodney turned his attention to Olivia. "What happened to your hair, gal?" he said.

"Nuclear accident," Olivia said.

He looked at her as if trying to decide whether she was kidding or not. "No, really," he said. "Were you trying to dye it blond or something?"

Olivia laughed and sipped at her beer. "It was intentional," she said. "I dyed it blue on purpose."

"Where are you from?"

"New York," she said.

"No, I mean where are your people from?"

Oh, crap. Jade tensed.

"Eastern Europe," Olivia said.

Fireball grabbed Rodney by the arm. "Let's shoot some stick," he said.

"Girls want to play?" Rodney said.

"You go on ahead," Jade said, in deference to Olivia. "We'll wait here."

"I'll be back," he said, and followed his two friends to the empty pool table in the back. Jade heard the *clunk-whish* of the balls dropping and rolling.

Now that the farm boys were occupied, Jade thought she was ready to bring up the child situation. She cleared her throat. "Hey, Olivia, I wanted to talk to you about—"

Rodney reappeared at Jade's side and said to the bartender, "How about a round of Jack Black shots?"

"You know what?" Steve said. "I think you all've had enough."

Jade stared at him. Yes, the guys were tipsy, but they weren't can't-serve-you-any-more drunk.

"What happened here?" Rodney said. "Used to be you could get any kind of liquor at this place before everything closed and—"

"Sir, I'm going to have to ask you and your friends to leave."

"What the hell, man?" Rodney said, getting red in the face.

Quick as a flash, one of the guys from the other pool table rushed up and shoved Rodney's face into the bar, twisting his left arm up behind his back, forcing a squeal of pain from him.

"Hey," Jade yelled. "What are you doing?" Her eyes drifted downward and she saw the pool player had a holstered pistol on his hip.

"Rodney," she said, in as calm a voice as she could manage, "you and your buddies need to go. All right? This man has a gun. Do you understand me?"

"This is none of your concern, miss," the player said.

"Jade," Olivia said in a small voice. "Just mind your own—"

"I'm trying to help," Jade said. "Dave. Fireball. Get Rodney out of here. Now."

They dashed forward, and Jade saw what was about to happen in slow motion in her mind's eye. "Stop!" she shouted, and stood between them and the gun-carrying pool player. Everyone froze, the pool player's hand inches from his piece.

"They're leaving now," Jade said. "Aren't you?"

No one said anything, the only sound panicked breathing.

"Right? You're taking off. Everything's cool. Okay?" She slowly put her hand on the pool player's arm and he turned and eyed her. His arm relaxed, and he let Rodney up and backed away.

Dave and Fireball each took one of Rodney's now-bruised arms and led him out of the bar.

The pool player went back to his table, and everyone else stood staring, until Olivia, her terrified face flushed and damp, stepped forward and slapped Jade's arm. "What the hell were you doing? You could have been killed!"

Jade turned toward the pool player, who lined up a shot back at the table as if nothing had happened. No sweat, no panting, cool as a cucumber. He didn't look at her. She turned back to the bar, where Steve the bartender stood looking up at the television.

The car with no muffler started up out in the street, music blaring again, the engine being revved over the red line, the engine screaming, and then the tires burning rubber out of there.

"I think we'd better go," Jade said to Olivia, who followed her out the door.

She looked up and down the deserted dark street.

Olivia got into the Volt's driver's seat while Jade climbed into the passenger side and stared out the windshield.

What was with this town?

Why did it seem less like reality and more like a reality show?

Chapter 9

THEY SAT IN the Volt in front of the bar, and Olivia kept turning to look at Jade, as if she had something to say but wasn't sure she should. Then she said, "Jade, we have a responsibility here. The project is largely in your hands. You realize that, right? Putting yourself into a dangerous situation like you did tonight, you could have gotten hurt. Even killed. And if something happened to you, then what does that mean for the project and all of us?"

Conflicting emotions warred inside Jade. She did have a responsibility to her coworkers. But she could also take care of herself. She didn't believe the guy with the gun would have shot her. She felt scolded and manipulated simultaneously, because Olivia knew she carried a lot of people's burdens for them, and now she was loading up a few more—the team. The project. Their futures. All up to her.

"Listen," Jade said. "The situation needed to be defused. I did that. I saved that hayseed Rodney's life. And do not throw my family in my face again. I know what my responsibilities are."

Olivia didn't react to this, just started the Volt, backed out into the empty street, and drove toward the county road. Jade stared out the window at nothing, drained. She didn't want to talk about the peculiarities of the town anymore.

This had been, without a doubt, the weirdest day of her life.

Until the road next to the car got brighter.

Jade looked back at a vehicle coming up fast behind them. Olivia's eyes darted back and forth from the rearview mirror.

"Guy came out of nowhere," Olivia said, her eyes on the rearview. "Must be doing seventy at least."

"Maybe slow down and let him go on by," Jade said.

Olivia eased her foot off the gas and the other car slowed down too. Olivia sped up again, and the other car followed suit.

"What are you doing?" Jade said. "Just let him go around us."

"I tried, but he—"

"Pull over, Olivia," Jade said.

Olivia pulled over, rolled down her window, warm air whooshing into the car, and stuck her arm out, signaling for the guy to go around. But the car kept pace with them until Olivia stopped altogether, continuing to motion with her hand for him to pass them.

The car behind them stopped too.

Jade glanced behind them again. A figure stepped out of the driver's side.

Her mouth wouldn't work, as if she had ALS and couldn't speak, as in a dream. But she finally shouted, "Go! He got out of the car! Go!"

"But maybe—" And then Olivia's eyes got wide. "It's them," she said. "Isn't it? It's those guys from the bar."

"It's not them," Jade said. "Just go!"

Olivia floored the accelerator, spinning the wheels on the dirt road, and lurched forward.

Jade kept looking back as the car started up and gained on them again.

"Oh shit, oh shit, oh shit," Olivia said, eyes tracking back and forth from the rearview to the road.

Then Jade felt the impact, the car's front bumper striking their back bumper.

"Fucking environmentally friendly hemp burner!" Olivia said, pounding the steering wheel. "Go faster, you piece of shit!"

The speedometer showed they were going seventy miles an hour, and still the car behind them kept ramming.

The dashboard light illuminated Olivia's frightened face. "What do I do?"

"I don't know!" Jade shouted.

About a mile ahead, she could see the lights of the Compound.

"Can we get in there before he—"

Jade didn't finish her sentence before the car behind them gave one final mighty push. As if the steering wheel had been ripped from Olivia's hands, it started spinning of its own accord. She lost control of the Volt in the gravel and slid sideways toward the shoulder. Everything slowed down as the world outside Jade's window spun crazily and her own head followed its trajectory, wrenching her neck as the Volt tipped and then slammed over sideways, all the loose items inside flying through the air. Jade's head smacked into her window and then jerked backward as the Volt came to a stop on the passenger door.

Jade's ears rang but she could hear dust settling and the engine clicking. Olivia hung above her, held in place by her seat belt and the middle console.

"Are you okay?" Jade asked her.

"I hit my head," Olivia said, her voice hollow and strained. "There's blood coming from somewhere."

"Let me get out of my seat belt and then I'll get you free. Just hold on."

Jade unbuckled her seat belt and knelt on her door. She reached up and tried to undo Olivia's seat belt.

Through the broken glass of Olivia's window, Jade heard running feet. The Volt began to shake and then rock. The man was trying to right the car, to bring it back to its wheels. But one man alone couldn't do that. Which meant there was more than one of them.

Once the car was upright, what were they going to do?

"Do you have that pepper spray you talked about?" Jade asked Olivia.

"I don't know where it is," Olivia said, her voice rising in hysteria.

Jade heard talking outside the Volt.

"Jade Veverka," a man's voice said.

Olivia looked frantically at Jade.

"Who is that?" Olivia said.

"I don't know."

The Volt rocked and Jade realized they would be successful in righting it, so she scrambled into her seat and hung on until the car came over straight and Olivia undid her seat belt.

"What are we going to do?"

"Jade," the voice said again, coming from a dark figure who

stood at Olivia's door. "Get out of the car. You're coming with us, right now, and—"

And then Jade heard *pop-pop-pop* nearby.

Gunshots.

Jade folded in half as Olivia fumbled for her hand and squeezed it until Jade yelped and Olivia let go.

Scuffling feet, flesh hitting flesh, grunts, shouts, but no actual words Jade could make out.

A body falling to the ground.

Jade put her hands over her ears. Someone was getting the shit kicked out of them.

Now the body was being dragged away.

Jade made out the shouted words, "Shut up!"

In all the confusion that followed, huddled against Olivia in the front seat, Jade couldn't see what was happening, but it appeared several men were standing across from each other shouting and brandishing weapons.

"Oh my God," Olivia said. "What is going on?"

Finally Olivia's door opened and a flashlight beam shone in their faces.

"Come out of there," a voice said.

"No," Olivia said, shielding her eyes. "Who are you? What do you want?"

"Jade, Olivia," another man's voice shouted. "You can come out now. We got them."

But Jade couldn't make herself move, and neither, it seemed, could Olivia.

Jade's door opened, and she cowered as another flashlight beam illuminated the inside of the Volt.

They were still bent over, heads nearly touching their knees. With her face right next to Jade's, Olivia shrieked, "No!" so loud Jade was temporarily deafened in her left ear.

"It's all right, ladies," the voice said. "We got them. It's okay."

A man in camo with a rifle crouched down next to her open door.

"Who the hell are you?" Olivia yelled.

"We're the good guys. You can—"

"What do you want?" Jade said, shielding her eyes.

"Sit up," the man said. "It's okay. We got them."

"Who?" Olivia demanded. "Who did you get? What happened?"

Jade heard a siren in the distance. The rifleman's head turned toward the sound. "You are not to talk to county law enforcement," he said.

"According to who?" Olivia demanded. "By whose authority?"

"Is the car drivable?"

"We're not moving or doing anything else until you answer my questions," Olivia said.

"Then I will shoot you," the man said.

Jade believed him.

"Start the car and drive it to the Compound. Now."

Olivia obeyed, and the other men got out of the way and let Olivia drive past more men in fatigues, and one farmer. Or a man who looked like a farmer.

Jade's head thrummed. She had a sudden urge to tell Olivia to keep driving, to stay away from the Compound.

Don't talk to county law enforcement?

Who were these people?

Chapter 10

Jade couldn't seem to catch her breath as Olivia pulled the Volt into the garage. A metallic clanging under the hood sounded like the engine had a busted fan. They got out of the car and Jade nearly fell over, dizzy and disoriented.

Her thoughts were jumbled, bouncing around like tennis shoes in a dryer, her brain unable to retain anything for very long.

Jade and Olivia held on to each other, as much to stay vertical as for comfort.

A Humvee parked in front of the house, and two men in fatigues carrying rifles got out of it. "Come with us," one of them said.

Jade and Olivia obeyed silently, arms still around each other, and followed the soldiers to the fitness center. Jade glanced over her shoulder and happened to see Elias peering out one of the house windows and beckoning frantically to her. She looked ahead to the fitness center's entrance, where Martin and Greta stood, their arms crossed, then back at Elias, who seemed to be mouthing something she couldn't make out. She shook her head at him.

Martin opened the door, his face strained, his lips in a thin line, and Greta looked nonplussed as well. Jade's stomach bottomed out. Disapproval. They were not happy. Why? Because they wrecked one of the Volts? Or was something else going on?

As they approached, Martin snapped, "Come inside." They followed meekly behind him and Greta. Now Jade's head really began to throb with pain and fear.

Martin and Greta led them into the clinic, which Jade hadn't even known existed, where bright fluorescent lights shone, and a male nurse in scrubs asked them to take a seat.

Olivia said, "You're bleeding," and touched Jade's face. Her fingers came away with clotted blood and small glass shards. Jade was only now aware of the stinging pain on her forehead. But this didn't interest her as much as the fact that soldiers with guns had herded them into their place of employment.

"Mr. Felix," Jade said.

"We'll talk after you're patched up," Martin said in a clipped voice.

"You can't keep me here!" a man's hoarse voice croaked outside the clinic. Then he made an *oof!* sound as someone must have jabbed him in the gut.

A door off the hall outside opened, feet shuffled inside it, and the door closed again.

Jade glanced at Olivia, who looked as scared as Jade felt.

They each sat on a cot, and the nurse examined them. Pupillary response, blood pressure, temperature, pulse, oxygen uptake.

"Who is that across the hall?" Jade asked.

"I don't know." The nurse removed the pulse oximeter from

Jade's finger, then closely examined her forehead. "You're going to need a few stitches." He opened an alcohol swab and cleaned up the cuts, the stinging pain making her eyes water. He gave her a shot of Novocain and then stitched her up.

"What's going on?" Jade said.

"I don't know," the nurse said.

"What *do* you know?" Olivia snapped from the other cot.

"I'm just the medic," he answered, then turned back to Jade. "Do you feel sore anywhere?" Jade moved her shoulders and elbows, rolled her neck, which was indeed sore. The nurse palpated her joints, her neck, and vertebrae. He did the same to Olivia and then said, "I don't think either of you broke any bones, but I want you to come back tomorrow morning in case we need to x-ray you. We'll see if there are any residual problems. Martin wants you to meet him over at the office building."

Outside the fitness center door stood another man in fatigues Jade had never seen before, who silently led them to the office building. Jade had a sudden urge to run.

But she wouldn't get far, not with all these men with guns around.

"What is going on?" Jade whispered to Olivia. "Who are all these people? Is this a military takeover or what?" She wanted to look at her phone and search for any world news she should know about, but of course now that she was on campus, the Internet was blocked so she wouldn't be able to find out anything anyway.

They got into the elevator and went up to the third floor conference room. Berko sat there looking bewildered and trying to appear brave. Elias, on the other hand, was on red alert.

Martin stood at the head of the table and Greta sat at his right looking grim.

"Have a seat," Martin said.

They did and waited for him to speak.

"Are you two all right?"

Olivia and Jade traded looks, and Jade touched the bandage on her forehead. She didn't trust her voice, didn't trust she wouldn't burst into noisy, wet sobs, so she just nodded.

"Yeah," Olivia said. "A little banged up. What are all these soldier-types—"

Martin held up a hand. "What exactly did you two do in town?" He crossed his arms.

Jade wondered if she should explain about the grocery store near-abduction, since she wondered if one of the guys in the vehicle that drove them off the road was her would-be kidnapper.

But Olivia spoke up first.

"We went to the bar in town," Olivia said. "There was a problem with some locals. But I really don't think—"

Martin waved his hand, effectively cutting her off. He turned to Jade. "Did you see anyone you knew there?"

She didn't think Rodney counted, but she wanted to give all the information she had. "A guy there recognized me."

"Did you *know* him?" Martin nearly barked out.

Greta leaned forward, as if this would somehow compel Jade to spill whatever beans they thought she had.

There was none of Martin's usual bumbling about tonight. His movements were as precise and controlled as they normally were clumsy and goofy. And it occurred to Jade then that the awkward act may have been just that—an act.

But why?

"No," she said, taken aback, nervously rubbing her tattoo. "But he knew who I was."

Martin paced, Greta watching him, and it seemed to Jade that he was trying to decide how much to tell them.

Jade, Olivia, and Berko all traded mystified glances. But Elias stared straight ahead. *He* knew something, all right.

Martin zeroed in on Jade again. "Did you . . . tell anyone what we're working on here?"

"Me?" Jade said, stunned.

"You didn't tell, say, your autistic sister because you didn't think she could understand what we're doing, did you?"

Jade sat straighter, this peculiar allegation raising her hackles. "No, sir. And she could understand it. *If* I told her. Which I didn't. And I don't appreciate your insinuation."

Berko looked toward a clearly seething Elias then back at Martin.

"Are you accusing her of corporate espionage?" Berko said. "Is that what we're talking about here? Because—"

"No, it's much more serious than that. Much more serious."

From the corner of her eye, she saw Elias give a tiny nod. As if to say, *You're damn right it's more serious.*

"Will you quit being so cagey and tell us what you're talking about?" Olivia burst out. "What the hell is going on here?"

"If one of you violated the NDA," Martin said. "The consequences will be severe. Do you understand?"

Olivia opened her mouth to say something but Jade placed a silencing hand on hers.

"Here's what's going to happen," Martin said. "You will all stay on campus for the remainder of the project. No one will leave here until our work is complete."

Everyone started talking at once. But Elias gave a shrill whistle and silenced every voice.

"Are you going to tell us why?" Elias said, enunciating every syllable.

"We can have no more slips," Martin said.

"You can't keep us here," Olivia said.

"It's in your employment contract, and if you'd actually read it, any of you, you'd know that. In case of emergency, you can be sequestered on the Compound grounds."

"And that's all you're going to tell us," Elias said.

"That's all I *can* tell you," Martin said. "According to what you've all told me, it shouldn't be much longer anyway. And then you can leave whenever you like." He smiled around at them. "Everything you need is here, so it's not so bad, is it?" He departed the room, and Greta followed him.

Why had she even been in the room? She'd never attended any of the meetings in the office building before. And she'd added nothing to the interrogation.

Everyone stared around in disbelief. Except Elias, who drummed his fingers on the table. And then he left the conference room.

"What is up with Elias?" Olivia said.

Elias returned and sat in his chair. "Martin's gone down to his office," he said. "I watched the elevator stop on the first floor."

"Okay," Berko said. "So . . ."

"Yeah, I'm not going to beat around the bush like old Martin there. I'm going to tell you exactly what I found after dinner. Berko wanted to read, so I was on my own, and I decided to go to the lab."

"And?" Olivia said.

"This is going to sound crazy."

Olivia and Jade glanced at each other and then at Berko, but his eyes were fixed on Elias's pale face.

"I found some hidden directories on the servers."

They all looked at each other again.

"How'd you do that?" Olivia said, skeptical.

"I scanned the system for vulnerabilities with a utility I designed when I was an undergrad. You know, for fun."

"For fun," Berko said. "That's what you do for fun."

Elias ignored him. "I found a vulnerability and ran a fuzzer to find hidden files. The fun of breaching a vulnerability is just knowing you can do it."

Jade understood. It was just a smarter-than-thou exercise, harmless if the person doing it didn't have nefarious motives. She trusted Elias.

Didn't she?

But why would he be looking for vulnerabilities now? He'd been here for twelve weeks.

"So you were spying on SiPraTech?" Berko said.

"Not spying. Snooping. It's harmless."

Berko's expression said he didn't think it was so harmless. But he listened, his mouth set in a rigid line.

Elias took a deep breath and said, "This isn't just some random tech company we're working for."

"No shit," Berko said. "I kind of picked up on that after the militia descended."

"Who are we working for, then?" Jade said, not sure she wanted to hear the answer.

Elias looked around at everyone.

"The National Security Agency."

Chapter 11

JADE FELT ALL the air rush out of the room.

"That would explain why they won't let us leave," Olivia said.

"And all the military people out there," Berko said, giving what sounded like an involuntary gulp.

"And how they can get away with holding us virtual prisoners here," Olivia said.

"Ain't nothing virtual about it," Berko said.

"I didn't sign up to work for the federal government," Olivia said. "If the military's involved, then they're going to militarize Clementine. It's like we're in a bastardized version of *Ender's Game*."

"Why though?" Jade said. "What would they use it for?"

"To infiltrate terror cells, maybe?" Berko said.

"And why build this campus in the middle of Kansas and pretend to be something they're not?" Jade said.

"We have to confront Martin," Elias said. "Tell him we know what's going on. Demand all the details." He grinned. "And demand more money."

Shocked, Jade said, "Demand more money? I don't want more money. I just want to go home. We could have been killed tonight."

"Don't you get it?" Elias said. "That's why they offered us so much money. Because they aren't going to let us leave. Someone ran you off the road, someone who clearly knows something about what's going on inside this Compound, and they're trying to stop it. Which means there are more of them out there, they know who we are and they're not going to stop coming after us. All of us."

"But—"

"Our own government has put us in grave danger. They've lied to us about what we're doing. And by God they're going to pay."

"But how do we know this is actually the NSA?" Berko said. "Just because you found some files?"

"That's why we're going to get Martin up here," Elias said. "He's going to tell us exactly what's going on."

"What if he doesn't admit to it?" Olivia said.

"I'll show him the files, that's all," Elias said.

They did need to confront Martin. And also to find out why he believed Jade had breached the NDA.

Elias pulled out his phone and dialed. "Martin? We're still all up here in the conference room. Yup. We'd like you to come back because we have a couple of questions for you. No, I think you'll want to do it right away. It could be a matter of national security."

He clicked off.

"That'll get him up here faster than shit through a goose."

Olivia laughed nervously.

"Hey, man," Berko said, looking at his friend with respect. "Thanks for telling us alone instead of springing it on us in front of him."

"I knew I had to consult you all first," Elias said. "Come to a consensus regarding course of action. We're a team, you know."

Berko slapped him on the back and shook his hand.

Martin entered the room, a wary expression on his face, the words *national security* probably still ringing in his ears. "What is it? It's late, and I have work to do."

"We know," Elias said. "But we've taken a vote, and we've decided you need to tell us who we're really working for."

Martin scanned the room. "I don't have time for this."

Olivia stood. "Look. Either we get some answers, like, now, or we're all walking."

"You'll be in violation of the NDA," Martin said.

"I don't give a shit," Olivia said. She pointed. "There are men with guns crawling all over this place. We are clearly in danger. Good God, I never thought I'd have to say this sort of movie dialogue in real life, but there it is."

Elias also rose, as did Berko, and then Jade, even though she was shaky on her feet.

"We're going to leave, and Jade will take her program with her," Elias said.

They hadn't discussed that portion of the threat, but it made sense to Jade. With a bravery and conviction Jade didn't feel, she headed toward the door. "I'm going down to the lab right now and pulling Clementine off the system," she said.

Two armed soldiers appeared in the doorway, blocking her way. She turned and Martin said, "Clementine belongs to us now, Jade."

"Who the hell is 'us'?" Jade said.

"Martin," Elias said. "We know who we're working for. Just say it."

Martin stood gaping at them, speechless.

"All right then," Elias said. "I'll say it for you. The NSA."

Martin's expression didn't change, but his Adam's apple bobbed as he swallowed.

"So why don't you tell us what we're really working on."

Martin appeared to be thinking this over.

"Why did you lie to us?" Berko said.

"Like Elias said, it's a matter of national security," Martin said. He sighed. "Here's the situation. We are expecting—reliable intelligence indicates that . . . China is set to attack us."

Jade gasped and put a hand over her mouth.

"Reliable intelligence," Olivia mocked.

Ignoring her, Elias said, "A nuclear attack?"

"Cyber," Martin said. "They plan to bring down our electrical grid."

"That's not even possible," Olivia said, uncertainty creeping into her voice.

Martin addressed Olivia directly. "The Chinese have been working on an AI program similar to Clementine. The program is very good at overcoming obstacles and will be uploaded to the federal government's servers, and from there it will filter down into the infrastructure."

"I'm very suspicious of that sort of language—they're 'going to,'" Olivia said. "If they are going to, why haven't they already?"

"That's a good question," Martin said. "For one very specific reason. September eleventh."

Jade traded glances with her teammates. What did that have to do with anything?

"They're going to attack on September eleventh—"

"Wait," Berko said. "This September eleventh? Three days from now?"

Martin nodded. "They know if it happens then, regardless

of *how* it happens, the Arab world will be blamed. Once all our systems fail, we'll be helpless, vulnerable, in chaos. The Chinese will step in and say to the federal government, oh, you're having trouble with your power grid? We can help. We have this great program that will allow all the stations to operate separately while still remaining connected, just like the systems of the body, so this will never happen again. We'll have everything up and running within three days. We'll even bring in some military to help you restore law and order. Just one little stipulation, they'll say. It's going to be expensive, transporting personnel, helping straighten out your food and water supplies, shipping, et cetera. And you already owe us a lot of money. So we'd like to cash those loans in for land and tangible assets to offset our costs. And we'd like to help you with your political system, which is a mess."

"So you're saying we have *three days* to finish," Berko said.

Jade started to shake. This had to be a joke. This was not happening.

"You're sure it's China," Elias said.

"Yes. Our intelligence says they've been preparing for quite some time. The special agents who discovered the plan had been embedded for four years there and . . . didn't make it out of the country."

Jade's breath came faster.

"For the last six months, we've been tracking power grid outages around the country, and the number has nearly tripled from twenty-five per week to seventy. Consistently."

Berko scoffed. "Of course power grid outages are going to increase because of aging infrastructure, weather, population growth. How do you know the Chinese are responsible?"

"Patterns have emerged," Martin said. "I can show you the

documentation, if you like. There's also been an unprecedented number of simultaneous multistate outages."

Jade remembered seeing something about this on the news before she came to SiPraTech, but the Chinese were never mentioned, of course.

But Olivia put her hands on her hips, skeptical.

"The time is right," Martin went on. "The country is divided. The political system is in chaos. Our national debt is crushing. Our current president has alienated our allies and angered our enemies. We're so dependent on technology that the country will be crippled by the loss, even for a few weeks, of electricity. It's the perfect way to hold the country hostage."

"It's sort of like ransomware on a massive scale," Berko said. "It's brilliant."

Martin shot him a scorching look.

"So what do you think we can do about it?" Jade said, her voice cracking.

"Maybe we should let them do it," Berko said. "Maybe they can do a better job governing us than we can."

Elias gaped at him, horrified. "You can't be serious. You think communism is the way to go?"

"No," Berko said quietly. "But you have to admit they've got a point. This country's a mess."

"The best mess on earth," Elias said.

Martin raised his voice. "Save the political debates for later. If the Clementine Program can do what you say it can—reroute the connections in the power grid, reconnect everything that becomes disconnected and do it continuously—then we can prevent the lights from going out. And if the program isn't able to do what you've said it can, you'll have to *make* it work."

Berko consulted his watch. "Three days. We have so many more tests to run. I don't see how—"

"Solve the problem," Martin said. "Make it happen."

Jade searched the faces of her teammates as the weight of what lay before them bore down on her consciousness. From their expressions, she gathered they were feeling the pressure too.

"So I can count on you all to stay put, yes? Until we're done?"

Jade waited for Elias to ask for more money, but looking at his face, she knew it wasn't going to happen. The seriousness of the situation had wiped his mind clean of any such demands.

But something still bothered Jade. "I'll say yes to that as soon as you tell me why you're so convinced I violated the NDA," she said.

"That's the primary reason we need you to stay in the Compound," Martin said. "There are people out there who've learned about the project, and they want to stop it. I just don't know how they found out. The only connection to them is you. Olivia told me about the man in the grocery store."

"Yeah," Jade said. "But I don't know the guy."

"Think, Jade," Martin said. "Who is he?"

"I told you," Jade said. "I don't know him."

He continued staring at her, and she suddenly felt guilty, as if she had spilled about Clementine to the man she didn't know, and just didn't realize she had.

"I don't know him," she whispered.

"Well, he knows you," Olivia said. "He said your name."

Martin straightened on hearing this news.

The room seemed to shrink with all eyes on Jade.

Martin got close to her, again staring her down. "Think, Jade. Who is that man?"

"I don't know," Jade said.

"Who have you been in contact with?"

"No one!"

Martin looked around at everyone, then back at Jade. "I'm not sure we can trust you're telling the truth."

Jade gasped. "Of course I am! Why would I—"

"Maybe this group got to you before you ever arrived on the Compound," Martin said.

"Got to" her? Hot, sharp panic set her skin on fire. She looked at Elias, who gazed at her suspiciously. But he was with her at the grocery store! Did he think she'd cooked the whole thing up with the baseball-cap man?

"Where did you go on your drive this afternoon?" Martin said. "Was it to meet him?"

"Martin, I was with her," Olivia said.

Martin kept his eyes on Jade, ignoring Olivia. "Where did you go this afternoon?"

Olivia kept her eyes on Jade, who knew she wouldn't tell. Jade needed to admit where they'd gone to clear this whole thing up.

"Olivia and I went to Ephesus to visit my family."

Martin threw his hands in the air. "I thought I made it clear you were not to go beyond Miranda?" He surveyed the group. "Didn't I make that clear?"

Jade stood and slapped her hands down on the tabletop and shouted, "I don't give a shit about what you made clear, Martin. My mother is *dying.*"

That shut everyone up. And then, of course, Jade was crying, snot and tears running down her face, but she didn't care.

Her mother was dying.

Berko walked over to her, pulled her to him, and held her while she cried.

Martin continued in a softer voice. "They must have been watching your parents' house, and you led them straight here."

Olivia grabbed a box of tissues off the sideboard, pulled a few out, and handed them to Jade.

"You okay?" Berko asked her as she dabbed her face and blew her nose. He didn't let go of her until she answered him.

"I'm all right," she said. She hugged him gratefully then sat back in her chair. He squeezed her arm.

"Well, why in the hell did you set up the project here?" Elias said. "If you knew there was a group—"

"They're not just here in Kansas," Martin said. "They're everywhere."

That sounded paranoid and ridiculous, although having just been hit by an SUV made it seem less so.

"But why don't you just tell them about the upcoming attack?" Berko said. "I'll bet they wouldn't be so excited to stop the project if they knew."

"They do know."

This fell on Jade's head like a rock. "They want the Chinese to take over? Seriously?"

"It's not that they want the Chinese to take over," Martin said. "They don't want the US government to have access to this kind of technology. They're afraid the NSA would abuse it, use it to spy on the population, put a stranglehold on the Internet or worse."

"Sounds reasonable to me," Berko said.

Population. Something about that word. Miranda, population 800. Homogeneous population . . .

Jade covered her mouth with her hand. "That's why there aren't any children or elderly in town," she said through her fingers. "The town is populated with soldiers. By the NSA. That's why you didn't want us going anywhere but the Compound and Miranda. That's why the town was boarded up just nine months ago. It was a dead town, and the government bought it. Right?"

"Yes," Martin said. "The soldiers are there to protect you and this computer system. But we believed you to be a rule-follower, Jade. We didn't expect you to sneak away."

"I didn't sneak," she said, her voice rising again. "I just didn't tell you. And if you'd given me the whole story at the beginning, I wouldn't have gone home."

"If they'd told us why they really recruited us," Olivia said, "none of us except sailor boy over there would have willingly come here at all."

"Hey," Elias said, straightening.

"Am I wrong?" Olivia said.

Berko shook his head, and Jade had to wonder if she would have agreed to work on the project had she known. She didn't think so. It was too big. Too heavy.

"The point is," Martin said, "we could have quietly completed this project and subverted the cyber-attack if it hadn't been for your little road trip, Jade."

He was right. This was her fault. They'd been found because of her. And now they couldn't leave because of her. And the Chinese might take over. Because of her.

"And that's why we need you to stay on the campus," Martin said. "No more going into town."

"But you just said the whole town is militia. Isn't it their job to protect us?"

"Do you really want to take that chance?" Elias said. "They couldn't protect Jade and Olivia on the road back to the Compound."

"It's a precaution," Martin said. "Otherwise, we'll have to line the road with soldiers, and that will attract attention, one way or another. We can only protect you if you stay here until the project is completed."

But what if Jade couldn't control the program? If she couldn't control it, steer it somehow, she needed her fail-safe, the cartridge that could neutralize the core of the program. She called it her AIP cartridge.

But it wasn't here.

It was in Ephesus, because it didn't occur to her that she'd need it. She'd thought they were working on a theoretical scenario, not real life. Plus, if the anti-AI people were out there, watching her parents' house, neither she nor anyone else could retrieve it.

"Why aren't you working with real live adults?" Olivia said.

"Because in your midtwenties, your brains are more elastic. You're more likely to think outside the box."

"Bullshit," Olivia said. "You chose us because you can ruin all our careers before they even start."

"Yes," Martin admitted. "You have much to gain. And much to lose."

Clearly insulted by this, Berko said, "And if we refuse to help?"

"Then the Chinese shut us down," Martin said, letting his arms drop to his sides. "Simple as that."

"We're not going to refuse," Elias said. "We have no choice here. Because we want this country to go on, however screwed up it may be, it's better than the alternative. You know that, right, Berko?"

"Is it?" Berko asked. "Does anyone believe the UN would allow the Chinese to do whatever they want once they 'restore' our power? That's not how the world works. You know that, right?"

"Do we really want to take that risk?" Elias said. "Once they establish a significant foothold in our infrastructure, where does it end?"

Berko made no answer, just stared at his hands folded on the table in front of him.

"What are you going to do with the guy who ran us off the road?" Jade asked.

"We're going to interrogate him," Martin said. "And then we're going to turn him over to the FBI."

"Oh, I'm sure you are," Olivia said. "Two of your militia pals told us *not* to talk to law enforcement."

"Right. *County* law enforcement," Martin said. "They're not aware we—the NSA—are here. They would be more of a hindrance than a help. All right? Now let's all get some sleep."

"Like anyone's going to sleep tonight," Olivia muttered.

Martin rose from the table, stretched, and left the room.

They sat silently, sneaking peeks at each other, the silence pregnant with questions.

Jade imagined she would wake up from this nightmare, that this couldn't be happening. She wanted to talk to Dan. She wanted to talk to her mom.

She wanted to go home.

But if they didn't get this right, there might be no more home to go to.

Chapter 12

September 8

JADE FINALLY FELL asleep around four after flopping around in her bed for hours. She'd forgotten to turn off her alarm, which woke her up at six forty-five. She got out of bed and went to the bathroom. The sight of the bandage on her forehead in the mirror seemed to remind the wound to throb. So it would be a dry-shampoo day. After a careful shower, she got dressed and went outside, the heat already crouched and waiting to spring at the edges of the sunrise.

She walked around the Compound, now spotting at least three armed soldiers scattered around the fence's perimeter. The sight gave her a chill. She tried to ignore them and just listen to the early-morning birds and gaze through the chain-link fence to the wheat fields and prairies beyond. She wanted to go home.

Jade heard the front door of the house open and close, and she turned to see Olivia jogging toward her, her face grim.

"Hey," Jade said.

"I don't know about you," Olivia said in a quiet voice, "but I did not sleep last night. I kept thinking about how we were . . . fooled into working for the federal government. I kept thinking how I am fundamentally against all the sketchy things the NSA has done, and how I would never work for them voluntarily. This is all wrong."

"Yeah," Jade said. "But what can we do?"

"What can we do? We have all the power here. We have what they want. Or you do. And anyway, how do we even know this is for real?"

Jade hadn't even considered that.

"I want to talk to someone outside of this Compound, outside of SiPraTech, or the NSA, or whoever we're actually dealing with. I want confirmation this is real and not some weird scheme some crackpots have cooked up."

"I don't think 'crackpots' typically have the deep pockets to pull off something this elaborate."

"Whatever. The point is, they can't keep us here against our will. They can't *force* us to work for the government. There are laws."

This hadn't occurred to Jade, probably because her upbringing taught her that if you were told to do something, you did it. You didn't question authority. But this was a good time to break away from that mind-set.

"I need to get my head on straight," Olivia said. "Do you want to go over to the fitness center and do that yoga DVD? It might help us feel better."

They went back to the house, changed into workout gear, and walked over to the fitness center. After the hour-long yoga practice, Jade did feel better, but she still needed to burn off some nervous energy, so she got on the elliptical machine for another forty-five minutes while Olivia lifted weights.

"Let's see if the guys are up, we need to be together on this," Olivia said.

"Right," Jade said, and they walked back to the house.

Berko and Elias were unloading the refrigerator and freezer into a cooler, both of them looking haggard and exhausted.

"What are you doing?" Olivia said.

"Refrigerator's out," Elias said. "Don't know if we can save any of this, but—"

"It needs a new coil or something," Berko said.

"They've sent one of the maintenance guys to the big city of Great Bend, so they'll replace it as soon as he gets back."

"When you're done with that," Jade said, "we need to talk to you." She and Olivia sat at the table.

Elias closed up the cooler. "What's up?" He and Berko sat at the table.

Olivia gave them the same spiel she'd given Jade. They looked apprehensively at each other.

"So you want proof we're working for the NSA?" Elias said. "I told you about the hidden files I found."

"I know," Olivia said. "But how do we know those are authentic? How do we know any of that stuff about the Chinese is true and not just some—"

"Let's talk to Martin and politely ask for confirmation," Jade said. "Information about China's AI tech, or maybe—I don't know, some satellite spy photos or something."

"Even if this is really happening, I'm not sure I want to stay anyway," Olivia said. "They don't need me—I'm just the med research person. It appears the brain research part of the project was a sham. I truly do not know why I'm here."

"They don't *need* any of us but Jade," Berko said, concentrating on the bowl of cereal in front of him. "I'm not crazy about the idea of working for the NSA either. Not gonna lie."

"They have Clementine—that's all they want anyway," Olivia said. "But really, Jade, it's not theirs. It's yours. And if you don't want the NSA to have it, then you can just pull it off the system like you said last night."

"But if the Chinese really are planning to shut down the power grid, then I need to give the program to the NSA to help stop them. I'd rather do that than be their prisoner here."

Everyone looked at Elias, who hadn't said a word. He stroked his chin. "I agree," he said. "We didn't volunteer for this. I *would* have, if they'd told us the truth from the beginning. Happily. But we need to meet with Martin and tell him we're handing over Clementine, and then we're leaving after they give us everything they promised. Because we were lured here under false pretenses."

"But what if they don't give us what they promised?" Berko said. "I need that money."

"So do I," Jade confessed. "But regardless. We have no business being here."

Olivia walked over to the wall, picked up the house phone, and dialed. "Hello, Martin—we'd like to meet with you in the conference room at—" Here she checked the clock. "—noon. Yes, we're all busy, but it won't take more than a few minutes. All right. See you then."

She hung up. "We're all set."

At five 'til noon, the four of them trooped into the conference room and took seats around the large table, fidgeting and waiting. The clock said lunchtime, but Jade had no appetite.

Finally, Martin came striding in, his face tight, his jaw clenched. "All right," he said. "What is it now?"

They'd elected Olivia to speak for the group. "Here's the deal, Martin. None of us signed up to work for the government. We accepted employment in a privately owned company. We feel very strongly that we were duped into working on a project. We'd like to hand over the Clementine Program to you, and we would like to receive payment, and we would like to leave as soon as possible."

"I'm happy to train a replacement on the program," Jade said. "I'm confident another computer scientist would have no problem—"

"I thought we'd worked all this out last night," Martin said, impatient. "You know what's at stake."

"We've had time to think about it since then," Elias said, "and we realize we're not comfortable with the situation. You crossed a line of ethics by lying about who you are."

"You should know this better than anyone, Elias," Martin said. "In times of war, sacrifices must be made." He smiled around at them all. "Honestly, you think you *volunteered* for this?"

The silence in the room echoed inside Jade's head. What was he saying?

"No," Martin said. "You've been drafted. You've been selected to do the most important job the NSA has ever undertaken. You're not volunteers."

"But by definition," Berko said, "sacrifice is voluntary. What you're talking about is indentured servitude."

"You can't keep us here," Olivia said. "You can't keep us against our will. That's against the law. That's kidnapping."

"Remember you're being compensated—debt paid off, cash prize, prestigious positions, all that. But you're required to finish the project, and you're required to stay here."

"This is ridiculous," Olivia said. "This is illegal search and seizure. This is unlawful imprisonment."

Martin stood silent, his arms crossed.

"Let's put everything out in the open," he said. "I'm sure you're aware it's standard procedure to run security clearances on NSA employees. In the course of those clearances, we naturally run across certain intel."

Intel? What did he mean?

The puzzled expressions on her teammates' faces mirrored Jade's own bewilderment.

Olivia said, "All right, but I don't see what that has to do with—"

"Let me be clear," Martin said. "If you want to leave, you give up certain privileges. Such as the privilege of keeping your personal business private. Your *family's* personal business. Do you understand what I'm saying to you?"

"You and I must have a different definition of 'clear,'" Olivia said. "Because what you just said is what I'd call cryptic. And those are *rights*, not privileges, guaranteed by the US Constitution."

"If you leave—and you're right, we can't keep you here, but if you leave, information will be released. That's all I'll say. Information will be released." Then he smiled around at everyone, and Jade had never been so chilled by a grin before. "Now, I want you all to take the rest of the day off, because for the next three days, there will be very little rest. So make the most of it."

And he left the room.

Elias held his hands out. "What information will be released?"

Berko said, "Is he talking about blackmail?"

"This is ridiculous," Jade said. "The US government doesn't blackmail people to get them to work for them."

"Sure they do," Olivia said. "They can justify just about anything with a compelling enough national security interest. And this is about the most compelling reason I've ever heard of." She pressed a finger to her lips, then said, "Elias, did you see any personnel files in that hidden directory you found?"

"I didn't go through everything—there's a buttload of stuff in there."

"Why don't we go see if we can figure out what he's talking about."

They took the elevator down to the lab. There was none of Jade's and Elias's usual jostling to see who could get their keycard out first. Berko opened the door and they went inside.

"The script is on this," Elias said, sitting at his desk and opening a drawer. He tossed a flash drive to Jade.

Jade plugged it into a USB port on her CPU.

"Just log in normally and then click on the file marked FUZZ," Elias said over his shoulder. "As soon as it's done running, you can eject it and give it to the other two."

"Got it," Jade said.

The hidden drive came up on Jade's monitor, a long directory with abbreviated labels. She ejected the flash drive. "Olivia," she said, and tossed it to her as soon as she turned around.

"Thanks," she said and plugged it in.

Jade scrolled down through the list of files until she came to one labeled PRSL. Personnel? Personal?

"Berko," Olivia said.

"Thanks," he said.

Jade clicked on *PRSL* and a photo of a middle-aged couple appeared. *CONFIDENTIAL*, it said.

"Found it," she called out, her competitive streak activated by finding it first. "It's the one called *PRSL*."

A chorus of *Thanks* rang out and then the clicking of computer keys.

David Harman, b. 1960, ethics professor, NYU, retired. Allison Harman, b. 1962, French Department Chair, NYU.

Jade scrolled down and found medical histories for Olivia's parents. She didn't read through it but scrolled down.

Olivia Harman. Convicted of disturbing the peace at Baltimore gay rights protest. Questioned and released, never charged, on suspicion of prescription medication theft from her employer, Greater Baltimore Medical Center.

Never charged. But the NSA knew about it anyway.

Jade gasped, her hand over her mouth.

"What is it?" Olivia said.

"Stop," Jade called out. "Stop. Don't open it. Don't read it."

But then she herself couldn't stop reading.

Alicia Renee Deloatch, b. 1969, employed by American Rental Car, Atlanta, GA.

Four live births, two miscarriages. Type II diabetes, diagnosed 2010. Deep vein thrombosis, diagnosis 2012.

Jade felt as if she was peeking into someone's bathroom window, reading this. She scrolled down.

Berko Deloatch, b. 1993, student.

Acute appendicitis, 2000. Appendectomy, no complications. Chronic migraines, diagnosed 2005.

Jade scrolled down.

Juvenile conviction, sexual assault, female cousin, age nine. Record expunged, court files sealed, 2004.

Stunned into paralysis, Jade stared at the phrase *sexual assault*. She couldn't look away from it.

She heard from behind her a loud gasp. She swiveled around and saw Berko, his face slack and his hands noticeably shaking, his eyes wide behind his horn-rim glasses.

"I can explain," he said, his face drawn, seeming thinner.

"Berko," Jade said.

"You have to listen," he said, his voice pleading. "We went swimming."

"What's he talking about?" Elias said, but went silent as he read, and then frantically scrolled down.

"No," he whispered.

Olivia turned around, her hands over her mouth. She looked at Berko, horrified. And then at Elias the same way.

Jade couldn't stop herself. She turned back to her monitor as Berko babbled behind her.

"I was helping her go to the bathroom," he said.

"No," Elias said again.

"Later her mom accused me of fondling her, which I *did not* do," Berko said, his voice cracking and frantic. "My record was expunged, which is why I'm completely baffled as to how it got in here—how they . . . found this information. My aunt and my mom always had a contentious relationship. Since they were little, my aunt tried to get Mom in trouble. This time she succeeded."

Nausea clogged Jade's gut. She wanted to scrub her eyes with steel wool. She didn't want to know any of these things, not about sweet, studious Berko. And then Jade couldn't help herself. She read Elias's record.

Juan Diego Palomo-Gutierrez, b. 1967, Mexico City, d. 1996, Reno, NV. City councilman.

Elias Juan Diego Palomo, b. 1990, ensign, United States Navy.

Hit-and-run accident, county road, New Mexico, 2007. Car repaired, no accident report filed. Driver of other vehicle killed.

She turned slowly and Elias sat with his back to the keyboard, his legs splayed and head back, hands on either side of his face.

Olivia stared at him, openmouthed.

"You *killed* someone?"

"It was an accident," Elias said. "I was visiting my uncle in New Mexico. I was helping him on this ranch he was working on. We'd been working our asses off and I was driving down a country road, and I was so tired. And I fell asleep. The next thing I know my uncle's pulling me out of the driver's seat and shoving me in the passenger side, and then he guns it and we tear ass out of there. Tio had weed in the car, and he panicked. He told me I had to keep it a secret. If I was arrested for careless driving, I couldn't go to the Academy, and if I didn't go to the Academy, I wouldn't be able to support my mom and my brothers and sisters. I was a kid. I was scared. It wasn't until a week later that I found out the other driver died."

He covered his face with his hands, leaned forward, and began sobbing.

This was so awful. Everything was stripped away. They were all exposed.

Well, three of them were.

Jade turned back to her monitor and scrolled down, her skin covered with hot, painful prickles.

Pauline Marie Brazier Veverka, b. 1968. Arteriolateral sclerosis, diagnosis 2016.

Prescription: Prozac. 350 mg. January 1999-present. Prescribed due to severe postpartum depression after first delivery. Taken through second pregnancy.

Possible causal link to second child's autism.

Chapter 13

BERKO CONTINUED TALKING behind her, but she couldn't understand any of the words.

Was it true? Her mother had never mentioned she'd taken antidepressants during her pregnancy with Clementine. She remembered Pauline telling her, "I couldn't stop crying. I couldn't do anything but take care of you. You know how a lot of moms want to harm their children when they've got postpartum? I was the opposite. I couldn't let go of you. Couldn't put you down. Couldn't be away from you. But that meant I didn't shower or cook or even talk to your dad."

No wonder her mom felt so guilty about Clementine. No wonder she'd fought so hard to secure her treatment and benefits.

But then, like a low-simmering pot of water, her rage at Robert and Pauline for depending on her to figure out how to communicate with Clementine came to a full rolling boil. Because she believed deep down she would indeed be stuck with Clem forever. She'd never let this thought creep into her conscious mind before, and now that it had broken through it brought another, uglier thought with it. The wish that Clementine would be killed in some accident. The wish that Clementine had never been born.

Jade squeezed her head between her hands, her eyes clamped shut, willing these thoughts back into the attic. But they refused to get out of the living room. They were here now to stay, with their feet up on the coffee table. And Jade herself was pure evil. Pure. Evil. Clementine couldn't help what she was. It wasn't her fault. It was Pauline's.

It was Jade's for causing the postpartum depression that compelled Pauline to take the meds during her second pregnancy.

She started to cry.

This was the selfishness Jade never knew existed in her mother. She'd been willing to risk Clementine's health and welfare for her own comfort and well-being.

Maybe that wasn't fair. Jade had never experienced depression, but she wondered if it was a real thing, or just self-indulgence? Was it a bid for attention? Jade didn't know. But she'd never doubted her mother like this before, and she didn't like it.

Why did the NSA have this information? Had Mom's doctors provided it, or had the NSA gained access to her medical records?

This meant they knew everything about everyone.

No one should know this much about people, no one but God.

Scrolling down.

And there it was.

Jade Veverka. Twelve payments to essaymills.com during attendance at Carnegie Mellon University.

Shame choked her. She'd been stretched so thin in undergrad, needing to maintain an A average and work part-time jobs, so she'd cheated. If this information got out, CMU would most likely take her degree away.

If her parents found this out, they'd never look at her the same way again.

But didn't everyone cut corners in college? Fudge the facts? Do whatever it took to get their degree?

She had devolved into an excuse-making phony. But at least her transgression paled next to Elias's and Berko's.

This thought stopped her cold. Who the hell did she think she was? A privileged white girl whose biggest problem was an autistic sister and the desperate desire to be better and smarter than everyone else. It was pathetic. Jade turned back around, and her friends were in varying states of panic and despair.

"So it looks like . . . we're staying," Jade said, the eye of the storm, calm, or maybe in shock.

"You had to push it, didn't you?" Berko said to Olivia, his eyes red. "You had to ask why we had to stay. Why didn't we just finish the project like we promised? And now you all know . . ."

Olivia's face was devoid of color, but she turned on Berko and snapped, "This is not my fault."

"You have to believe me," Berko said, looking around at everyone.

"We do, Berko," Jade said. "It was a misunderstanding. And Elias, what happened to you could have happened to . . . anyone. Seriously." She didn't know what to say to Olivia, who turned her eyes toward Jade.

"If this comes out," Elias said, "my life is over. I'll lose *everything*."

"Everyone will be ruined," Olivia said. "Except Miss Whitebread Goody Two-shoes Homecoming Queen Jade."

Jade gasped at this.

Why was Olivia pissed at *her*? She didn't do anything.

"My BS could be rescinded," Jade said, defensive.

"Bitch, please," Olivia said. "The only bad thing you've ever done in your life you did just to make yourself look good."

"You're such a reverse snob," Jade said, anger rising. "Getting arrested for protesting did the exact same thing for you. You're a radical, getting arrested to fight for someone's rights. I'll bet you begged the cops to cuff you."

"You and your small-town myopia," Olivia said, "can go straight to hell."

"I may be small-town," Jade said, "but as far as myopia goes, you can't seem to see past whatever the trendiest cause is. What is it this month? Keystone species? Alternative energy?"

How quickly they'd all turned on each other. Having their secrets revealed had turned them all into rats.

"I'm going to call Dan," she said quietly. She picked up the landline phone and pressed the receiver to her ear. It was silent.

"My phone's dead," she said.

Everyone picked up their receivers. They did exactly as Jade had, listening, looking, listening again.

All chairs turned slowly toward the center and the four of them contemplated each other, Jade's own feelings again reflected on her coworkers' faces.

This wasn't an outage or an interruption of service. This was a deliberate attempt to keep the team from outside contact.

"Let's go back to the house," Berko said. "Let's try the phone there."

But Jade assumed the landline in the house was as dead as the ones in here.

They all walked out and got on the elevator. A tense, brittle, electric silence descended as they avoided each other's eyes while the elevator car rose. It was the longest ride of Jade's life.

Outside, the sky had darkened and a thunderstorm threatened, but it would likely push off to the south. Lightning flashed on the horizon.

They trotted toward the house and went inside. Jade strode into the kitchen and was startled by a man she'd never seen before in workman's coveralls facing the back of the pulled-out refrigerator.

"Oh," she said, her hand to her throat.

He turned around, his hand going to his hip, and for a split second Jade thought he was going to pull a gun on her. But he reached toward the kitchen island, on which his tool belt rested. He twisted a dial on a walkie-talkie strapped to the belt then turned back to her. "Sorry," he said. "Didn't mean to scare you. I'll be out of your hair in a minute."

"It's fine," she said, catching sight of the keycard on a lanyard around his neck, which read *Connor Lemaire*. "Thanks for taking care of this, Connor."

"Sure," he said, startled she'd used his name. "I'm almost done."

She turned and as casually as she could, picked up the wall phone. It was dead. She didn't want him to know they suspected the phones were cut off on purpose, so she said, "Oh, hey, the phone's out. Can you fix that too?"

Without turning around, he said, "I'll let them know in the main office."

Jade walked out of the kitchen and said, "Guy's here fixing the fridge. He'll be done in a jiff."

All four of them gathered in a knot in the living room. "No phone here either, huh?" Elias murmured and Jade shook her head. "I'll go upstairs and grab my satellite phone. We'll wait until he leaves to use it."

Jade brightened, grateful they had a military man on their team. Elias mounted the stairs and Jade made eye contact with Olivia, which made despair germinate inside her. Jade wished she could take back what she said to Olivia, about begging the cops to cuff her. She wished she could grab it and stuff it back in her mouth, gag herself with it. She also wished she hadn't gotten a glimpse of what Olivia really thought of her.

A heavy scraping noise issued from the kitchen, and Jade figured Connor was putting the refrigerator back in its proper place.

Jade heard rumblings upstairs. She heard clunks and bangs. The noises came louder and more frequently, followed by "Shit!"

The maintenance man appeared in the doorway, wiping his hands on a towel. "All done," he said. "You can put your food back in there."

"Thanks," Jade said, hoping Elias wouldn't say anything more from upstairs as more bangs and clunks sounded on the second floor.

Connor exited out the front door, and Jade walked into the kitchen as Berko shouted up the stairs, "What's the problem?"

Jade heard Elias come charging out of his room above her head. "It's not here," he said. "It's gone."

In the kitchen, Connor's tool belt was still curled on the island. Jade picked it up and headed for the front door. "Be right back," she said.

Outside, Jade ran down the front walk and searched the greenbelt, but she couldn't see the maintenance man. She walked back toward the house and decided to leave the tool belt on the front porch in case Connor realized he didn't have it. She had the urge to go through pockets on the belt but decided against it. This guy was a lackey, a tool like them. She dropped the belt on the porch and went back inside. She opened the front windows so she could hear if he came back. She didn't want him lurking around outside eavesdropping.

When she turned around, Elias stood at the top of the stairs. "They fucking took it," he said.

"The phone?" she said.

As the words came out of her mouth, she had the feeling her ears were plugged, and she moved her jaw. Every sound in the house seemed to be on a millisecond delay, as if she were hearing everything twice.

"Is there a radio on somewhere?" she said.

Olivia ran toward the stairs and took them two at a time. "Come on," she called over her shoulder. "Let's help him look."

Ookookook

"It's not here," Elias said. "I told you."

Ououou

What the hell?

"Do you hear that?" Jade said.

"I'm going to help you look," Olivia said in a tone that didn't invite discussion. She disappeared into his room, and Berko followed.

The noise Jade heard seemed to be echoing in from the open windows. She looked out at nothing, then went to the front door and went outside. She closed the door behind her, but she could still hear the other three talking, as if they were right next to her.

Elias's voice: "They took my phone because they're not going to let us call out."

Berko: "Shit just got real."

Jade glanced down at her feet and there lay the tool belt, and the walkie-talkie, which had landed facedown. She lifted it and her friends' voices came clearer.

Olivia: "Oh, yeah? It wasn't real enough to see all your secrets puked up all over everybody?"

Jade twisted the dial on the receiver, and the voices got louder, first through the windows then a microsecond later from the walkie-talkie.

Her insides seemed to melt and drain toward her feet, making her legs weak. There were microphones in the house. There were probably cameras. She had to shut everyone up and let them know what she'd discovered without actually saying it. How was she going to do that?

Jade twisted the dial on the walkie-talkie, set the tool belt down, and paced in front of the house.

She didn't know Morse code, and even if she did, she had no idea if any of the others did. They needed to communicate in code. Jade ran through various ideas in her head—pig Latin, semaphore, windtalking.

And then she remembered the paper she'd written on atypical communication represented in popular culture, and her premier example had come from the ultimate nerd resource—*Star Trek: The Next Generation*. The 102nd episode of the series was often regarded as its creative peak, in which Captain Picard finds himself unable to communicate with an alien race until he comes to understand they communicate by citing examples of their mythology. The episode was called "Darmok."

She and the others could communicate through their own

mythology—that of popular nerd culture. She had to hope whoever was watching and listening wasn't a supernerd. Jade reen-
tered the house.

"Hey, guys," she called up the stairs. "Come down here."

Olivia appeared at the top of the stairs, her posture impatient.
"What is it?"

Jade willed Olivia to come down, staring hard at her, her lips
pressed together.

Her brow furrowed with curiosity, Olivia looked over her
shoulder then back at Jade. "Hey, guys, Jade needs us downstairs."

Her tone of voice did the trick, because both men appeared at
the top of the stairs, and Jade gestured them down.

"I'm sure you just misplaced the phone," she said emphatically.

Berko and Elias glanced at each other, suspicious, but they followed Olivia down the stairs. Jade indicated the sofa and chairs
with her hand then sat in one.

Though confused, everyone went along with it.

Jade cleared her throat, gave each of them a meaningful stare,
and said, "Darmok and Jalad at Tanagra."

Berko's confused expression morphed into a wide grin and he
nodded excitedly at her, sitting in the chair opposite.

Olivia sat at one end of the couch, Elias next to her, and crossed
her legs. "What in the hell are you—"

But Elias touched her arm, and said, "Picard and Dathon at El-
Adrel. Mirab, his sails unfurled."

Olivia's mouth dropped open, and she said, "Darmok." She
smiled, her eyes glittering.

Jade said, "We should watch a movie. Have you guys ever seen
THX 1138?" She hoped this wasn't too obscure a reference. It was

possible none of the others was this deep a film nerd. But she hoped the fact it was the student film of George Lucas, the father of *Star Wars,* would ring some bells.

"I've seen it," Berko said, concentrating hard on Jade's face. "But I don't think it's in the library." He flicked his eyes toward the other two, who stared in confusion.

"Yeah," Jade said. "Remember SEN fifty-two forty-one and LUH thirty-four seventeen?"

Those were the names of two characters who were in charge of surveillance in the film's dystopian future world.

Elias and Olivia traded glances, and Elias shrugged.

Berko said, "If they ever made a movie of this situation, Elias, what actor would play you? I'm thinking Will Smith would play me, and Gene Hackman could be you. What do you think?"

Jade hoped they'd recognize the reference to the electronic surveillance movie *Enemy of the State.* From their identical expressions of understanding she saw they did.

"Maybe we could watch *Lord of the Rings* again," Olivia said. "Although I'll have to leave the room whenever the Eye of Sauron comes on screen. So creepy."

They got it.

It appeared Elias was trying to inconspicuously scrutinize the ceiling.

This dawning realization made everyone go still. Of course they were being monitored. That's what the NSA did.

The four of them sat in silence, trying to work out what to do in their own minds. They needed to get in touch with Dan, and the only way to do that was to escape the Compound. How could she relate this to the team though?

"We could rewatch *Firefly,*" she said, "watch Captain Tightpants lead the Browncoats. If the Browncoats can track him down, of course."

Elias laughed at this nod to Joss Whedon and the one-season series about a group of independent soldiers fighting against the corrupt Alliance.

"But . . ." Berko said. "What would happen if Captain Tightpants turns out to be Cypher?"

Cypher was, of course, the traitor in *The Matrix*.

Jade's face flamed.

Elias made a *psh* noise and said, "More like Giles the Watcher, right?"

Jade laughed at the *Buffy the Vampire Slayer* reference, and realized Dan was indeed her Watcher.

"And anyway," Olivia said, "it's straight up Leia and Obi-Wan."

The *Star Wars* line dropped into Jade's head. "Help me, Obi-Wan Kenobi. You're my only hope."

Their only hope, their only choice, was to reach out to Dan. Everyone knew it.

"How about some *Shawshank* action?" Elias said.

The other three looked at each other.

"Well, you know what I always say," Jade said. "Get busy living, or get busy dying."

That was of course a line from *The Shawshank Redemption*, a movie about a prison escape by tunneling through a wall.

"We don't have twenty years," Olivia said.

"Not to mention," Berko said. "It could be *Burn After Reading*."

Yes, it could. The NSA could indeed release the information they'd gathered on each of them.

"Right, Berko," Olivia said. "But Captain Tightpants definitely knows *All the President's Men*."

Berko's expression brightened. Dan had contacts in every area, including the media. They could release their own story before the NSA could release theirs. He smiled at Jade.

Jade thought. She had to reference a movie where the escape happened by going over a wall, i.e., the ten-foot chain-link fence that surrounded the Compound.

"He also knows Rocky the Rhode Island Red."

This was a reference to the stop-motion animation film *Chicken Run*, in which the chickens escape a factory farm by catapulting themselves over the wall.

Olivia nodded, but the other two didn't understand.

"All right, we could watch *Game of Thrones*, then," Jade said. "And now their watch begins."

Everyone nodded, but their faces all said, how and when are we going to do this?

"Who wants to play Dominion?" Berko suddenly said.

Elias smacked the heel of his hand against his temple, shook his head, and fluttered his eyelids as if this were an outlandish suggestion. But he rose and retrieved the board game from a cabinet in the corner of the living room and everyone gathered around the dining room table.

They were being too quiet, acting suspiciously, so Jade needed to talk about anything, try to draw them all in. When they'd first met, one way they bonded was giving "best-of" and "first" lists.

"Best superhero movie," she said. "Top three. *Mystery Men. Iron Man. The Incredibles.*"

Berko went through the cards and pulled the ones he wanted, then laid stacks of ten in front of each of point of the compass.

"*Mystery Men* is not a true superhero movie," Elias said. "*The Dark Knight. The Avengers. X-Men: Days of Future Past.*"

Berko took three moat cards end to end in the center of the table. He placed a militia card in front of Elias. He laid a witch card in front of Olivia, an adventurer in front of Jade, and a bureaucrat card before himself.

Olivia wrinkled her nose at Elias then studied the cards on the table. "Yes, *Dark Knight*. No *X-Men* at all. *Deadpool*. And . . . *Guardians of the Galaxy*."

"No," Jade said. "No outer space movies."

"You didn't specify," Berko said.

"Okay," Olivia said. "Fine. *Spider-Man 2*."

"Yuck," Jade said, and pulled three random cards from the deck by Berko. Then she tapped the top of her left wrist and laid the cards facedown, two vertical, one at an angle at two o'clock to indicate the time she figured they should attempt their escape.

Elias nodded, pressing two fingers to his temple, looking to Jade for confirmation, and she nodded back, glancing at the other two, who also nodded. Elias swept up the three cards and put them back on the deck. "*Batman v Superman: Dawn of Justice*," he said. "*Avengers. Iron Man*."

"Copycat," Jade said. "And *Dawn of Justice* sucked."

Elias shrugged.

Olivia gathered up the four cards in front of each of them and lined them up on one side of the three moat cards.

"First video game you ever played," Berko said, even though they'd done this one weeks ago. But Jade appreciated his attempt to keep the conversation going. "Mine was *Lego Lord of the Rings*. The best part was the battle at Mordor's gates. That's where I excelled."

Jade knew this not to be true, since that game came out in 2013. But she also knew the battle at the gates of Mordor was a diversionary tactic to distract the Eye of Sauron. Berko was saying they needed to draw the guards' attention. But how?

She couldn't help it. "But how?" she said.

He laid his hand on her wrist and stared hard at her. "It's what I was best at. Always."

She blinked. "Okay."

He considered the other two and they nodded. "Well," Olivia said, "you should absolutely do what you're best at. My first game was *Tetris*." She selected her witch card, held it up for all to see, then passed it over the moat and set it down on the other side. She put the adventurer over next.

Elias slapped his hand down over the cards and shook his head vehemently. "I hate *Tetris*," he said, and put the witch and adventurer cards back.

Unruffled, Olivia repeated putting her and Jade's cards over the moat and looked hard at Elias as she passed the bureaucrat over then picked up the militia card and showed it to him. "*Y: The Last Man* was also a favorite." She was referencing a comic book series in which every living thing on earth with a Y chromosome died, except for one man. Then she laid down Elias's card next to the other three. "Yorick's mom—" she touched Jade's adventurer card "—was the only reason they ever found Dr. Mann in the first place." She touched the witch card. "And of course, I loved Nintendo DS *Buffy the Vampire Slayer: Sacrifice*. Willow usually went before Buffy, remember? Can't hurt to have some mojo to slow the vamps down." She took her hands away and went silent.

Elias set his elbows on the table, staring down at the cards, seeming to work out the logic of this. He finally gave a terse nod. "Then all we need is Dean's baby, or at least the roadhouse."

Jade was surprised to hear a *Supernatural* reference from Elias.

Yes, they'd need a car or somewhere with a phone, and they would run through the fields and prairie until they found one or the other.

Their shared fear gave Jade strength.

"Have fun storming the castle," said Olivia, forcing a smile.

Jade made herself laugh and endeavored not to think of the next few lines in *The Princess Bride*. She gathered up all the cards. "*Guitar Hero*," she said and dealt Dominion for real.

Chapter 14

AFTER THE DOMINION game, Olivia found a pen in the junk drawer in the kitchen and wrote on her hand, then showed it to Jade and then the other two: *Let's go find out where all the Reavers are.*

Another *Firefly* reference, but she was talking about the guards and where they were stationed around the perimeter of the fence.

Aloud, she said, "Jade, you want to go for a walk? Stretch our legs?"

"Sounds good," Jade said and followed Olivia out the front door.

Once they were away from the house, and presumably away from the microphones, Olivia said, "We need to go to the lab before we head for the fence." She held up a hand to prevent Jade's objections. "If we're caught, we say we couldn't sleep and decided to check on the simulation. Then you lock them out of the system so they don't have access to our work. Once we talk to Dan and everything comes out, maybe we'll be able to salvage what you've done."

Jade slumped. "Won't they just blow up the supercomputer?"

"Are you kidding?" Olivia said. "The government wastes money, but I can't see them wasting *that* much. Then we'll walk out and take different routes to the fence corner and make our getaway."

Olivia was right, Jade decided. They had to prevent the NSA from accessing their work. No telling what they'd do once they found out the team had escaped.

They walked in silence for a bit.

"Hey, Jade," Olivia said. "I'm sorry for what I said in the lab. I get mean when I'm scared. You *should* be mad at me. But I'm sorry."

Jade said, "I'm sorry too. But it's obvious they're using Dr. Heller's Blame Thrower." A *Mystery Men* reference, which made Olivia laugh. But Jade was shocked by how easily they had turned against each other.

They walked along the fence, and as they neared a guard in camo, he walked the other way.

"I'll bet you'd never be friends with someone like me under normal circumstances," Jade said. "Would you?"

"That's not fair," Olivia said.

"Would you?"

Olivia snorted. "Probably not."

Jade nodded, satisfied with honesty.

"Here's what you need to know, though," Olivia said. "I have always been the smartest in the room, even at Johns Hopkins. But what you've accomplished with the Clementine Program has got me gobsmacked. I am one hundred percent in awe of you. In the stress of the moment, I wanted to lash out and bring you down to my level, and that's the truth."

Jade saw in her eyes that it was.

"And then you defused that situation at the bar in town like such a badass. I *pretend* I'm tough, but it's all just talk."

"Olivia, you *are* tough. You scare the hell out of me."

Olivia laughed as they came upon another guard.

By the time they made the rounds, they'd counted five guards, all with rifles, and determined the best place to go over the fence—the southwest corner that faced away from all the windows of the office building's living quarters side.

Jade leaned into Olivia as they stared out over the beautiful greenbelt, the pool, the park benches, and trees. "I'm really scared," Jade whispered.

Olivia hugged her, and she whispered back, "Don't be. What are they going to do if we're caught? Shoot us?"

Jade couldn't help but feel that yes, they might shoot them. But . . . the guards wouldn't actually shoot them, Jade kept assuring herself. *They're here to protect us. And to scare us into staying, because national security depends on us staying and finishing. If they kill us, the project is unfinished.*

When they got back to the house, Jade could smell frying meat and vegetables, and she was famished. She scratched at her neck, where some sort of heat/stress rash had appeared. "Well, this is great," she said, showing it to Olivia.

"Put some alcohol on it," Olivia said, and then poured Jade a tall gin and tonic. Jade didn't often drink gin, but tonight she would make an exception.

As they sat down to dinner, Jade was surprised at how high everyone's spirits were. Maybe the idea of doing something so naughty, of defying the National Security Agency, energized them, the thought of sneaking out in the middle of the night. And maybe having all their secrets revealed lifted a weight from them too.

They tried to eat, but nerves got the better of them and they couldn't quite seem to choke down much, except for Elias, who ate everything on his plate, and then everything left on Jade's and Olivia's plates.

"You're a beast," Jade said to him. He smiled and wiped his mouth with a napkin.

Jade and Olivia cleared the table and did the dishes while Elias and Berko set up the board game The Settlers of Catan. Through the rest of the evening, they argued over anime and comic books, sending each other into giggle fits every so often.

Jade couldn't quiet her heart, which was on full alert, banging away in her chest. She could practically hear it thumping and thudding.

She'd give anything to talk to her mom. To Dad. To Clem. But especially to Dan. He'd know what to do. But she consoled herself that she would be talking to him in a few hours, once they were safely away.

Olivia glanced at her phone. "I'm exhausted," she said. "I'm going to bed."

"Good night," Jade said. "I think I'll hit the hay too."

They all nodded at each other, eyes terrified and alert.

"Good night," Elias said, stretching melodramatically, so much so that Jade worried he'd dislocate his shoulder. "See you in the morning."

"I'm tired too," Berko said. They trooped up the stairs and they gave each other meaningful glances as they each disappeared into their rooms.

Jade paced her room. Set her phone alarm for one forty-five a.m. Then she took off her shoes and stretched out on her bed, but she expected sleep to elude her.

Next thing she knew, her phone was buzzing silently in her

pocket. She had indeed fallen asleep, but now she was as awake as she had ever been. She slipped on her shoes and admired her room. This had been home for weeks, and now she was leaving it. She despaired as she realized she'd have to leave her posters, family photos, and books. But all those could be replaced. She was sad to leave, but sadder she'd been fooled into doing this at all.

She slowly and quietly opened her door and tiptoed out into the dark hall. Elias and Berko were already there. Elias tapped his watch and pointed at the other door. Jade went to Olivia's and knocked as softly as she could. The door opened and Olivia held up a one-minute finger in Jade's direction. She put her phone in her pocket and tightened her shoelaces, then followed Jade out the door. They filed down the stairs as silently as possible.

Jade feared the door would trigger an alarm, but Elias opened it with abandon. No noise erupted and they left the house. Berko peeled off from them and went behind the house, having been tasked with creating a diversion. The other three walked toward the office building. They'd predetermined they would take the stairs, since the noise of the elevator could have woken up their jailers. Jade didn't even know where the stairs were, but luckily Elias did. They all followed him to the door, and he placed a silencing finger to his lips before slowly turning the doorknob. For some reason, Jade was afraid she would burst into laughter.

She also started to wonder how they were going to get away. They were miles from anything, and very little traffic went by the Compound. She'd seen a propane truck or two, some tractors, some pickup trucks, but not much else. She should have packed some food and water. She guessed they could raid the conference room refrigerator.

The eerie hum of the lab, electronics and fans, met their ears as they exited the stairwell. Elias went to flip on the lights, but Olivia put a hand on his arm and shook her head. They'd need to work by monitor light. They stole into the lab and sat at their workstations. Jade booted up her computer.

A new password screen appeared. Apparently the higher-ups had been busy little bees last night. Jade brought up the terminal and typed several different commands into it, which took her into the back end of the system. Did they really think they could stop her from getting in? She navigated to the work directory where they stored all their files.

It was blank.

Empty.

Nothing.

She typed in the command to access her and Elias's system back door. It was gone. The NSA files.

All gone.

"Oh, shit," she murmured. She turned to Elias, who was typing. He turned and met her gaze. He'd discovered the disappearance too.

Olivia wheeled over to her. "What is it?"

Jade pointed at the screen.

"What does that mean?" Olivia whispered.

"It means they've removed our files. They're not here."

Olivia stared at her, the glow of the monitor making her skin appear dark green. "You must be looking in the wrong place."

"No. This is the directory."

"Can you do a search?" Olivia said. "Surely the files aren't gone, just moved. After the near-mutiny today, maybe they figured they'd better move everything in case we tried something like this."

Jade did a search and found nothing. She opened her drawer to pull out the backup drive, but to her horror, it too was gone.

"Elias," she whispered. "Do you have your backup drive?"

He opened all the drawers of his desk. "No," he whispered. "They're all gone."

"Does this mean they have other coders and engineers shadowing us?" Olivia asked.

"Doing their own tests with the program? Have they figured out how to use it and don't need us anymore?"

"That would mean we're dead already," Jade said. The poisonous thoughts that circled her brain threatened to immobilize her. "There's nothing we can do. We have to go now."

She traded glances with the other two, and the haze of fear strangled her.

"Okay," Olivia whispered. "Let's go."

They shuffled out of the lab and to the stairwell and ascended the staircase to the ground floor.

Outside, they trooped around to the back of the office building, where Berko stood with a controller in his hands.

What was he planning to do? Jade couldn't think about it, had to trust he'd come up with a suitable diversion.

"Ready?" he whispered. "This is going to get loud, but don't let it distract you, no matter what you hear. As soon as you hear the noise, proceed."

Olivia nodded. "As soon as you do whatever you're going to do, I'll go first, and Jade, you're second. Wait until I'm over and out of sight before you start for the fence. Got it?"

She turned to leave, but Jade caught her arm. "Maybe—maybe we shouldn't—"

Olivia smiled at her. "It's going to be okay. Trust me. It's going to be fine. No matter what happens. You'll see."

Berko walked away from them to the east side of the building and Jade heard the whir of drone blades moving away from them toward the other end of the Compound fence. Berko came back into view, guiding the drone with his controller.

They watched as Olivia walked toward the house and go around it. She reappeared again on the other side.

BOOM!

Jade retracted her head into her shoulders, looking around, and realized Berko's speaker was blasting out the sounds of warfare high over the Compound. Immediately several sets of feet were pounding off in that direction, away from them.

Jade whirled around and watched Olivia run toward the fence, away from the racket that had easily drawn all the guards.

Olivia approached the fence, and glanced over both shoulders before she rubbed her hands together and reached for it.

At that moment, with the sounds of automatic gunfire, TNT blasts, rocket explosions, and atomic bombs detonating behind her, Jade was overcome with fear the fence would electrocute her friend. She opened her mouth to shout, but Berko slapped a hand over her mouth, painfully.

Olivia reached out, grabbed hold of some links, and hoisted herself up.

Jade began breathing again as Olivia ascended quickly higher and higher. And then she was at the top and jumping to the ground on the other side of the fence. She ran and disappeared into the darkness.

Elias watched in the opposite direction. "Hurry," he said to Jade. "They're not going to be fooled for long. Go!"

Euphoric, Jade pushed off and ran. Halfway to her goal, Olivia burst from the darkness, running back toward them, sprinting really, a look of terror on her face. Her blue hair flew out behind her.

"Someone's out there!" she shouted and sprang onto the fence, climbing faster than the first time and made it all the way to the top.

Then Olivia went rigid, and Jade spun around, expecting to see guards running toward them, but she saw nothing. Turning back, she saw Olivia clinging to the top of the fence. A Rorschach of red fanned out on her chest, her mouth wide in a silent scream.

Time stood still as Olivia hung there. A spotlight illuminated from across the Compound, and in that bright light, Jade watched the Rorschach grow on the front of Olivia's white shirt. Olivia stopped moving, and then she dropped to the ground beyond the fence.

In the chaos of the fake explosions, Jade hadn't detected the real gunshots that had ripped into Olivia's torso.

Jade screamed and the boys yelled. They all ran toward the fence when an electrically amplified voice said, "Stop! Don't go any farther. Stay where you are."

Jade couldn't stop screaming. Her friend. Her friend needed help.

When Jade ran out of breath, the Compound went eerily silent. No more explosions or detonations. She now heard footsteps coming from the northeast and two men in fatigues ran toward her. One of them shouted, "Go in the house!"

They did as they were told, stumbling in shock toward the back door of the house.

Martin was coming in the front door as they came in the back.

"Are you all right?" he asked them. "What happened? Where's Olivia?"

Berko stared dumbfounded at Martin. "She was . . . shot! She's shot!"

Jade looked out the kitchen window, trying to ascertain what was going on out there.

Martin's face clouded. "I warned you. I told you to stay in the Compound. That's what I've been trying to tell you—there are people out there who are trying to stop this project, and they'll do anything to accomplish that goal. Up to and including—I thought I made this clear—*killing* you all if necessary."

"You never," Jade said, turning away from the window, her words coming out in bursts, "*ever* said they would try to kill us. You never said that." She wanted to bash his face in. She wanted to destroy something. Her friend had been shot.

He pulled out his phone and dialed. "Did you find them?" he demanded, then his eyes tracked back and forth as he listened. "What? No. Oh shit." His eyes flicked to Jade's and then away again. He turned and murmured something into the phone she didn't catch. "All right. Keep me posted."

From a distance, Jade heard chopper blades.

Martin listened. "Good. The medevac is almost here. They'll take her to the nearest hospital."

"Who were you talking to just now?"

"Guards," Martin said tersely.

Jade stood crying, uncomprehending what had just happened. This had to be a dream. This couldn't be happening.

Berko put his arms around her, and Elias looked enraged, clenching and unclenching his fists at his sides. Veins throbbed at his temples and sweat covered his face. Jade collapsed against Berko and sobbed.

"Why was she trying to climb the fence?" Martin asked them.

"Take a wild guess," Elias said. "How can you even ask that?"

Jade heard the helicopter land, its bright lights shining through the back windows, and Jade ran to them and peered out.

The bright beams blinded her and, for an interminable time, the blades sliced up the light as they presumably loaded Olivia into the chopper. Finally, the helicopter lifted off and the roar and light lessened until they disappeared altogether.

"I want to go home," Jade said. She grabbed at Martin's shirtfront, twisted the fabric in her fists. She was a little girl and she couldn't think or speak coherently. "I want—to—go—home! Let me go home. Please!"

"Jade," Martin said gently, "I'm sorry about this. I am. It's horrible."

The anguish on his face scared her more. He took her wrists in his hands and she let go. Elias stood behind her and she turned toward him and he held her.

Forty-five minutes later, they were all sitting in the living room, waiting for news, and Jade's sobs had devolved to gulps and stupid noises she couldn't stop making. She sat between Berko and Elias, holding both their hands, and Elias whispered alternating Our Fathers and Hail Marys. No one had said anything else since Jade had begged to go home.

Martin's phone buzzed and he jumped to his feet. He pressed it to his ear. "Yes?" He listened, nodding. "I see. Thank you."

He clicked off and sat back down. "They located the sniper in the field across the road," Martin said, then hesitated.

"There's something else, isn't there?" Berko said. "What is it?"

Martin's face contorted. "They couldn't save Olivia. She's gone."

Chapter 15

JADE STRUGGLED TO take a breath. But as if she'd been left outside of the airlock without atmosphere, she failed.

Olivia was dead.

Berko stood with his arms wrapped around his midsection, breathing in gusts and spurts, trying not to cry and failing. His glasses were fogged up and sweat beaded on his forehead.

Jade clawed at her throat, trying to force it open and let in oxygen, but her body had been shocked into forgetting how to function.

Elias put his arms around her. "Breathe, Jade. Just breathe."

Oxygen hit her lungs like poisonous gas, burning, and Jade let out a wail. "No!"

Elias glared at Martin. "What did you get us into?"

Martin's barely controlled fury made him talk through clenched teeth.

"What did *I* get you into? After the girls were run off the road, it didn't occur to you that going beyond the fence was dangerous?

I made it abundantly clear you were to stay here, but apparently, you four kids put your heads together and decided the guards were here to keep you prisoner, when I *expressly* said they were here to protect you. Olivia's death is on your head. On all your heads."

Elias's face fell. "You're right," he said. "I should have gone over first. Why didn't I insist on going first?"

"Because Olivia always made the rules," Jade said. She addressed Martin. "Did you call her folks?"

Apologetic, Martin said, "We can't until . . ."

"The project is complete," Berko said.

"That's right. But they may be able to take some comfort that their daughter died in service to her country. We won't mention she was AWOL."

"She wasn't *AWOL* because she wasn't a *soldier*," Elias shouted. "She was a med student. She was . . ." He broke down crying.

"Our friend," Jade finished for him. She put her arms around his shaking shoulders. He clasped her to his chest, nearly squeezing the breath out of her. But she let him until he was cried out. Then he drew away from her as if embarrassed.

"Why is all our work gone?" he demanded. "Why did you take it off the server?"

Martin turned to him. "Because we knew what you were planning to do."

Icy fingers wrapped themselves around Jade's nerves. The NSA had been watching everything. All their plotting now seemed like a child's fantasy destroyed by the real world.

"The tests are still running," Martin said. "We locked you out and moved the files. Your log-ins will be restored, and we'll restore the files because, Jade and Elias, you'll need to determine how long the program will need to propagate. We're not going to wait for September eleventh—as soon as it's ready, we're going to inject it."

"Berko's done his part," Jade said. "Why don't you let him go?"

Martin shook his head. "Until the project is successful, no one is going anywhere. He'll be intercepted by the terrorists, and no telling what they'll do with him. Once it's over and the Chinese attack is thwarted, you'll all be national heroes. We'll let you tell your story."

"But wait," Berko said. "We'll still be hunted by these domestic terrorists, right? Why would they suddenly lose interest in us? We're going to be targets for all time." His fists clenched. "You should have told us. *You should have told us.*"

This sank into Jade's brain. What did that mean? Did it mean they'd never be safe again? That her family wouldn't be safe?

"How are you going to protect us once it's all over?" Jade said. "You can't. What are you going to do, put us in the equivalent of witness protection? That's why you're paying us so much—because our careers are all over. We'll have no careers, no lives. This is it for us. You son of a bitch."

"In wartime," Martin said, "sacrifices must be made. In any event, until the project is completed, there will be guards posted at the front and back doors of the house. They will walk you to the other buildings as necessary. No one is to go out alone. Do you understand?"

They all nodded.

"Now get some sleep," Martin said. "I'm going to restore the system so it'll be ready for you in the morning."

"But what if the program doesn't work?" Elias said.

Martin shrugged. "You'd better pray it does." And he walked out of the house.

Jade walked over to Berko and put her arms around him and hugged him. He was stiff at first but he relaxed and returned the hug. Then they went upstairs to their rooms.

Olivia was gone. Her friend.

Jade couldn't concentrate, couldn't think. She kept walking in circles in her room like a dog trying to find a place to bury a bone. She finally lay down on her bed, staring at the poster of Imperator Furiosa, because every time she closed her eyes she saw Olivia dangling from the fence, blood spreading like ink over the front of her shirt. Exhaustion won out around sunrise.

September 9

JADE WOKE UP, eyes stinging and head throbbing, and for a moment didn't remember Olivia was dead. But that fact seeped into her consciousness, and she sat up and stared, bleary-eyed, out the window at soldiers roaming the field across the road, on high alert for more snipers or saboteurs.

In the bathroom, Jade peeled the bandage from her forehead, exposing the black stitches and angry red skin. Had it only been the night before last they'd wrecked the car? It seemed so long ago.

Jade didn't bother to shower or eat breakfast. She opened the front door and a rifled guard stepped to the side.

"Hi," Jade said.

"Ma'am," he said. "Can I escort you somewhere?"

"I'm going to the lab," she said. "You can come if you want."

"I'm required to," he said.

They walked across the Compound, the guard to her left and a little behind her. It felt creepy, having these shadows everywhere, but this was the new normal.

"Do you have any idea what's going on here?" Jade said to the guard. "I mean, are you aware we're being held prisoner here? Against our will? Does that bother you at all?"

"I don't know anything about that, ma'am," he said.

She went down to the lab, and Elias was already there, looking glum. She supposed she did too.

Jade seated herself at her desk and moved her mouse. "Is the system back up?"

"Yes," he said, turning from his monitor.

Jade swiveled toward him. "Where's Berko?"

"He's not feeling well," Elias said. "He developed a migraine and was up all night throwing up."

Poor guy. "I'm surprised I wasn't too, honestly."

Elias turned back to his keyboard and typed as Jade faced hers.

The command prompt screen appeared on her monitor, and she worked not to react. It was covered with gibberish code, interspersed with actual words.

Our back door is still there. If they'd found it, they would have closed it.

So, obviously, was Elias's chat program. Prickles of warning flashed over her skin as more code and words appeared on her monitor.

You need to write some code to lock up the program so they can't use it unless you start it up. I'm not sure everything is as it seems.

She desperately wanted to turn and look at Elias but knew they were still being watched. More code popped up, and Jade's eyes watered with the effort of not crying out.

Because I'm convinced that gunshot didn't come from outside the Compound. It came from inside.

Chapter 16

How could he know that? She couldn't ask him. She had to trust he knew what he was talking about. Or was he under so much stress that his paranoia meter had jumped off the scale?

And what did that mean? That the *NSA* killed Olivia?

And if they shot Olivia, what would stop them from shooting *all of them* once they got what they wanted?

And what *did* they want?

What she did know was she had to work fast so they could get out of here.

If the NSA was going to let them leave.

She minimized the command prompt window and then she got to work, first confirming the back door was indeed still there. Even in the midst of all the craziness, Jade was eager to see if Clementine worked. But she did as Elias had asked—put a virtual padlock on the program. Then started wading through the results of the tests. She made sure she had an alternate screen to click over to in case Martin popped in for a surprise inspection.

Berko came in around noon, looking faded and wrung out. "How's it going?" he asked, sinking into his desk chair.

"Okay," Jade said.

He slid his glasses onto his forehead and rubbed his red eyes. "I dreamed I was back in Palo Alto," he said. "It was a great dream. You ever been there? I love it there. California is great. Beautiful. Nobody ever shot at me there. I wasn't a prisoner at Stanford. Do you suppose we're being punished for being greedy? For wanting to make the big money and all that?"

"I don't think so, Berko," Jade said. "I think pretty much anyone would have done it."

Berko shook his head and put his glasses back on.

"When I get back to Palo Alto, I'm going to kiss the ground. I'm not kidding."

"Have you eaten anything?" Jade said.

"Don't know if I can keep it down," he said. "My meds didn't work. If I don't catch the headache within fifteen minutes of its start, there's no stopping it. But it's starting to recede."

"Speaking of food," Elias said. "I'm going to grab something from the kitchen. You want anything, Jade?"

"Yeah," she said. "Do they still have those pizza bagel things? You think you could pop one of those into the microwave for me?"

"Sure," he said and left the lab.

"Take a look at this, Berko," Jade said, beckoning him toward her computer. She brought up the fake command prompt and pointed out Elias's messages. Berko did a good job of keeping his expression neutral. "What do you think?"

"Looks good," he said. "I think we're right on the money there."

They locked eyes, and she couldn't help herself. She hugged

him. And once again, he let her, but it cost him. He groaned in pain and returned to his workstation.

The door flew open and Elias, out of breath, came running in. He sat back in his chair and typed.

Jade's command prompt appeared.

They didn't turn baseball-cap man over to the cops.

Jade typed a question and sent it.

"There weren't any pizza bagels in the freezer," Elias said. "Sorry about that." He typed some more.

Went down to the storeroom and passed a closed door, heard tapping. That hall is lined with doors. Almost didn't stop, heard whispering from inside the door. I say Hello?

Jade turned to Berko and said, "Hey, can you take a look at this?"

Berko wheeled over to her desk, adjusted his glasses, and leaned in then sat up straight.

"What—?"

"I know," Jade said casually. Berko shut up, his eyes riveted to the monitor.

Elias typed on.

Voice says, I'm Harry Gilby, I'm being held prisoner.

Locked in a room in the basement?

Not done interrogating? Jade typed.

He wants to talk to you.

Me? Why me?

More text popped up on the screen.

He's the one from the grocery store.

Berko and Jade stared at each other before looking back at the screen. So the baseball-cap man *was* the same guy who ran her and Olivia off the road.

Elias typed.

The guy with him didn't run away. THEY SHOT HIM DEAD.

Berko's eyebrows shot up and Jade said, "Bullshit," out loud.

Elias kept typing. Another line of text popped up on Jade's monitor.

He said we're not working for the NSA, and there's no Chinese threat.

Jade's heart nearly stopped.

The door opened and in strode Martin.

"Status?" he said.

Jade kept her eyes on him but clicked her mouse and brought up the fake screen just before Martin focused on her monitor.

Martin's eyes tracked to hers and then to Berko, who sat frozen, his mouth ajar. Everyone remained silent.

Jade had to hold her breath so her hyperventilating wouldn't be evident.

Elias cleared his throat and said, "We're writing the code right now for the power grid. You'll be the first to know when it's done."

Berko stared down at the floor, and Martin cased the lab.

"I'll just hang out in here with you all for a bit, okay?" Martin said. "Take a look at some of the code."

"Sure," Jade said, and she had a terrifying urge to giggle. As if any code they could write would make any sense to him at all.

Martin's eyes went to her monitor again, and Elias turned back toward his.

Berko wheeled back to his workstation and said, "Martin, if you need help translating any Chinese correspondence, let me know."

Martin didn't answer him. He turned to Jade and said, "Let me see where we are."

She rose from her chair so he could sit down and stare at the fake coding screen. He did, and her eyes lit on the minimized command prompt tab at the bottom of her screen. She hadn't had time to close it out. She shut her eyes and prayed he wouldn't click on it. She turned and looked at her teammates, who stared tensely at her screen.

"There's no way to tell how long it's going to take you?" Martin asked without turning around.

"No, sir," she said.

He swiveled toward them. "You wouldn't lie to me. Would you?"

"No, sir," she said again, hoping her face didn't betray her. She'd been told before she had a glass head—everything she thought showed in her face. She hoped this wasn't true.

He continued gazing at her, and it took a superhuman effort not to start laughing, maniacal, hysterical, terrified laughter bubbling at the base of her throat.

Martin walked idly around for another five minutes before he left. The tension left the room with him. And poor old Berko ran out shortly thereafter. When he returned, he said, "I don't know how much more of this my guts can take."

"Ditto," Jade said, her stomach sour and burning.

Elias waited a few minutes before typing, and Jade maximized the command prompt screen.

Should we wait until after dark to visit Harry Gilby?

Berko cautiously rolled back over to Jade's desk and read Elias's message. He pointed at the keyboard and Jade slid it his way. He typed, *How are we going to get in there?*

Elias turned around and lifted up the lanyard around his neck, waggling his keycard at them.

Hopefully they didn't reprogram that door so we couldn't get in, Jade wrote.

That was a big if. And she was burning with curiosity—who were they working for if they weren't working for the NSA? The Chinese? Or someone else?

Elias typed, and Jade turned back to her keyboard and read, *Let's plan on coming back here at midnight. Guards will walk us over, but they never come in with us.*

Jade closed out the command prompt window and then worked until dinnertime. She still had about a quarter of the testing data to go through. It would have to wait until tomorrow. She was fried. And she still had the nocturnal visit with Gilby to dread. Plus Jade kept thinking of things she wanted to tell Olivia, and every time it happened, her stomach bottomed out and tears threatened.

After the guard walked them back to the house, Jade went up to Olivia's room, which was just as she'd left it. Colorful throw pillows covered her purple bedspread, one with a Minecraft creeper and another that said MAY THE $d/dt(mv)$ BE WITH YOU!

Jade covered her mouth with her hand in attempt to quell a sob. A poster emblazoned with a feline face framed by the words WANTED: $100,000 REWARD, SCHRÖDINGER'S CAT, DEAD OR ALIVE hung above her bed. Framed prints decorated the other walls, and then Jade's eyes landed on what she wanted, what she was going to take: the framed photo of Olivia shaking hands with Ruth Bader Ginsburg. Jade trusted that Olivia would want her to have it. She plucked it off the wall and took it to her own room where she set it on her nightstand.

Jade went downstairs into the kitchen and looked in the freezer.

"Szechuan beef or rigatoni?" she called out to her teammates in the living room.

"Either," Elias said. "I'm going to go and get in a quick workout before dinner."

"Okay," Jade said. "How long will you be?"

"No more than thirty minutes," he said and opened the front door. "How's it going?" she heard him ask the escort guard as the door closed behind him.

"Berko? Rigatoni or Szechuan beef?"

"Doesn't matter to me," Berko said, lying on the couch with his eyes closed and his glasses on his forehead.

"But you need to eat something," Jade said. "We need you to be strong."

He waved a weak hand without opening his eyes.

"I'll try to eat," he said. "This is so humiliating."

"Don't worry about it," Jade said. "I doubt any of us have been under this kind of pressure before."

"I know," he said. "But Elias is this rock, and you're—a slightly taller rock. And here I am puking my guts out like a little girl."

"You can't help that you get migraines. This situation is untenable. It's not your fault."

He opened his eyes. Without his glasses she could see how pretty his eyes were and was reminded how handsome he actually was.

"But my brothers took my migraines as a sign of weakness, you know? And then after my brush with the law as a kid, it scared me so much I made up my mind I was going to stay on the straight and narrow. Lucky for me I had a real facility with language."

This was the most personal Berko had ever gotten, and Jade appreciated it. "I wish we'd met under different circumstances," she said.

"Me too," Berko said. "You really are one of a kind."

Jade's face reddened. She wasn't sure how to take that. "Well, thank you," she said. "I think very highly of you as well."

That came out much more formally than she meant it, but he'd caught her off guard.

He laughed the first genuine laugh she'd heard from him in what seemed like ages.

"What I mean is," Jade said. "You're one of a kind too. You're the only linguist I've ever met, and from what I can tell, you really know your stuff."

Berko put on his glasses and sat up, placing his feet on the ground.

"The whole reason I originally became interested in linguistics was because of my name, and I wondered why the Ghanaians put these particular sounds together in that order to mean firstborn. Why the Akan language exists at all."

"It's fascinating stuff," Jade said. "You're going to do great things."

"Am I?" Berko said, the defeat in his voice breaking her heart.

"Yes," she said. "You are."

When Elias returned, Jade pulled the frozen rigatoni out of the freezer and put it in the microwave, reasoning a spicy Asian dish might ratchet up Berko's suffering.

Jade had a hard time eating but forced herself to. She needed her strength. Berko did the best he could, eating like a determined toddler, tiny bites, lots of water. As usual, Elias had no problem scarfing down any food put in front of him.

"I'm going to bed," Berko said.

"I'll be your wake-up call," Elias said. He winked.

"You want to watch a movie, Jade?" Elias asked.

"Sure," she said. Anything to pass the time until they went back to talk to Gilby.

At midnight, Elias went to Berko's room and woke him up. They came downstairs and Jade followed them out the front door.

The guard held out an arm. "Sorry," he said. "My orders are that you're no longer allowed out of the house after ten p.m."

They all traded glances. "But we wanted to go get some more work done," Jade said.

"Sorry," he said. "Those are my orders."

"But—"

The guard shrugged. "You can talk to Mr. Felix in the morning about it, ma'am. Good night."

They trooped back inside, alarmed at this new development.

The noose was tightening.

Chapter 17

September 10

JADE AWOKE FROM a dream about Olivia running ahead of her in a wheat field. She kept looking over her shoulder at Jade. "Come on," she said. "Hurry! Come on!"

I'm trying were the words Jade woke with in her head. "I'm trying."

As she rubbed the sleep out of her eyes, she thought, *I have to tell Olivia about this dream.* And then she remembered.

Everything that happened, Jade would think, *I have to tell Olivia,* and then she'd remember Olivia was dead, and feel it all over again. It was like when her grandmother with dementia would ask for her husband, and they would tell her he was dead, and it was always like hearing it for the first time.

Jade missed Olivia. She'd known her only three months and had never made such fast friends with someone. Now it seemed like a dream that she was ever here at all.

Today Jade would get through the simulation data by lunchtime. Maybe she would be home by dinner.

She didn't really believe that though. She had the distinct feeling she might never see Ephesus or her family again.

She took a shower, careful not to wet her stitches, then got dressed and had breakfast. Before she left the house, she retrieved the framed photo of Olivia and RBG to put on her desk in the lab. She carried it out the front door and a guard fell in step with her—a different one from last night, of course. With a start, she realized she recognized him. The maintenance man who'd fixed their refrigerator, Connor Lemaire. But she didn't feel friendly today. Not after everything. He walked behind her so she didn't have to make small talk.

When they were halfway between the house and the office building, Connor muttered something.

"What did you say?" Jade said, stopping dead.

"Keep walking," he murmured. "I said, Colonel Stevenson is on his way. Just act casual."

Dan? Dan was on his way? Such a surge of relief and hope rolled over Jade that her knees buckled and she almost dropped Olivia's photo.

Connor caught her. "Careful," he said in a normal tone of voice, now walking beside her.

After the initial swell of hope, Jade began to wonder if they'd let Dan into the Compound. Why would they? Unless he brought an armed contingent with him.

"You left your tool belt on purpose, didn't you?" she whispered.

His lips curved into a slight smile. "Just go about your business and don't tell Elias or Berko what I've told you. All right?"

Why not? They were her team members. But he was probably

afraid the listening devices would pick up this bit of info, and then *they* could better prepare for Dan's arrival.

He opened the door to the office building. "Have a nice day, ma'am," he said in a normal tone of voice. Then walked away.

As soon as he did, Jade wished she'd asked him about Gilby. She and the guys needed to go down to the storeroom hall together to find the prisoner, but how would they do that without attracting the attention of Big Brother?

The first order of business, however, was to finish going through the data, and she needed all her powers of concentration to do that.

She sat at her desk, set the photo of Olivia next to her monitor, and got to work, optimism ballooning inside her.

The guys straggled in, but Jade was focused and took little notice. She wanted this done before Dan got here.

If he was really coming.

The fake command prompt popped up.

Didn't want to say anything until I was sure, but I found the surveillance program in the system. I took a screenshot of the hallway outside the lab, the hallway where Gilby is, and inside the elevator. I've also recorded thirty minutes of us sitting at our desks working. I'll program both to display when we go to see the prisoner. We'll have thirty minutes to talk to him and get back here.

This day kept getting better and better. Elias was a genius. But . . .

Jade typed and sent a response.

But surely they saw/heard your interaction with Gilby, right?

Elias's reply popped up.

They'd have confronted me about it if they'd caught it, don't you suppose? I dropped a handful of change on the floor so I'd have plenty of time to crawl around and gather it all up. They must not pay too much attention to what happens in the halls.

That made sense, but she couldn't help feeling trepidation.

Another screen popped up that took her breath away. She stared at it. Was it possible? Yes, it was.

She had to restrain herself from whooping, from jumping up and doing a fist pump. Instead, she typed her reply and sent it.

Elias gasped loudly behind her. Message received.

"What?" Berko said.

Elias rose from his chair and charged to Jade's workstation, leaning in over her. Berko joined them. Jade watched their faces as they read her words.

IT WORKS.

Berko dropped his book and Elias squeezed her shoulders so hard she yelped.

"Sorry," he said.

Jade pointed out Elias's and her exchange about the surveillance system to Berko. He straightened, pushed up his glasses, and stared at Elias, who grinned at him.

"I think I'm having a panic attack," he whispered. "Are you sure?"

She nodded and typed.

Simulation's done. It prevented all seventy stations from going down. ALL seventy. But act casual. They're watching. Now, Elias, do your magic, and then let's go see this Gilby character.

The guys went back to their workstations and Jade sat anxiously staring at her monitor, waiting for the go signal from Elias.

Jade looked at her phone. It was two forty-five. The sounds of Elias's clacking keys intensified her jitters as she waited and hoped.

"Let's go," Elias said.

Jade and Berko rose from their chairs and followed Elias out the lab door.

All three of them stood a little straighter as they rode down the elevator, and Jade was jumpy with nerves, relief, and excitement all at once. Berko looked better than he had since all the drama began.

Jade and Berko followed Elias down the dim hall. He stopped in front of a door and tapped softly on it. "Mr. Gilby," he whispered.

No answer.

"Maybe he's asleep," Berko said.

"Mr. Gilby?" Jade said in hushed tones. "It's Jade."

Still no answer.

Elias lifted his keycard to the electronic lock and the light turned green.

And suddenly, Jade was terrified at what they'd find inside. Because if they *had* shot Gilby's companion, then . . .

The door clicked open and swung inward. Jade groped the wall inside until she found a light switch and flipped it.

The room was empty.

Elias walked inside and examined the walls, the floor, the corners, as if there were some secret passage or false wall that might be hiding Gilby.

There was a sink, a toilet, and cot with a thin mattress on it, but no Gilby.

"Are you sure it was this room?" Berko whispered.

Elias didn't say anything for a moment. "No," Elias said.

"But it was this hall," Jade said.

Elias gave her a stung look. "Yes."

"Maybe we should check the other rooms to be sure," Jade said.

"There's no need for that," came Martin's voice from the doorway.

Jade jumped, and all three of them turned around to see Martin accompanied by an armed guard, whose name badge said Hobart.

"Where is he?" Elias said.

"I told you we would be turning him over to the authorities," Martin said, "and we did, early this morning."

Jade watched Elias try to decide whether he should say what Gilby had told him, but before he could make up his mind, Martin said, "What works?"

Chapter 18

JADE GULPED, CAUGHT. She'd left the command prompt window open on her monitor. Martin must have popped into the lab.

Both her coworkers' faces were slack with surprise and dismay.

Jade straightened, rose to her full height, and said, "Clementine. It's ready. The simulation is done. It works. So you can let these two go, and I can go over the specifics with you or—"

"Not necessary," Martin said. "We just need you to remove the lock on it."

"Before I do," Jade said. "We'd like you to tell us who we are actually working for. And we want our money deposited in our accounts. And we want assurances you're not going to . . ."

She gulped again.

"We're from the government," Martin said, a twinkle in his eye. "And we're here to help." He herded them out of the room as Hobart turned off the light and closed the door behind them.

"Come with me," Martin said. "I want to show you something."

Jade traded glances with Elias and Berko, who was trembling. Elias walked stiffly, with his military bearing.

They walked down the hall toward the elevator behind Martin, who whistled tunelessly between his teeth. Hobart brought up the rear. On the ride up two floors, Martin kept his eyes on the ascending numbers, and Jade wondered what he wanted to show them.

They walked down a hall Jade hadn't been in before. She didn't like being followed by a man with a rifle, and she glanced around at Hobart, who stared impassively straight ahead. Martin led them into a small, dark room with a large window. Light flooded a room beyond the window, and once her eyes adjusted, she saw two men seated in chairs facing the window, and another standing beside them.

With a shock, Jade recognized both seated men. It was Dan and Connor the guard. And both their faces were bloody messes. Their arms were tied behind them.

Before she could react to this, another guard, a very large man, wound up and punched Dan in the jaw.

His head snapped back and a low moan escaped him.

"Dan!" Jade screamed. "No!"

She turned to Martin and grabbed his arm. "What's going on? Why are you doing this?"

The guard punched Connor in the stomach, causing him to double over as much as he could with his hands behind him. He sagged to the left.

The guard went back to Dan and punched him in the mouth, making blood fly.

Berko gagged and put his hands over his own mouth.

"Stop him," Jade said to Martin. "Stop this."

"We need that password, Jade," he said. "Do you want to be responsible for the fall of the free world? You can stop it, Jade. Give me the password."

"You're not from the government," Elias said. "The government does not beat people up."

"Tell that to the guys detained at Abu Ghraib and Gitmo," Martin said. "This is SOP for hostiles."

This was patently untrue. Jade now saw Martin was a loose cannon. "But Dan isn't a hostile," Jade said. "I am!"

"We need *you*," Martin said. "We only need Colonel Stevenson to *motivate* you."

The guard picked up some implement from a table, moved behind Dan and stooped over, wrenching at something.

Dan began to scream.

"Stop!" Jade said. "Stop it!" She began to cry, seeing the agony on Dan's face as the guard must be pulling out her mentor's fingernails.

"What is wrong with you?" Elias said. "This is insane! Can we sit down and talk about this? We can come to some sort of agreement that you—"

"Give me the password," Martin said to Jade. "Give your country the password."

"My country does not torture citizens!" Jade screamed.

Dan's head lolled on his shoulders, his chest rising and falling quickly in gasped breaths, maybe with broken ribs, and he gazed through blackened, swelling eyes at the window.

"Sacrifices must be made, Jade. But Colonel Stevenson doesn't have to be one of them. You can stop it right now if you give me the password."

"There's no threat from the Chinese," Elias said. "Harry Gilby told us—"

"Gilby," Martin spat. "Of course he'd say that. What he really means is that letting the Chinese take over is not a threat. That it's a good thing."

Berko wept openly, and Elias's red eyes watered, his face a shade of red Jade had never seen on a face before.

"This is not right," Elias said. "This is *not right*." Then he turned to Jade. "But do not give them the password. No matter what happens in there. Don't give it to them."

Berko stared at him, his mouth open, and Jade said, "We can't let them do this, Elias."

"We can't let them have the password. They're not the NSA. I don't know who they are, but they are *not* on our side. The Chinese are *not* going to attack."

Nothing made any sense. Jade tried to code what she was seeing, what she was hearing, what she was feeling, but her brain was a jumble of inflamed neurons that couldn't put together a cogent thought.

Who was right, and who was wrong? What was real? Who were these people?

"What should I do, Berko? What should I do?"

The guard got behind Dan again, presumably to pull out his remaining fingernails.

"I don't know," he whispered.

"You will not give the password," Elias said.

Dan howled in pain, the sound echoing into the deepest part of Jade's mind, the same howl her sister would give when she felt most disconnected from the world, her existential torment equal to Dan's physical suffering.

"Sure, it's not *your* friend, your mentor being tortured in there," Jade shouted. "What if it was your mom?"

"I'd still say no," Elias said.

"That's a lie," Jade said.

"Jade," Martin said. "Gilby has been in contact with the Chinese, and they are ready to attack. They're not going to wait until the eleventh."

"Don't listen to him, Jade. He's the one who's lying."

"That's right, Jade, listen to the hit-and-run murderer instead of your instincts. Your instincts are right. The Chinese will attack, and your program can stop them. You said so yourself."

Jade was frozen with indecision.

"All right," Martin said. "You know we can run a password decryption program. It'll just take longer. And if I have to do that, then we're going to kill Colonel Stevenson."

Jade inhaled so hard she choked. "No," she said.

"If I tap on that window—see the gun on the table?—Lieutenant Hobart will pick it up, aim it at Connor's heart, and pull the trigger. And then he'll shoot Colonel Stevenson. So it's up to you who lives . . . and who dies. Your choice."

"Colonel Stevenson is an airman," Jade said. "He fought for this country in Iraq. He has a Purple Heart."

"Yes," Martin said. "And he's serving his country right now by helping persuade you to do what's right."

Jade sobbed, crying so hard she couldn't get her breath, dizzy, in danger of falling over.

Martin leaned forward and tapped on the glass.

Chapter 19

THE GUARD PICKED up the pistol and aimed at Connor's heart, and before Jade could say anything, he pulled the trigger.

"No!" Jade screamed.

Connor and his chair pitched over, a fine red mist hanging where he'd sat milliseconds ago.

"The password, Jade," Martin said.

As if she were inside a nightmare, she couldn't move or speak. She opened her mouth but all that emerged was a thin stream of saliva since she could no longer swallow.

"Jade," Martin said.

The image of Olivia hanging from the fence wafted before her imagination, how time stood still, the way it did now.

She was aware Elias and Berko both chattered away beside her, but she was inside a bubble of cement.

Martin tapped on the glass a second time.

The lieutenant then aimed the pistol at Dan's chest and shot him, and blood poured out, darkening his shirt. He slumped forward.

Jade fell to her knees and the room went dark.

When she came to she was staring at the ceiling and Berko was throwing up in the corner. Elias had his hands around Martin's neck and Hobart pulled out a sidearm and aimed it at Elias's head.

"Stop!" Jade screamed and struggled to her feet, throwing herself in between Elias and Hobart, the gun now aimed at her head, and she didn't care.

She could not watch another one of her friends die. Not one more.

Elias let go of Martin. Everything stopped.

"Put the gun away," Jade said to Hobart with a calm she didn't feel. "Put it away."

Behind her she heard Berko grunt.

She turned. Martin held a gun against Berko's head.

"Who else will have to die before you do the right thing, Jade? Give me the password, or Berko dies too."

"Okay! Okay!" Jade said. "You can have it! It's right here, I've got it right here, just please don't kill Berko! Please!"

The lieutenant let go of Berko and he crumpled to the floor, landing in his own vomit.

"Let's go to the lab. I want you to type it in yourself, Jade."

Rage simmered up in Jade's gut. "You son of a bitch. You are going to burn in hell for this."

"Let's go."

Martin herded them out the door, that bastard Hobart following them.

Jade noticed Berko and Elias were keeping their distance, as if a toxic cloud surrounded her.

In a way, it did.

"What have you done?" Elias's whispered words drifted toward her.

She turned on him. "They would have killed Berko, Elias!"

"A lot more people are going to die instead when the power goes out. People in hospitals who need life support. Elderly people. Babies. You know they are. And you could have prevented that."

"You wouldn't be saying that if they'd aimed the gun at you," Berko said.

"I *did* have a gun pointed at me, " Elias said, "and I'm saying it."

"Elias," Martin said. "Just so you know. We would have shot Berko, and then you, and we have people stationed near the Veverkas' house, ready to execute her whole family if necessary."

Of course they did. Jade imagined Clementine in her blue nightie and fox ears, trying to understand why there were men with guns in her house, why they wanted to hurt her and her mom and dad, and how she would die in confusion and pain.

Elias wouldn't even look at Jade. He was done with her.

She didn't blame him.

They rode the elevator down to the lab, and Berko shook violently, clutching his stomach. "I need to use the restroom," he said.

"You can wait," Martin said.

"No, I really can't," he said. "I'm going to throw up again."

"Will you let the man go to the bathroom?" Elias said. "Send your merc with him, but for the love of God, let him go!"

Martin turned to Hobart and nodded. When the elevator doors opened, Berko stumbled out toward the men's room, and Hobart followed, his rifle pointed at the floor.

Jade opened the lab door and Martin and Elias followed her in. She sat at her workstation, logged in, and navigated to the back door. She sat staring at the password box, the blinking cursor, and typed in the password.

She hoped and prayed the Chinese actually planned to attack.

That she had done the right thing, but a feeling of doom enveloped her. Because if there was no Chinese attack, what were these people planning to do with Clementine?

She stood and let Martin have her chair, and the screen lit up his smiling face. He bowed his head as if in prayer, then got up and patted Jade on the arm. She wanted to kick the crap out of him. The place on her arm where he touched her felt poisoned.

"You're a good girl, Jade," he said. "I knew we could count on you."

Elias faced him and looked him in the eye. "You're not part of the government," he said. "Are you?"

"No," Martin said. "But we soon will be."

"You shot Olivia."

"An accident," Martin said, his hands up. "That was not supposed to happen."

"And there's no Chinese threat, is there?"

"No, but they certainly have been helpful with funding. They paid for all this. What they don't realize is we're going to use this program against them. The Russians too."

"You're communists. Or socialists. Or whatever you people are calling yourselves these days."

"Some of us are, yes, but this is a truly bipartisan effort. Our country has been slipping for decades. It's a disgrace, but what could anyone do? The government itself is so huge it employs one-tenth of the population, and that's not counting the private-sector jobs that depend on government contracts. This was not what the Founding Fathers had in mind.

"You remember your Declaration of Independence, don't you? Sometimes in the course of human events, it becomes necessary to overthrow the government by the people, for the people, of the people. Because the people are too stupid to choose appropriate representatives. We're going to start over, and we're going to do it right."

"You're one of those, huh?" Elias said. "Everything was perfect back in the good old days of slavery, right?"

Martin shook his head. "Not at all. We can do better, but the only way to change things is with a war or another cataclysmic event. That's what Clementine is. We've had analysts going through the program since you first loaded it on the mainframe, Jade. We think we've figured out how to get it to do what we want it to."

What he didn't know was the program was a lot like her sister. Unpredictable. Driven by unknowable motives. Its mind worked the way Clem's did—in ways no one could truly understand. And the fact they had the hubris to believe they were smart enough to control the uncontrollable would be their downfall.

It had definitely been her biggest weakness. Believing she was the smartest one in the room. That she knew best. Wanting to impress people with her intelligence and cleverness.

Berko and Hobart entered the room, Berko wrung out and wobbly.

"Get him some water," Jade said.

Too weak to resist her, Berko allowed her to help him to his chair. His clammy skin dampened her hands.

Jade hoped Hobart would go for the water so . . . what? So they could overpower Martin? He had a gun, and even if Elias could get it away from him, what then? There were more soldiers outside, the place was crawling with them.

"I'll get it," Martin said. He left the room, and Hobart leaned against one of the workstations.

"You will be court-martialed," Elias told Hobart.

The guard ignored him.

"And then you will be shot."

Still nothing.

"You're not even military, are you?" Elias said.

"Not officially," Hobart said.

"So you're all mercs, is that it?"

Hobart said nothing.

When Martin returned, he handed Berko a chilled bottle of water and set four more on a desk. Jade opened his bottle and handed it to him. He took a long drink and then laid his head on his arm on the desk.

"What did you do with Gilby?" he asked Martin in a faint voice.

"He has been moved," Martin said. "Don't worry about him. He'll be fine."

"So what happens now?" Jade said.

"You've written up the documentation for the program, correct? I'll need that, and if I have any questions, you'll be here to help me."

"And then you'll let us go home?"

"At some point," Martin said. "Yes."

At some point. Maybe she'd end up chained up here in the lab, peeing in a bucket, writing code for crazy people.

She wished they'd turned the gun on her. She wished she was the dead one instead of Dan and Connor. And Olivia. Because how could she live with herself knowing she could have prevented two deaths if she'd handed over the password sooner?

This wasn't like in the movies, where the villain gives the hero several chances, almost pulls the trigger then the cavalry swoops in and stops them. Dan *was* the cavalry. And now there was no one to save them.

And . . . the other thing. There would be no one to get her mom into a stem cell study.

How crazy was her mind that she continued to think selfish thoughts like that? Two men were dead because of her.

She looked at the tattoo on her forearm, in her mother's handwriting. *I love you.*

This was all she had left, because she was certain she would never see her family again.

Chapter 20

THE HARD WORK done, Martin relaxed into full lecture mode. "We're going to bring back family farming," he said. "We're going to revitalize the agricultural economy, decentralize food production. Why do you think we chose Kansas? So many ghost towns and abandoned family farms. We're going to teach the country how to farm again, without so much dependence on technology. No more patents on seed strains and the constant threat of patent suits if one of their seeds drifts onto your land. Your dad will get to go back to real farming."

"So no more technology?" Jade said.

"No, we still have the technology. It'll just be in the hands of people who know how to use it. Trained people. One of the things that's torn this country apart is the anonymity of the Internet. The ability to say whatever you want without consequence. We're forcing people to gather in person again, to be part of communities in the real world. We've got personnel in place all over the country, ready to take over. We're breaking down the bureaucracies. We're reopening the factories around the country. No more offshore manufacturing. It will all be done right here."

While Jade liked the idea of the resurrection of family farming, she couldn't understand how this group could accomplish what Martin talked about. It was all just a dream. The country would fall apart, and China could come in and take over if they wanted to. And why wouldn't they want to? "Won't the military just—stop you?" Jade asked.

"If the power grid goes down, the military can't use their equipment. Sure, the older stuff, but who knows how to operate anything anymore without the aid of technology? And we've got plans in place to take over the energy industry. We'll require the use of nuclear power, of solar, and wind, and hydroelectricity. We've got people in place in every sector. No more special interests, no more lobbyists buying favors, and forcing the use of fossil fuels. The US will stop contributing to climate change. We will be a shining example to the rest of the world."

Martin had seemed like such a normal guy when she'd first met him. The thousands of systems it took to keep the country running couldn't just be taken away.

They stood at the lab door while Martin waved his keycard in front of the keypad. "Once all the tech goes down, the power goes out, we'll step forward and say we have a solution." The door clicked open and they all filed inside. "We'll say we can help. We know what to do, because we've been planning for this contingency for twenty-five years. We had the foresight to put a plan into action at the end of the last century."

"The last guy to try this," Elias said, "had the military behind him. And his plan was to exterminate two-thirds of the population of his country to take it back to 'year zero.' Is that part of your plan too?"

Martin laughed. "Pol Pot was an ignorant, bloodthirsty madman. And you may have noticed we do have a military—ex-military, trained mercenaries, et cetera, who we've been sending to the four corners of the country."

Would Martin's plan be all that bad?

Of course it would, because as in every utopia system ever devised, only the "right" people would have power.

"Listen," Martin said. "You'd be up at the top of the food chain with your computer science genius. Berko and Elias would be up there too."

The aristocracy in what would surely become a wasteland, with anarchy and chaos reigning supreme.

"Martin," Jade said. "It will never work."

"The American experiment has failed. Democracy has failed. Look what it's brought us to. The candidates in the last election? A reality TV star and a career bureaucrat under indictment for fraud? Are you kidding me? And even aside from that, lifetime politicians whose only interest is staying in power, completely unable to accomplish anything, locked in a battle of wills against each other. No progress at all, the dumbing down of the educational system—all those things are endemic to our process here. Government by a small but benevolent, highly educated, intelligent group—oligarchy—is the last best hope of this country."

"It's not going to work," Elias said. "Even if it could, you're talking about the overthrow of the US government. A coup."

"A peaceful coup," Martin said.

"But you've already killed people!" Jade shouted.

"And there'll be rioting, and you know it," Elias said. "More people will die. There's no way around that."

Martin shrugged. "Sometimes the herd needs to be thinned. We're way past due." He stood, resembling an excited kindergarten teacher. "We've accomplished great things here, and we won't forget. There will be special perks for all of you once we've taken control."

"So we'll be the new royalty," Berko said. "The privileged few."

Martin shook his head impatiently. "You're missing the big picture. There will no longer be a privileged few. We will have true equality."

"That's not possible," Elias said, staring. He turned his gaze on Martin. "You're an educated man, Martin. You know this. True equality is impossible. Like the scripture says: 'The poor you will always have with you.'"

Martin's face clouded. "Don't you quote scripture to me, boy. But yes. You're right. We're educated. We have history to show us what has worked, and what hasn't, and why it hasn't. We're going to do it right."

"There's the fallacy," Berko said. "That's what everyone who's ever overthrown a country has thought—that they had special knowledge. That they were extraordinary. Anointed, even. With gifts no one else had, so they were the only ones who were entitled to lead the people."

Martin's smile was patronizing. "I also have the benefit of age, and watching the country deteriorate bit by excruciating bit. When I was a kid, Lyndon Johnson set a precedent—guns and butter. We could have our war and eat it too. No sacrifice required. No skin in the game, and therefore no support for the troops in Vietnam. Then Nixon set another—that the president was not bound by the law of the land, that he was the Übermensch to whom rules and law did not apply. Forever degraded the highest office in the land and forever dismantled the respect that office once commanded. And underlying all that, unprecedented prosperity that raised up generation after generation of spoiled, idle, entitled kids who demanded that standards be lowered to meet them until our education system is nearly useless. The difference is my friends and I aren't interested in power for its own sake. We are deeply interested in restructuring the country so it works, so it raises up citizens that are engaged, productive, satisfied. Reintroduce the idea that sacrifice and hard work are the only things that make life truly worthwhile. That's what we're interested in."

Chapter 21

"THIS IS YOUR fault," Elias said to Jade. "You did this."

She sat in despair. He was right.

Martin held up his hands. "Now, now," he said. "You're all going to be national heroes. Once we bring down the power grids, we'll offer Clementine to save the day, and everyone will know you were the designer. Jade, you did the right thing. And all that's left is to upload it to the power grids."

"Wait a minute," Berko said. "Once it's on the Web, there's no telling what it will do."

"We've got it under control," Martin said.

"No you don't," Jade said.

"Don't worry," Martin said.

The three looked at each other again, horrified.

"But you're not interested in power," Berko said, sarcasm dripping from his words. "You're not interested in being emperor of the universe or anything."

"We're interested in only one thing—making this country better, making it work again. When the power goes down, *we'll* step in and say we have a solution."

"But the program is unpredictable," Jade said. "I told you that. Once it's on the Internet, it will propagate its own culture, communicate across the Internet in a language no one outside of it will be able to understand. You know how fast it computes. You know no human mind can analyze data as fast as it can, and it will begin to make its own decisions, like—"

"Decide what the world needs is to be cleaned up permanently. Detonate nuclear bombs," Elias said. "What if that's the determination it makes?"

Martin waved his hand. "We have the best minds in the country to control it."

"The best minds would not only understand how harebrained this scheme is, but have the humility to understand it can't be controlled. Not in the way you think. No one can control it," Jade whispered. *Just like no one can control the real Clementine.*

"Sure we can," Martin said. "We have a few more things to line up before we can upload it, but it will happen soon."

"How soon?" Jade said.

"That would ruin the surprise, now, wouldn't it?"

Did that mean he believed something *could* be done to stop it? But he also believed he could control the program.

"I've got to take off now. I'll see you on the other side of the revolution."

And he walked out the door, Hobart behind him.

"Okay," Elias said. "We have to find a way out of here tonight. We have to inform the FBI about what's going to happen."

"They're not going to believe us," Berko said. "And with all the soldiers crawling over this place, we can't get away."

"No way we're going to sit here and let this happen," Elias said. "I'm going to have to break into the system and shut it down."

"How are you going to do that?" Berko said.

"All I need is the IP address of the main processor in the server room, and then . . . I don't know," Elias said. "But I have to try." He rolled back to his desk. "Between Jade and me, we can figure this out."

"We need to go to my parents' house," Jade said. "I have a program that'll scramble Clementine. That's what we have to upload to the main processor."

"How come you never mentioned this before?" Elias said.

"I didn't think I'd need it," Jade said.

"You should have brought it with you," Elias said, suddenly angry. "You should have thought ahead."

"Well, I'm sorry, Elias," Jade said, matching his ire. "I guess it didn't occur to me at the time SiPraTech wanted to overthrow the United States government. Forgive my lack of foresight. It doesn't matter anyway—they've locked us out of the system again. If I had the AIP here—"

"The AIP?" Berko said.

"That's the name of the program that neutralizes Clementine," Jade said. She turned back to Elias. "If I had it here, I wouldn't be able to upload it anyway, because we're locked out."

"So you're not even going to try?" Elias said, turning away from his keyboard.

"What can we do if we can't access the system?"

"I'll find my way in."

He typed on his keyboard and Jade tried to think of a solution. She sat down at her desk and reached out for her keyboard.

Then the lights went out.

Chapter 22

JADE SCREAMED.

"What did you do?" Jade heard Berko's thin voice from across the room.

As the monitors died, the light died with them, leaving them in a darkness so complete it seemed as if the air had been cut off too.

The CPU fans shut down, and silence descended.

"Is it just a power outage, you suppose?" Jade said.

"Have we ever had one before?" Berko said. "Of course it's not a power outage. It's deliberate. We can't use the computers without power."

"Well," Elias said. "That's one way of keeping us out of the system."

A small LED emergency battery-powered bulb near the ceiling illuminated, a sickly green glow that barely gave any light at all.

Jade got her phone out and turned on the flashlight. She stood, but her balance was thrown and she almost pitched over.

"Come on," she said. "Let's go back to the house to wait for the New World Order."

"That's not even close to funny," Elias said.

"It wasn't meant to be." She shone the beam of her phone in the guys' direction as Elias helped Berko stand. She directed her beam to the floor in front of them so they could see where to go. She led the way out the door into the dark hallway. She walked to the elevator.

"If there's no power, Jade," Elias said, "there's no elevator. Let's take the stairs. You think you can make it, buddy?"

"Uh-huh," Berko said, and stumbled. Elias lifted Berko's arm over his own shoulders and walked him to the stairwell door.

Jade reached for the doorknob and twisted it.

It wouldn't budge. It was locked. She'd assumed once the power went out, the electronic locks would disengage. This door didn't have an electronic lock though. It had an old-fashioned one. She rattled the knob.

"What's the matter?" Berko said.

She stepped back from the door, and Elias reached out and twisted it. Then he disentangled himself from Berko, who leaned against the wall, and tried the knob with both hands. Then he shook it violently until his whole body was in on the action and ended up slamming his palms on the door and then kicking the bottom of it again and again.

Then they stood in stunned silence.

"It's dead-bolted from outside," Elias said. "There's no way out of here."

Jade stood in the dark and the silence, with no more whirring CPUs around her, disoriented, as if she might topple to the ground.

"They knew we'd try to get into the system," Elias said. "Of course they did."

"Listen," Berko said.

They did, and Jade heard fans.

"They can't shut down the servers," Berko said. "They need them for the uplink. They must have a backup generator or an alternate source of power. We need to get into the server room and shut everything down."

The screen of his phone illuminated his face. He turned on the flashlight feature and shone it in front of him.

Jade's mental paralysis shocked her, how this hadn't occurred to her. Berko was a steely-eyed missile man, she now saw, even as sick as he was. She stood and bumped into Elias.

"Sorry," she said. They walked single file toward the server room. Berko got there first.

"It's locked too," he said.

"No shit," Elias said. "How are we going to get in there?"

"We're just going to have to . . . break the door down," Jade said.

"Yeah? How are we going to do that? These aren't wooden doors. They're reinforced steel. Unless you have a blowtorch I don't know about, there's no way we're getting in there."

"So what are we going to do?" Berko said.

"Nothing," Elias said. "We're not going to do anything." And he dropped to the floor, sitting against the wall, resigned.

"You've got to be the one with the solution," Berko said. "You're military. Don't they do like survival training or something like that? How to escape stuff?"

"I didn't go to magician school," Elias said, irritated.

"There has to be a way out."

This was too heavy for a group of twentysomethings to bear.

In future history books, she would be remembered as the woman who destroyed civilization.

Again. Her own self-importance. Her, her, her.

She wanted to punch herself in the face.

And who was she kidding? History books? How was that going to work? With no control over Clementine, the country would end up a *Matrix*-style wasteland, but the computer would not set up any cozy little tanks for them. No, it would be Cormac McCarthy's *The Road*. Since she'd never experienced true catastrophe, her only frame of reference was pop culture. And that would be a thing of the past.

Without technology, Jade was worthless. She couldn't do anything without it. She had no real-world skills she could use. She thought about the AIP cartridge at her folks' house, and how far away it seemed. But without power, without access to the computer system, what good would it do them?

Elias stood. "I'm going to go down to the kitchen and see how much food and water we have. Figure out how we're going to ration it."

"What difference does it make?" Berko said. "Do you really think they're going to ever let us out of here? Because I sure as hell don't."

"I'll be back," Elias said, as if Berko hadn't spoken. "I'll also look for something for your head, Berko. Turn off your phones to conserve the batteries." He walked away from them down the hall.

Jade's impulse from another life, another time, would have been to make some crack about who did Elias think he was, giving them orders? But jokes now seemed pointless.

Across from the lab was a sitting area with two chairs, an end table, a useless lamp, and a ficus tree. Berko walked over to it and sat in one of the chairs.

How long would it take without tech for the country to dissolve into chaos?

What would Martin tell her family—if he planned to tell them anything at all? And Berko's, and Elias's? How would they explain to Clementine what had happened? Tears came to Jade's eyes at the thought of her mother further deteriorating, and dying without ever knowing what happened to Jade. And Dad would have to go it alone in the awful new world with Clem.

Chapter 23

As JADE AND Berko sat in the dark silence, Jade sensed air moving, and thought of standing in a ripe wheat field, the wind blowing. Remembered being out in the fields, riding the combine with her dad when she was little. Riding in his pickup truck on the way to . . .

She sat straight up and listened. Then heard a sound unlike the electric whirring of the server fans. Barely perceptible—a quiet but discernible whooshing sound.

She grabbed Berko's wrist. "Do you hear that?"

"What?" came Berko's listless reply.

"I hear air," she said.

"What are you talking about?"

Elias came walking back down the hall, packets of peanut butter crackers and water bottles in his arms. "I think we have enough food to—"

"Ssshh," Jade said. "Come here. Listen."

Elias didn't argue. He froze in place and cocked his head. "What is it? I don't hear anything."

"Air," she said. "Ventilation shafts." Jade remembered riding in her dad's pickup truck on the way to one of his HVAC jobs, replacing a furnace. Crawling through the dusty ducts and sneezing.

"The ventilation system has to lead to the surface," Elias said.

Berko started breathing hard. "Unless they plugged all that up at the surface," he said, sounding panicky.

"We need to figure out how to get into it," Elias said, crouching and setting the food and water on the floor in front of Berko. "We need to look for vents. There's one of those LED emergency lights in every room. I'll go grab three so we each have one. No telling how long they'll last though." He dashed down the hall, disappearing into the darkness.

"How are you feeling, Berko?" Jade said.

"Okay," he said.

"Why don't you try to eat something?" she said, opening up peanut butter crackers for him.

He took small bites followed by sips of water.

Elias reappeared with LED lights.

"Okay," Jade said. "Let's everybody be quiet for a minute. Listen for air. Listen and feel for it. That's where the vents will be."

"But the vents will be too small for us to get into," Berko said.

"Then we'll have to enlarge the openings," Jade said.

"What are we going to use to enlarge them?" Berko said.

"Let's find them first."

"What are these walls made of?" Berko said. "Because if it's concrete, I believe we are royally screwed."

"Berko, no offense," Elias said, "but if you ask one more question, I'm going to punch you."

They fanned out, searching for the larger registers. Jade found the first one, down near the baseboard in the hall across from the lab. "Here we go," she said. "Is there a wrench or a screwdriver in the lab?"

"I'll go look," Elias said.

He returned with both, and Jade got down on her knees and loosened the screws holding the register plate in place. She removed it and stuck her head inside.

The duct would not accommodate her shoulders. She twisted and bent herself but it was no use. The hope that had been building inside her evaporated. And she remembered the last time she'd been inside ductwork she was around ten years old.

"It's not big enough," she said.

Elias groaned. "But you said—"

"I know what I said, but—"

"How big is it?" Berko said.

"No more than eighteen inches across," Jade said.

"I can do it," Berko said. "I'm the smallest. I'll go."

"You're not small enough," Jade said.

"Let me try," Berko said. "I can't do anything else. I want to contribute somehow."

"You'll get stuck in there," Elias said. "We'll just have to pry the elevator doors open somehow and go up through the trapdoor on top." He walked over to the elevator and attempted to wedge his fingertips between the doors. His attempts became more frenzied, and still the doors wouldn't budge, and finally he was just pounding his fists on the metal.

He turned, looked wildly around, and let out a roar. He picked up the unoccupied chair, lifted it high over his head, and smashed it repeatedly into the wall, until he crashed through the drywall and splintered the two-by-fours behind it.

As debris settled, Jade and Berko stood stock-still, as if moving might make Elias turn on them in his wrath. He dropped the chair, breathing hard.

Jade realized she heard debris falling with an echo. She lifted her LED light and stuck both her head and the light through the hole. Behind the wall another wall curved, made of concrete, about five feet beyond the drywall. That was weird.

"Take a look," she said.

Elias held his light to the hole, then pulled on the drywall, until the studs were exposed. Then he shone the light into the cavern beyond and stuck his head in. She heard him whistle.

He reemerged from the hole, drywall dust whitening his hair, looking like a warrior painted up to go into battle. "Something else was here before this building."

"Something else?" Berko said. "What do you mean?"

"I'm not sure," Elias said. "But it's a good thing, because there's room for us to move around behind these walls."

He stuck his head and arm back in. "Holy Mary," Jade heard him say inside the hole. "There's a ladder built into the wall back there."

"There is?" Jade said, feeling a thrill of hope, and then an immediate crash. Where did the ladder go?

"It's to the right." Elias backed away so Jade could take a look. She leaned through the opening. She looked the ladder up and down but couldn't see a terminus at either end in the dark.

She pulled out of the hole and said, "How far up is it, do you think?"

"No way to tell," Elias said. "So there's one level beneath us— where the storage rooms are."

"Okay," Jade said. "We're going to need to make another hole. We can't reach the ladder from here." She walked over to the sitting-area chairs, where she thought the ladder might be closest to.

Berko stood and had to grab the wall.

"Sorry, buddy," Jade said. She moved the chair, the end table, and the ficus, then removed a framed abstract print from the wall. "Right about here, I think."

Elias picked up the chair again and bashed another hole in the drywall, this one six feet high by sixteen inches wide.

Jade investigated inside the hole. It would be a close fit.

"I'm going up first," Elias said. "Berko, you come next, and then Jade last."

Jade wanted to argue but for once decided she'd just go along.

"Wait," she said. "We need to take this food and water with us."

"My backpack is under my desk," Elias said.

"I'll get it. Okay if I empty it out?"

"Sure," he said.

She went into the lab and to Elias's desk. She cast about underneath it and found his backpack, then upended it on the floor. His tablet fell out, and she briefly wondered if she should bring it. But it was replaceable. As she headed to the door, she spied something that wasn't: the photo of Olivia and Ruth Bader Ginsburg. She slid it into the backpack and exited the lab.

Out in the hall, Jade put the water bottles and food into the pack, then slung it on her back.

She wondered what would await them at the top of the ladder.

Elias disappeared into the hole, then turned back and said, "It's going to be a reach. I can just barely grab it." He looked back at

Berko, the smallest of them, and Jade wondered if his arms were long enough.

"When I'm on the ladder, Berko, you're going to need to reach in and grab my hand, and I'll pull you over. Okay?"

"Okay," Berko said faintly.

Then Elias squeezed sideways through the hole, his right hand clutching the two-by-four stud as he swung to the right. The wood groaned as it bore his weight and then Jade heard a metallic tone as he grabbed on to the ladder.

"Wait," Berko said, turning to Jade, his eyes feverish with fear. "I'm going to have to swing in backward. Reach backward to get the ladder."

"I guess so," she said. "Elias will help you."

"How am I supposed to get my foot on there?"

"I've got my light stuck in my shirt," Elias said. "You'll be able to see. We've gotta go. Come on."

Berko took a shaky breath and slid through the studs and held on to the farthest right one with his right hand. "Whoa, it's a long way down."

"Don't look down," Elias said. "Look at me. Grab my hand."

Once he disappeared, Jade stuck her head in so she could see what was happening.

Berko dangled from Elias's arm, his feet bicycling frenetically.

"Berko. Stop. Bring your right foot to the ladder." Elias's voice strained with effort. "You need to be calm."

Berko kicked his right leg out and it hit the ladder but bounced off again. He tried again, and this time Elias yanked him forward, where Berko took hold of the vertical edge of the ladder with his left hand.

"Okay, buddy, I'm going to let go—"

"No! Don't let go!"

"You've got this. You're okay. So you let go of my hand and put it on the ladder. Okay?"

Berko finally did as Elias said, and Elias shook out his arm and clenched and unclenched his fist.

Berko's breath came in quick, ragged gasps as he hugged the ladder.

"All right, buddy, now you need to start going down."

"Down?" Jade said.

"Yes," Elias said. "We need to go find Gilby. We can't leave him here."

"He'll be fine," Jade said. "We need to get out of here."

"We're not leaving him."

Berko carefully picked his way down the ladder.

"What are we going to use to break through the drywall?" Jade said. "There aren't any chairs."

"You were a punter, right?" Elias said. "You're going to kick the drywall in."

Oh, am I?

But she held her tongue, and as soon as Berko and Elias were on the ground, she tried to squeeze between the studs, but the backpack held her out.

"I'm dropping the pack down," she said. "Somebody catch it."

When Elias was below her, she let it go and he caught it. Then she squeezed through the studs and looked down. It was a mistake, but she couldn't look away for a moment.

"Go on, Jade," Berko called up. "Piece of cake."

Before she made the commitment, she backed out of the hole

and took in the hallway, the place she'd spent the past three months, where her Clementine was, and the sharp sting of regret pierced her heart. For so many things. Then she leaned out into the darkness, her right hand on the stud, which creaked, and reached for the ladder.

She couldn't hold on to both. She'd have to let go of the stud to reach it. The wood was moist under her hand. She glanced below her, and Berko and Elias looked so small. It was a long way down.

"Come on, Jade," Elias said.

And she let go. Grabbed the ladder, her hand so wet with sweat it almost slipped right off the rung. But she clutched it and got her foot onto a lower rung, and she was descending.

When she hit the ground, her arms were shaking from holding on so tight.

"Okay," Elias said. "Go ahead and give this drywall a kick."

"Can't you just punch it?"

"All you're going to do is put that great big foot of yours there and kick harder than you've ever kicked in your life. As if your life depended on it. Which, in case you'd forgotten, it does."

So they had noticed how big her feet were. How could they not?

She looked behind her. "The concrete wall's too far away for me to brace my back against it."

"Okay," Elias said, getting between her and the wall, pressing his back to hers and putting his foot on the wall. "Let 'er rip."

Looked like she didn't have any choice. Berko stood well away, watching.

She put her left foot against the drywall and pushed on it, gauging how much pressure it would need to break through. The give was minimal.

"Kick it, Jade."

"I'm going to, just give me a second, okay?" she said, testy.

She pressed her back against Elias's solid one, bent her leg, aimed and pushed harder. She heard a crack, but it hadn't broken.

"Kick it," Elias said. "Picture Martin's face on it."

Jade backed up as far as she could, then pictured the Ephesus football field, pictured herself preparing to punt with nine guys rushing toward her. She did, and kicked with all her might.

"Wow," Elias said, turning toward the gaping hole in the drywall. "Good kick. Help me widen this hole."

He and Jade yanked pieces of drywall away until the hole was big enough to squeeze through. One after the other, they passed between the studs, and Elias put the backpack on once they were in the bottom floor hallway.

Elias led them, holding his LED light in front of him, the hall had a couple of these lights too.

"Gilby?" Elias shouted.

Jade heard a noise. She pressed her ear against one of the doors but heard nothing. Then she realized the sound came from across the hall. Jade knocked on the door. "Mr. Gilby?"

She heard muffled noises inside. She looked down at the door-knob and realized the electronic locks wouldn't work without electricity.

"How are we going to get it open?" she said. "I don't think I can kick it down."

"We're lucky the power's out, because I don't think our key-cards would work." Elias reached into his back pocket and pulled out his wallet, opened it, and selected a card—a library card from the looks of it. He held it up for everyone to see and then slid it in between the doorjamb and the door next to the knob. He wiggled it up and down, trying to push it in farther.

"Does that really work?" Jade asked Berko.

"Why are you asking me?"

"I'm just asking."

She heard a click and the door swung inward.

Chapter 24

THIS ROOM APPEARED identical to the one they'd entered—was it only that afternoon? It seemed like a lifetime ago. Gilby lay on his side on the cot. Zip ties restrained his hands and feet, and a strip of duct tape covered his mouth. His eyes rolled toward them as Elias shone his LED on the man's face.

"Is that him?"

"Yes," Jade said. She reached into her pocket and pulled out her pocketknife, and Gilby squealed behind the tape. "I'm not going to cut you," she said. Elias held the light while she inspected his bonds. Zip ties. These people meant business. She cut the wrist tie first, then the ankle.

Once Gilby's hands and feet were free, Elias helped him sit up, and he rolled his shoulders and flexed his feet. Then he reached up and carefully peeled the tape off his face, taking a good bit of his mustache off with it. He let out a burst of air, as if he'd been holding his breath the whole time.

"Give him some water, Berko," Elias said.

Berko reached into the backpack, pulled out a water bottle, opened it, and handed it over.

"Thank you," he said in a parched voice, then drank half the bottle in one swig. He wiped his mouth and set down the bottle, and then he sat and stared, his hands pressed between his knees, and rocked.

Jade and Elias shifted their weight from foot to foot, trying to give the guy a little time to get it together. Jade felt embarrassed for him and ashamed that she was embarrassed, because his friend had been killed, and he'd probably thought he would die down here in the dark, alone.

Berko sat down next to him on the bed and put his hand on Gilby's shoulder. "It's okay," he said. "We found you. But we need to go, and we need you to come with us. Okay?"

Gilby nodded his head and wiped his face. "I'm sorry," he said. He cleared his throat and drank more water, then capped it and stood. Then he groaned and pressed his hands into his side.

"Are you all right?" Jade asked.

"My ribs," Gilby said. "I'll be okay."

They filed out of the room and walked toward the hole in the wall.

"Mr. Gilby," Jade said.

"Call me Harry," he said.

"Okay. Can you tell us who you are? How you knew about the project?"

"Do you work for the government?" Berko said.

"No," Gilby said. "I used to work with Martin at a think tank. We studied government systems to come up with solutions for bloated bureaucracies. Over the time I was there, the organization began to split into factions—those who wanted to work within the system, and those who . . . didn't. Martin and a few others were always pontificating about how they'd run things if they ever got the chance, and I got tired of hearing it. They were laid off—a kind way of putting it."

They were in front of the hole in the wall now, and everyone paused to listen to Gilby.

"Anyway, our employer kept Martin and his group under surveillance. I know. It's not exactly legal, but we told the NSA about these folks, but they said they had bigger fish to fry. So we kept tabs on them. We got hold of some of their confidential emails—one of their members pulled a Hillary Clinton and put everything on a private server that was easy to breach. All of you were mentioned and the Clementine Program detailed."

He turned to Jade. "That's why I tried to get you to come with me in the grocery store in Miranda. I screwed it up. I'm sorry about that."

Jade's air left her. He'd been trying to rescue her from this situation. If she hadn't fought so hard . . . none of this would have happened. If she'd just gone with Gilby that day, maybe Dan, Connor, and Olivia would still be alive. They wouldn't now be trapped with little hope of escape. She'd be home with her family now.

"You're damn right you screwed up," Jade said, much louder than she'd intended. "Why didn't you say that? If you'd told me—"

"There wasn't time."

"And you nearly killed us when you ran us off the road," Jade said.

"I know," Gilby said, his voice rising. "You think I don't know that? Yes. I screwed it up. But I'm not a spy or secret service agent. I'm a political scientist. I have no real skills."

Jade let out a massive guffaw at this.

"This is going to sound a little crass," Berko said. "But why didn't Martin kill you when he caught you?"

"Because he wanted to use me to root out the rest of our group. He wanted to make sure he knew everyone's location, so once the 'revolution' began he could gather them all together."

Jade wanted to ask him if they'd tortured him the way they had Dan, but she didn't want to know. He looked banged up, but not to the extent Dan and Connor had. Her breath caught in her throat, thinking of them. But no time for that now.

"There's a ladder in there," Berko said to Gilby. "Do you think you can climb it?"

"I'll try," he said. "But I need to use the toilet first. I don't know how long it's been."

"Me too," Berko said.

Jade walked into the eerie darkness of the women's restroom alone, found her way into a stall, and took care of business. She set the LED on the counter and washed her hands and face, and searched her pockets for a hair band to tie back her hair but found none. She pressed her tattoo against her heart. "Help me, Mom," she said. "Help us, God."

She went back out in the hall where everyone else assembled.

"All right," Elias said. "Here's how it's going to go. I'll go up first, and then—"

"I think I should go up first," Gilby said, clearly feeling age made him the natural general of this makeshift platoon. "I'll lead the way, and then—"

"Excuse me," Elias said respectfully but firmly. "We've already been on the ladder, on the way down to find you."

"To rescue you," Jade added. "We've spent three months in this place, and we know a little bit more about it than you do."

"So you know where we are then," Gilby said.

Jade and Elias exchanged a glance. "Yeah," Elias said. "In the middle of nowhere."

"No," Gilby said. "I mean you know what this is. What this building is and how to get to the surface."

"What this building is?" Jade echoed.

Gilby looked at each of them. "They built this Compound, this office complex, inside an old Atlas missile silo."

"Does . . . does that mean they have a . . ." Jade said.

"A nuke?" Berko said.

Gilby shrugged. "Not yet."

"Not yet," Elias mocked. "There's no way they could . . ." He trailed off, obviously remembering what SiPraTech had accomplished so far. The supercomputer. The militia. The people they'd killed.

"At any rate," Gilby said, "I know how to get us out of here. I know how to get to the ventilation tunnels that lead beyond the Compound fence."

Jade was suddenly grateful to Elias for having the presence of mind to rescue Gilby. Who knew if they'd have ever found their way out otherwise.

"We'd better get going," Elias said. "So—I'll go first, then Berko, then Gilby, and Jade brings up the rear. Let's take it slow and easy up, okay?"

None of them could climb a ladder and hold a light at the same time, so they put their LEDs in the necks of their shirts as Elias had done earlier, so they each emanated a dim glow.

Jade's breath came fast now, her hands clammy. A light brightened above her, and Elias stood six feet up, shining the light to help Berko start the climb.

Berko reached up and pulled himself up one rung and then another. Elias continued his ascent one-handed to provide light for Gilby and Jade.

When Gilby's feet hit the rung that was two above Jade's head, she started up. She could hear his labored breathing above, and wondered if his ribs were broken or just bruised. Either way, all this exertion had to hurt.

"Okay, Elias," she said. "You can put your light away."

"Sure?"

"Yeah," she said.

Their voices echoed in the massive concrete tube.

She listened to Gilby's tortured breathing, and the climb was perilously slow.

"Come on, guys," Elias said. "Gotta save the world. Can't stop now."

Jade heard a clang and then was almost knocked off the ladder when Gilby's foot slipped off a rung and kicked her in the face. If she could see, she would have seen stars. She wrapped her arms around the ladder and willed herself not to pass out.

"Did I kick you, Jade?" Gilby said.

"What happened?" Elias said.

"My foot slipped," Gilby said.

"You okay?" Elias said.

"I'm okay," Jade said, feeling wetness on her face. He'd kicked her in the stitches and opened up the wound again. It throbbed, and now her right eye stung with blood dripping in it. Desperate to wipe it away, she couldn't let go of the ladder for fear of losing her grip and falling.

"Rub some dirt on it," her football teammates would say. "Quit being such a wuss."

Jade waited until Gilby was three rungs above her to continue.

Berko's breathing echoed in the silo. "Stop," he said, swallowing. "I can't go on."

"Come on, buddy," Elias said.

"I can't hold on," Berko said. "My hands—they're—"

"You have to, Berko," Elias said. "Stay with me, buddy. Come on."

"I can't—"

"Yes, you can. Do you want out of here? Do you want to go back to Palo Alto so you can kiss the damned ground? Then come on!"

Berko grunted and he continued on.

"Hold up," Elias said. "I got something here."

Jade heard his hand slapping concrete and then his light came on.

She took in what he had found. A horizontal tunnel.

"Just a few more, buddy," Elias said. "Just a few more then solid ground. Hoist yourself up here. Come on."

There was no guardrail in front of the tunnel, but there was a small narrow catwalk from the ladder leading to it.

Jade squeezed her eyes shut thinking of standing on that catwalk.

Elias made it into the tunnel, then set his light at the edge so the other three could see.

"Come on, Berko," Elias said. "Give me your hand."

It seemed to take an eternity for Berko to take his foot off the ladder and step onto the catwalk.

Elias held out his muscled arm, and Berko wrapped his arms around it and let Elias pull him into the tunnel, where he fell over and stayed there.

"Okay, Gilby. Come on."

He ignored Elias's outstretched hand and hopped into the tunnel, landing with a muffled grunt.

"Jade," Elias said. He held his hand out to her and she grabbed it with her left hand, but then she couldn't make herself let go of the ladder with her right. It had a mind of its own. And suddenly she was back on the balance beam in the Ephesus High School gymnasium in front of dozens of people, unable to let go of the beam after mounting it and start her routine.

"Come on, Jade," Elias said, pulling on her arm.

"No," she said. "I can't."

"Yes, you can. I've got you."

"I'm too big. If I fall, I'll take you with me."

"You're not going to fall," Elias said, the patience in his voice nearly making her cry. He should just let her fall.

"I can't."

"We need to get Berko out of here and get him some medicine, and Gilby's hurt too. Now, I can't leave you here, you know that. You need to come on and let's help our friend, okay?"

And then he yanked on her arm and she lost her grip on the ladder, and her right foot slipped.

Elias pulled her onto the catwalk and then into the tunnel, pulling her backward as if they were swing dancing, and then pulled her to himself where he held on to her.

"I'm sorry," Elias said in her ear. "Had to be done."

"I know," Jade said. "I'm sorry for being such a wuss."

When he released her he held his light to her face, concern etching his as he examined her wound. He pulled a handkerchief out of his back pocket and shook it out.

"It's clean," he said, then wiped away some of the crusted blood.

"Thanks."

"It's not bleeding anymore," he said. "But I think you're going to need new sutures."

"I'll get right on that," she said.

Gilby stood leaning against the wall, holding his side. The tunnel was about ten feet in diameter, another tube, only horizontal and forty feet long with a door halfway down on the right and one at the end. The tunnel was lined in corrugated metal, with its own LED emergency light, just large enough to walk through.

"What's this?" Berko said. "Where does this go?"

There were steel crossbeams, and it was all painted white. "I know where we are," Elias said in an awed voice.

"That's right," Gilby said. He guided them toward the door on the right.

Elias glanced back at Jade and Berko, his face eerie in the dim light, and then watched Gilby pull on the door handle.

To Jade's surprise, it opened. Gilby disappeared inside then stuck his head back out. "Want to see?"

Jade wasn't sure she did. But Elias went inside, so Berko followed and then Jade.

Elias and Gilby held out their lights. Inside the large room, the walls were lined floor to ceiling with metal shelves. And on those shelves was the most extensive collection of weapons Jade had ever seen in real life.

Chapter 25

THEY ALL STARED in awe at the dozens of rocket launchers, hundreds of grenades, assault rifles, boxes of ammunition, C4, gas masks, mortars, bombs, and other items Jade couldn't identify.

If she'd had any doubts about SiPraTech's intentions, this room wiped them all out. They were preparing for more than a cyberattack.

"We need to take some of this with us," Elias said. He reached toward an AR-15 but Jade grabbed his arm.

"Absolutely not," she said.

Elias shook her off but she stepped in front of him.

"No," she said. She shook her head.

Elias looked at Berko, who also shook his head.

"How are we supposed to defend ourselves?" Elias said.

"Elias," Gilby said. "We need to leave everything as is. This is evidence. We need to get the ATF and the FBI out here. You do not want to be caught with an assault rifle."

Jade could see Elias was wrestling with himself.

"Please, Elias," Jade said. "Let's go. We need to stay focused."

Gilby pulled out his smartphone and snapped photos all around the room.

Elias dropped his arms to his sides. "You're right. I'm sorry."

Jade took his hand and pulled him out of the room. Berko joined them, waiting for Gilby to finish documenting their find.

A few minutes later, Gilby exited, closed the door, and stuck his phone back in his pocket. He led them to the door at the end of the tunnel and opened it.

Beyond the door, a walkway led to a balcony of sorts, and he walked out onto it. He switched on his LED and held it out in front of him.

"Where are we?" Berko said.

"It's the launch silo," Elias said.

Jade walked through the door and gazed down the length of two stories, into darkness. "Wow," she said.

"If we can climb down that ladder below us," Gilby said, pointing, "we should hit one of the ventilation tunnels. During launch, that's where the gases escape so the silo doesn't blow up."

"We're not complete morons," Jade said.

"Sorry," Gilby said. "I know that."

"Another damned ladder," Berko said.

"The tunnels shouldn't be too far down," Gilby said.

"Just a little more and we're out of here," Elias said to Berko. "Okay?"

"I'm ready," Berko said. "Let's go."

Elias turned, got down on his stomach on the balcony, and held his light out.

"The ladder is to the left of us," he said. "Me first, then Berko, Gilby, then Jade."

Payback time. Of course she'd never kick Gilby in the face. If she did, his head would come clean off, make a racket on the way down, and give them all away. Jade nearly giggled, hysteria sweeping over her.

She was glad to be above everyone else, and took care going down. Her arms were sore and shaking from exertion and then being yanked on by Elias.

"There it is," Elias said below her.

This time Jade made it into the tunnel without Elias's help. She feared he'd dislocate her elbow this time.

This tunnel sloped steeply upward. How far? Impossible to tell. And how long had they been underground?

She pulled out her phone and was surprised to see it was seven forty-five. She assumed it was p.m., but who knew how long they'd been doing what they were doing?

"What time does the sun usually go down?" Jade asked. "About eight o'clock? We should wait until about eight fifteen to make sure we come out after dark. I don't want to be surprised by a bullet in my back."

They sat down on the slope.

Everyone waited silently, wondering what would happen. On autopilot, the enormity of what had taken place and what was before them had kept exhaustion at bay.

When it was eight fifteen by Jade's phone, they started the climb up the tunnel. Luckily, it was lined with corrugated metal too, so the going was easier than she thought it would be.

Berko fell and slid a ways before Elias went and got him, and piggybacked him the rest of the way. What would they do without Elias? They'd still be in the hallway across from the lab, most likely.

And then they were out, out in the sultry Kansas prairie evening, and Jade understood what Berko meant about wanting to kiss the ground in Palo Alto. Elias gently put Berko down, where he lay in the prairie grass, and Gilby sat next to him, his breathing ragged. They were now about thirty yards beyond the fence and a hundred yards from the Compound, which was entirely dark.

Elias pulled his phone out.

"Shit," he said. "With the power out, I'm sure the cell jammer is disabled, but I still don't have a signal. Does anybody?"

"I've got one," Berko said. He handed his phone to Elias.

"Who are you going to call?" Jade asked Elias.

"The police," Elias said.

"And tell them what?" Jade said. "We're wasting time. We need to get as far from this place as possible as soon as possible. We need to get the AIP from my folks' house and block Clementine from being uploaded."

"She's right," Berko said.

"How are we going to get there?" Elias said.

"We've got to—"

"Oh, shit!" Berko yelled.

"What is it, Berko?"

"They must have trackers on our phones," he said. "I can't believe I didn't think of it before. Remember the instant messaging app they had us download? Turn them off! Turn them off now. It may be too late. If they're not looking at it now, they're going to know soon. We're going to have to leave our phones right here. Right now."

"But—" Elias said.

"You guys are supposed to be the computer geniuses, not me," Berko said. "And you didn't think of that?"

If she didn't have her phone, she couldn't call her parents. But maybe their phones were tapped. Maybe she couldn't call them anyway.

"Damn it," Elias said, turning off his phone and throwing it to the ground. "Gilby, can some of your people come get us maybe?"

"My people are nowhere near here," Gilby said.

"We need to walk then," Elias said.

Berko looked around. "But where are we going to go?"

Jade said, "The closest place is a horse ranch about three miles from here that way." She pointed. "We need to go there and see if we can borrow a car. And then we're going to my parents' to get the AIP cartridge and Elias is going to hack into the system from there, and we'll load this program to stop Clementine."

"How are you doing, Berko?" Elias said. "Can you walk three miles?"

"I'll try," he said.

"How about you, Gilby?" Elias said.

Gilby gave him a thumbs-up with one hand while the other clutched his side.

Berko stood and stumbled. Without talking about it, Jade took one of his arms and put it over her shoulders, and Elias did the same with the other, and they set off for the horse ranch, Gilby falling in step behind them.

Chapter 26

Jade calculated having to drag Berko three miles should take them no more than three hours.

"You should leave me here," Berko said. "I'm going to hold you up. I can't do it."

"We're not leaving you," Elias said grimly.

They picked their way across what used to be pasture land and aimed toward the horse ranch. Jade hoped they were headed the right way. The darkness made it difficult to tell, and her eyes began to play tricks on her. She saw dark figures everywhere, and kept jerking this way and that, wringing grunts out of Berko every time she did it.

They stopped to drink some water before going on. No one spoke, and Jade was grateful for that. She found herself drawing her head into her shoulders, as if that could keep her head from exploding if a bullet hit it.

Jade's right heel had developed a blister, and the pain burned up her leg.

"Does anyone have a watch?" she asked.

"Yeah," Elias said. He lifted his wrist and pressed a button on the watch. It illuminated. "It's ten thirty," he said.

Berko pulled the last water bottle out of the backpack and cracked it open. "Sorry, guys," he said and drank.

"Not your fault," Jade said.

"I've always had a nervous stomach. This is the first time it's had a real reason to be nervous."

"Can't be helped," Elias said, and put Berko's arm over his shoulders.

Jade could see the light over the barn in the distance, but no matter how long they walked, it never seemed to get any closer.

Finally, they were walking behind a stand of large trees to the south of the house, trying not to be seen. She heard a dog bark sleepily inside, as if just going through the motions.

"What time is it?" Jade asked.

Elias looked at his watch. "Midnight."

Inside the dark house, the dog continued an intermittent bark.

"Should we knock on the door and ask to use the phone?" Gilby said.

"Okay," Jade said.

If these folks were like most ranchers and farmers, they'd have been in bed for a good two hours by now.

Jade stepped out from behind the trees when a pair of hands grabbed her by the arm and yanked her back behind the tree. It was, of course, Elias.

"Dude," she said. "You really gotta stop yanking on my arms. I'm going to need them someday."

"Wait a minute," he said. He stood thinking.

"What?"

"What if . . . these people are part of SiPraTech?"

"That's ridiculous," Jade said uncertainly. "I talked to the woman and . . ."

"But what if it's not?" Elias said. "What if these people were planted here to help keep an eye on us?"

She and Berko looked at each other. The sweat running down Jade's neck tickled, making her nerves even more jangled. This couldn't be the case. They were getting as paranoid as their captors. But she and her friends had good reason.

"So what do you suggest?" Jade said. "The next town beyond Miranda is fifteen miles away. It would take us all night, and Berko, you'd never make it."

"Why don't we hitchhike?" Elias said.

"Have you seen any cars driving by here?" Berko said. "Ever?"

Jade heard the horses in the barn nicker and shift restlessly on this hot night.

Horses.

"We could . . . borrow some horses," she said.

"We can't steal horses," Gilby said.

"Borrow, not steal," Jade said. "We'll write a note. Let them know we're going to leave them in the next town over—Niskuwe City."

"I'm not sure I can do it," Gilby said.

The jostling of a horse ride could definitely screw up Gilby's ribs even more. But what choice did they have? Leave him here and hope he'd be found by a friendly? Not likely.

"What if the horses won't come with us?" Berko said.

"I've been riding since I was big enough to walk," Elias said. "It's our only option."

Berko looked alarmed. "I can't ride," he said.

"Don't worry," Elias said. "We'll help you."

"No," Berko said. "You don't understand. I'm terrified of horses."

Jade tried to subdue her agitation. "Berko, I want you to think about what's going to happen if we don't get that AIP cartridge. We have to get away from here and find a car and . . ." The thought of all this exhausted her. She had a nearly irresistible urge to lie down behind that stand of trees and fall asleep. But she had to rally. "We can't let them upload Clementine. It's happening, and we'll be responsible."

But he shook his head, and Jade realized what was going on. If he only focused on his fear of horses, he wouldn't have to think about the real danger. Because if any of them thought about it too much, they'd be paralyzed.

"Just come with us to the horse barn," she said. "We'll just go over there and look at them."

They walked to the barn, Jade in the lead, and she tingled with excitement. This she could do. She was good at riding. But she wondered with trepidation how these horses would react to people they didn't know. She'd been around some horses in the past that wouldn't let strangers touch them.

"Wait here," she said.

Jade opened the barn door slowly. Inside, in the first stall to the right, a bay stuck her head out. The name plate on her door said SUGAR. Jade approached her slowly, assessing the horse's stress level. Sugar neighed at her in greeting.

"Hi," Jade said, and slowly raised her hand. She wished she had an apple or some carrots or a lump of sugar. But she talked in a low voice, and allowed the horse to sniff her hand. Then she petted her nose, the velvety smoothness bringing a special kind of calm to Jade. "How many friends you have in there?" she asked, peering around the bay.

There were four other horses inside, and she'd need to figure out which were the most docile. It would be tricky getting Berko up on the horse and able to ride away. It would take her and Elias a good thirty minutes to saddle and bridle four horses. Quietly. She went inside the barn and went around and said hello to all the horses. One was a pregnant mare, so that one was out. In addition to the bay, a palomino named Gabby, and a brown horse named Obadiah nickered curiously in their stalls. The last horse, huge and black, stamped and snorted at her, not happy with the strangers in his barn. She reached out slowly toward him and he snapped at her. She glanced over her shoulder, hoping Berko hadn't seen this. But she could tell by his wide eyes he had.

"Don't worry," she whispered. "I'll ride him."

But would he let her?

A chalkboard nailed to the wall offered a tiny piece of chalk to write with. She scrawled WE HAD AN EMERGENCY AND HAD TO BORROW YOUR HORSES. WE WILL LEAVE THEM IN NISKUWE CITY BY THE WATER TOWER.

She didn't know what else to do.

She saddled the bay first. Then she approached the black one. When she opened his stall door, he reared up on his hind legs. The wooden sign on his door said KODAK. She had to find something to give this horse to settle him down, so she searched the cabinets along the west wall. Nothing but brushes and currycombs and other horsey stuff. She reached into one and found a withered apple, but it would have to do. She rubbed it on her shirt and walked back to Kodak's stall.

"Kodak," she whispered. "You like apples? You want an apple? You hungry?"

She pulled out her pocketknife and cut it in fourths and held one of them out toward the suspicious horse. He snapped at her again but less convincingly this time. He wanted that apple. Jade held it with her left hand and reached up with her right to pat the horse's neck. Kodak sniffed the apple piece and then ate it out of her hand. "That's a good boy," she said, patting his neck. She reached for the halter and held it out for the horse to examine. She held out another apple piece in front of the halter so Kodak would put his head in it to get the apple. He shook his head and whinnied loudly.

"Yes," she said. "You can't have it unless you let me bridle you. That's that."

He argued some more, shaking his head, Jade nodding at him, until he plunged his head forward and took the apple and almost part of Jade's hand with it. She got the halter over his head. She placed a Southwestern patterned horse blanket on his back then pulled the heavy saddle off the stall side. She put it on top of the blanket and handed him the third piece of apple while she cinched it up. He held his breath to make himself bigger so the saddle wouldn't fit properly, but got too interested in the apple, so she was able to cinch it.

When she turned, Elias was saddling the palomino and had already done Obadiah. It seemed like months ago that she learned his uncle worked on a ranch in New Mexico, but it was only day before yesterday. Jade led Kodak out of his stall and out of the barn, holding on to the jingling parts of the bridle to keep them from making noise.

Gilby got up on the brown with difficulty, the effort further injuring his ribs. He waited, agony etching his face.

"Okay, Berko," Jade whispered. "Let's get you in the saddle."

"No," Berko said. "I can't go. I can't do it."

Elias made a cradle of his hands at the bottom edge of the horse's stomach. "Put your foot here and your right hand on the saddle horn. Put your left hand on my shoulder. Then step up and throw your right leg over the horse."

"Did you not hear what I said?" Berko said. "I can't."

Elias got close to his face and said, "This is not the time to nerd out. This is the time to be a superhero. This is your time."

Elias's words seemed to fill Berko with renewed determination. He followed directions and on the second try got his leg over the palomino's back. He sat like a sack of potatoes in the saddle, clutching the saddle horn and sweating, looking terrified. She felt sorry for him, but not sorry enough to let him stay here. Martin and his people would find him here. He had to come with them.

Elias got on Sugar, the bay, and she mounted Kodak, who made a half attempt at rearing. She still had a quarter of the apple to give him if things got rough. And now they needed to make their way to the town beyond Miranda.

"We're going to walk, Berko. You need to grip the horse with your knees. I'm betting Gabby will follow wherever these two go, so you don't need to move the reins. Hold them loosely. I'll lead, and Elias will fall in behind you. All right? We ready?"

Kodak jumped this way and that, trying to let her know he was in charge. He didn't know yet that she was. She murmured at him and gently nudged her heel into his side. He didn't budge, so she kicked harder and he reared, pawing the air, but Jade held on.

She heard Berko gasp as she leaned forward and threw her weight down to get him onto four legs. "Come on, Kodak. Let's go." He danced sideways and then in a circle. She yanked hard on the reins. The trick was to not feel any fear, because the horse knew if you were nervous and used that against you. She wasn't afraid of Kodak. She'd been on nastier horses than this.

She'd have to push him to a full gallop and wear him out a little to calm him down, so she dug her heels in. Kodak lurched forward and ran as fast as he could.

This felt good.

She lay flat against the horse's back, streamlining for greater speed, hearing the *clump-jingle, clump-jingle* as the distance disappeared beneath the horse's hooves.

After about a quarter mile of full-on gallop, she tugged at the reins to slow him, and he gladly did.

"Good boy," she said, slowing him to a walk. She walked him in a large circle, waiting for the other three to catch up, which took two minutes. By the time they caught up, Kodak's breathing had almost returned to normal.

She faced her companions, watching them come toward her, Gilby grim with pain and poor Berko tense and terrified, him also flat to the saddle, holding on for dear life. Elias looked natural and comfortable on the bay.

She pulled up beside Berko. "How are you doing?" she asked.

He didn't say anything, just looked grimly determined.

"You think you might be ready to try a canter?"

He shook his head vehemently. "What about a—what do you call it? Trot?"

"You don't want to do that," she said. "That'll rattle your bones and make you sore all over, especially your butt. Plus it's more wearing on a horse to trot than to canter."

"Galloping is much smoother. We can't wait. I'm sorry. We've got to get there."

Berko kept shaking his head.

Elias nodded at her.

She dug her heels into Kodak's sides again, said, "Hya!" and they raced forward. Elias did the same, and Gabby took the hint and galloped behind them.

"Stop!" Berko yelled. Luckily they were far enough away from the house now to not attract attention.

"No," Jade yelled over her shoulder. "We'll stop when we get there. Just hang on!"

They kicked up dust on the dirt road, and Jade was terrified they'd run into someone before they got to the lake park area where they could get off the main road and go through the back country.

They slowed to a walk and Jade suddenly had an urge to look back.

She did, and watched the Compound lights cycle on one by one. The operation was back up and running, which meant Martin and the militia had discovered Jade and her friends had escaped.

Chapter 27

When her comrades realized Jade had stopped, they all stopped too and wheeled their horses around.

"Shit," Elias said. "They're going to come for us. We need to get off the road, but where—"

"Follow me," Jade said. She dug her heels into Kodak's sides and whipped them with the reins.

"Let's go!" she shouted and didn't wait for anyone.

Jade guided her horse to a barbed wire fence alongside a pasture and urged him to a gallop. She kept looking back at the Compound, wondering how long until the Hummers went out onto the road toward them.

She almost missed it and had to double back to the makeshift gate, which was just a section of the fence that could be swung away and then put back in place with a loop of wire over one of the fenceposts.

Jade managed to reach the loop from horseback and popped it off the post. Then she peeled it back and motioned for the others to go on through.

"Is it safe?" Gilby said, panting. "Isn't this trespassing?"

"Is it safe to get caught by Martin and his pals? You can wait here if you want, but we're going across this pasture. We can't stay on the road."

They galloped across the pasture, the horses' hooves thundering across the prairie on this overcast, moonless night, Jade terrified one of the animals would stumble into a prairie dog hole and break its leg, but it couldn't be helped.

The next time Jade looked over her shoulder, two vehicles trundled down the county road in their direction and two were going the opposite direction on the county road.

They galloped toward Niskuwe City, Jade's mind whirring with static all the way, thinking the same thought over and over. Gottafindacargottafindacargottafindacar . . .

Niskuwe City was larger than Miranda, and the first chance they got, she directed the horse train toward the water tower a few blocks from downtown. The horses made an ungodly racket, blowing and breathing hard, their hooves clopping noisily on pavement.

Jade kept an eye out for citizens but saw only one car drive by at twenty miles an hour. Chances were good they'd attract a lot of attention if anyone saw them riding horses in the dead of night. But the town was quiet and dark for the most part, and Jade prayed this town would be like other little towns in regard to their cars—with the keys left in them.

When they stopped, Berko slipped out of the saddle and spilled onto the ground.

Jade tied their horses next to the base of the water tower, which had a livestock watering tank.

The horses dipped their heads into the tank and Jade patted

Kodak's neck. "Thank you, friend," she said to him. "Sorry for riding you so hard."

She was so thirsty she was tempted to take a drink from the dirty tank herself.

Elias dismounted and helped Gilby down, but the man toppled to the ground.

"Oh, shit," Elias said, crouching next to him. "He's out cold. He might be bleeding internally. We need to get him to a hospital."

Jade seized up in frustration. They didn't have time for this.

Gilby's eyes fluttered open.

"We need to find a car," Jade said.

Jade heard the distinctive sound of Hummer engines rumbling down the main street, two blocks over. The Hummers would no doubt work in a grid.

"Get him up," Jade said.

Elias did, and Gilby's limbs were floppy, his head lolling. Elias draped Gilby's good arm over his shoulder and dragged him along.

They kept to the shadows of the large trees lining the residential streets, but if one of the Hummer's occupants shone a flashlight on them, they would be caught.

Each car they came to, Jade tried the driver's side door.

"Do you know how to hot-wire a car?" Elias whispered, panting with the exertion of supporting a nearly delirious Gilby. "Because I don't."

"Don't look at me," Berko panted beside them.

"I don't think we're going to have to—" The door to the blue Camaro opened, the dome light came on, and the bell dinged. "Bingo," she said. "Get in."

But now that they were actually faced with stealing a car, Elias and Berko hung back, looking timid. "Guy just left his keys in the car?"

"People leave their keys in the ignition where I come from," Jade said. "In fact, on weekend nights, if you were out and about, you'd leave your keys in your car on Main Street, and if someone needed it, they'd take it. People always brought them back."

"Kansas," Elias said, shaking his head. As gently as he could, he helped Gilby into the front passenger seat. Gilby groaned. "Sorry, buddy." He closed the door then went around the Camaro, folded the driver's seat forward, and climbed in back with Berko. Jade got behind the wheel, shut her door quietly, and started up the engine. She turned off the lights and slowly pulled away from the curb. Once they were two blocks away, Jade turned on the headlights and hunted for a medical center.

They found one at the south end of town and drove up to the entrance. Elias helped Gilby out of the front seat.

"Can you make it inside by yourself?" Elias said.

"Yes," Gilby said, steadying himself against the car. "I'll contact my people, but I'm not going to call the feds until I'm away from here."

"What if Martin and—"

"I've got some false ID," Gilby said. "Just go. Like Elias said, you've got to save the world. Good luck." And he staggered toward the entrance.

Elias got in the front seat and Jade looked over her shoulder at Berko. "Maybe you ought to go in there too," she said.

"I'm fine," Berko said, his face resolute. "I'm not abandoning you now. Let's go."

Jade raised her eyebrows at Elias.

"Better do what the man says," Elias said.

"Should we find a phone and call the cops?" Berko said.

"Haven't we been over this?" Elias said. "What would we tell them? We just escaped an old missile silo and we've been prisoners there. And this shadowy domestic terrorist group is going to upload this AI program, and we thought we were working for the NSA, but . . ."

"All right, all right," Berko said.

"We have to try to stop them from uploading the program," Jade said. "That's all we can do now. It would take more time than we have to explain what's going on—if they'd even believe us. Which I doubt. Once we've hacked into the computer . . ."

Just thinking about the task before them wore Jade out. If it would work. If they could do what they had to do at all.

She drove out of town to the two-lane state highway and pointed the car toward home. Jade put on the cruise control to keep a steady speed on this deserted road. They'd be in Ephesus within forty minutes.

Berko lay down in the back and was soon snoring softly.

Jade had never been in a car so nice or so new, and it had a more powerful engine than she was used to. All she had to do was tap the gas for it to lurch forward, itching to speed. And she was itching to speed too, see how fast it could go, but she couldn't risk it, even if she'd rarely seen state troopers on this highway.

Elias kept shaking his head, trying to stay awake. It was two o'clock in the morning, and they had five hours and forty-five minutes, Jade guessed, before Clementine would knock out the power around the country. If, as Jade suspected, Martin planned to unleash the power outage at the exact time the first plane hit the north tower, at 8:46 a.m. eastern time.

Elias said, "How long before we—"

They both heard it at the same time. The siren behind them. A ways off yet, but coming up fast.

Jade glanced at Elias and he gave a tiny nod. She punched the gas.

She was gripping the steering wheel so hard her hands were numb. The road was hilly, so the sound of the siren ebbed and flowed. Elias faced backward in his seat, watching for the cop. "Should I find a place to pull off? Hide behind some trees or something?"

"No," Elias said. "Keep going."

Jade was afraid she would spastically jerk the wheel and drive them off the road. The speedometer, which topped out at one eighty, said they were going one hundred and ten.

Over the next rise, the lights hit them, the flashing reds and blues, and the cop flashed his brights at them.

"What do I do?" Jade said.

Elias remained silent as the cop car gained on them.

"Can you go faster?"

"Is that the best idea?" Jade said.

"What if the people in the cop car work for Martin?"

"All their goons were in Hummers, not police cars."

"But this could be—"

"I'm pulling over," Jade said, as she took her foot off the gas and flipped the blinker. Maybe she could explain to the officer.

The cruiser went around them, its speed increasing even more, and soon disappeared from sight.

Jade sat panting, unable to let go of the steering wheel.

"What just happened?" Berko said.

"Guess he was in a hurry," Elias said.

"Go back to sleep, Berko," Jade said, and pulled back out on the road.

They hit the city limits of Ephesus at two thirty, and Jade parked the Camaro a block away from the house just in case.

Her ears were ringing, she was so tired, and her vision was fuzzy.

When they reached Jade's street, Jade beckoned Elias and Berko behind a large elm and peeked out from behind it. The house was dark, as were all the houses on the street.

"Follow me," she whispered. She scrutinized the cars parked on the street to discern if they actually belonged there or if they were enemy cars, but she didn't live here anymore, so she didn't have everyone's cars memorized. She also needed to be careful. Most people had guns in their houses, and if they thought she and her friends were prowlers, they wouldn't hesitate to shoot.

They stalked from tree to tree, to the hedge that surrounded the house, and went to the back door. Jade found the fake rock in the garden with the key inside it, pulled it out, and fitted it in the lock. She turned the knob and was greeted by a *mrph* from Clementine's dog, a Lhasa Apso named Fearless. It always took her a few moments to remember Jade, acting timid and afraid, until Jade's scent registered. She crouched down and the dog scooted toward her a little at a time and then wagged her tail and gave her a lick. Then she *mrphed* at the guys, and they both crouched to let her smell them.

"Wait here," Jade whispered. She scratched the dog's ears, then went upstairs to her old bedroom.

Jade reached under the bed for her box of old Nintendo cartridges. But she couldn't feel it. She closed the bedroom door softly and flipped on the light, nearly blinding herself, and got back on her hands and knees and looked under the bed. The box was gone.

She looked in her closet. No box. She tiptoed into Clem's studio and looked in that closet. Not there.

Her heart stopped. The box and the cartridge were gone.

Now she ran to her parents' bedroom, threw open the door, and flicked on the overhead light. Her dad sat straight up, glancing around wild-eyed. "What?" he said.

Her mom was still fast asleep.

"Dad," Jade said. "Where's my—"

"Jade!" Robert said, rubbing his eyes, as if he couldn't believe what he saw. "What time is it?" He picked up his alarm clock and held it close to his face before putting it back again. "What happened to your head?"

Jade's hand went to her forehead, the dried blood. "I fell," she said. "Dad, where is my—"

"What are you doing here? In the middle of the night? In the middle of the week?"

"My box of Nintendo—"

"Honey, why are you—"

"DAD! Where's my box of Nintendo cartridges? And in particular the *Super Mario Kart* Nintendo cartridge?"

"Shush," Robert said. "You'll wake your sister."

Robert nudged Pauline, who gasped. "What is it?"

"Jade's home."

Her mother struggled to a sitting position.

Robert yawned. "Your Nintendo—"

"Yes," Jade said, her blood seizing with frustration. "It was under my bed. It's not there."

Her father looked at her like she was crazy. "You drove sixty miles in the middle of the night to—"

"Dad, there was something very important in there. I need it right now. Where is the box?"

Robert and Pauline looked at each other. "Did we sell them at the garage sale last month?" Pauline said.

Her mother's painfully slow speech irritated her like never before.

"We must have," Robert said. "We got rid of a whole bunch of stuff—remember, I told you if you didn't get your games and stuff out of the house we were going to go ahead and sell them."

Jade's stomach cramped up. "You . . . sold it?"

"I told you we were going to," he said. "I told you."

"Who did you sell it to? I have to get it back."

"What's wrong, Jade?" her dad asked.

"I don't have time to explain right now, Dad. Just tell me who you sold it to."

Her parents again looked at each other.

"Please, Dad," Jade said, nearly crying. "Who bought the box?"

Pauline said, "Honey—"

"MOM!"

"Don't talk to your mother that—"

"WHO BOUGHT THE CARTRIDGE? TELL ME NOW!"

"I think it was the Jenkins kid, wasn't it?" her dad said.

"Was it? I thought Mike Dougherty bought it."

Jade couldn't speak. Would she have to go to both places?

"That's right," Robert said. "It was Mike Dougherty. He said he'd been looking for old Nintendo games. I think he said he wanted to sell them on eBay."

Jade suppressed a scream. If he'd already sold them, then . . .

"I need to borrow the car," she said. If the Camaro had been reported stolen, they'd more likely be caught. Better to borrow Dad's Saturn. "I have to get that box and then I need to—never mind. Can I borrow the car? I'll bring it back as soon as I can."

"I guess it's okay," Robert said.

"Thanks, Dad," she said.

"Keys are in it."

As she descended the stairs, the ghostly appearance of Clementine in her white satin nightie, with Fearless close behind, nearly scared Jade out of her socks.

Clem hadn't spied the guys standing in the shadows. Jade hoped she wouldn't notice.

"Jade," she said.

"Not now, Clem. I'll talk to you when I get back. I have to go."

If I get back.

"Fearless has something for you." She pushed the dog toward Jade, who dropped something at her feet. Jade stooped to pick it up and began to laugh.

"What is it?" Berko asked.

Jade held it up, and Clementine smiled broadly.

"It's a potato," Jade said. She put it in her pocket, while Elias and Berko looked confused. She held out her arms and Clem slid into them, burying her face against Jade's neck.

"Who are they?" Clem said.

"Elias and Berko."

"It's nice to meet you," Clementine said, and shook each of their hands exactly once then wiped her hand on her nightgown. She said to Jade, "Go."

Jade gave her one last squeeze and led Berko and Elias out the door.

They got in Robert's silver Saturn and drove toward town.

"What was with the potato?" Berko asked.

"When Clementine was going through puberty, we weren't sure we'd survive," Jade said. "She regressed to the point of infancy almost. She destroyed things. We had to wrap her hands in gauze so she couldn't scratch herself. She ripped her room apart. She was obsessed with YouTube videos of dogs. She loved one in particular about a suicidal girl whose service dog was so upset one day because he somehow knew she was going to hurt herself. So he brought her a potato."

"Okay, I'm still not getting it," Elias said.

"Sometimes all you need is to know somebody cares, that somebody knows you're hurting and wants you to feel better, even if it's your dog. That dog saved that girl's life. So I trained our dog to take potatoes to Clementine, and she was just captivated by it. It means 'everything's going to be okay.'"

Berko stared out the windshield. "Jade, I don't know if everything's going to be okay or not."

"Me either," Jade said. "But if we don't do something, I don't think there'll be any room for people like Clementine in the new world order. So we have to try. A guy named Mike Dougherty bought the Nintendo box and he plans to sell them on eBay. We need to go to his house."

"Should you maybe call him first? Let him know we're coming?"

"Let's just go," Jade said.

She drove four blocks and parked the car on the street in front of the unkempt old house. The weedy lawn surrounded a sagging porch, and the whole place needed a fresh coat of paint.

They all got out of the car and walked up to the front door. Jade pulled back the screen door and knocked. "Mike?" she called softly.

"Try the doorbell," Elias said. When she didn't right away, he did. She knocked again.

A light inside came on, and the curtains drew back from the window. "Who's that?" came his voice through the door.

"Jade Veverka," she said. "Robert and Pauline's girl? You know me."

She heard the dead bolt draw back and the door opened. Mike stood there with pillow head in his T-shirt and boxers. "Everything okay?" he said. "Folks okay?"

"Yeah, Mike," Jade said. "Dad told me you bought a box of Nintendo cartridges at their garage sale last month."

"I did," he said.

Hope whooshed through her. "I need one of them back," she said.

"Sold some of them," he said.

"*Super Mario Kart*?" she said, holding her breath.

"Nope, still got that one."

Jade turned around and smiled at Berko and Elias.

"May I have it back, please?" Jade said.

He just stared at her.

"It's very important to me, and my parents didn't know—"

"You'll have to buy it back."

Jade's hands went to her front pockets but she had no money on her. She turned. "Guys? Got any cash?"

Both of them pulled out their wallets. Berko had a twenty and Elias had two fives. They handed them over.

"How about thirty dollars?" Jade said.

Mike stood looking at the money and said, "I don't think so."

"How much did you buy the box for?"

He didn't answer right away. "I'd rather not say."

"Come on, Mike," Jade said. "I need it back. How much do you want for it?"

"A hundred dollars."

"I don't have a hundred dollars. I'll get you the rest tomorrow from the ATM."

"Then I'll give it to you tomorrow after you get the rest of it from the—"

Elias slammed open the screen and grabbed the neck of Mike's T-shirt with both hands. "Listen," he hissed. "We need that cartridge. The lady offered you cash. Now you're going to show me where that cartridge is right now, or we're going to have a real problem. Understand?"

"Okay, okay," Mike said, his voice high and frightened. Elias let go of his shirt but followed him into the house.

"I just hope Mike doesn't have a gun or something back there," Jade said.

They returned, the *Super Mario Kart* cartridge in Elias's hand. He seized the three bills from Jade and threw them on the floor. "There. Thank you. Good night."

Chapter 28

WHEN THEY RETURNED to Jade's family home, the house was again dark. Jade led the way in, and they went into the den where Robert kept the family computer.

Jade booted up the computer and gave Elias the chair. Berko lay down on the futon they used as a sofa and a bed when company came.

"Do you want to go upstairs and sleep in my room, Berko?" Jade said.

"I'm not going to be able to sleep," he said. "I can drift off in here. I want to be available in case you need me."

"Okay," Jade said. "I'll be right back."

She went to the main floor powder room and found Excedrin Migraine in the medicine cabinet. Thank God. She pulled it out and put it in her pocket and then went to the kitchen and got three bottles of water and some mozzarella sticks from the fridge and took it all into the den.

"Here, Berko," she said.

"Thanks," he said, and accepted a water bottle and two mozzarella sticks.

She set four cheese sticks and a water bottle next to the computer keyboard.

Then she opened up a string cheese and scarfed it down. She didn't think she'd ever been hungrier in her life.

"Do I have your permission to download *Metasploit* and *PostgreSQL* to your folks' computer?"

"Yes," she said. "Whatever you need."

"Okay," he said, focusing on the screen, his heavy dark brows knitted in concentration. "Did I ever tell you I used to be in a hacking club? Nothing heavily illegal. But we learned how to breach a protected computer remotely. Information Warfare didn't teach us that."

"But you need the IP address for that," Jade said. This was not her thing at all. She didn't judge him though, especially not now, not when he was their only option.

"You do, but if we can figure out Martin's workstation name, we can ping it and find out his IP address."

Another big if.

Elias ate all the cheese while the software downloaded, and he downed the whole bottle of water.

"Would you mind getting me another?" he said.

Jade ran back to the kitchen and got out the rest of the string cheese, found a bag of grapes, and a package of crackers. She retrieved two more water bottles and carried everything back to the den.

Berko dozed on the futon, clutching a pillow.

"Okay, I'm logged into the network. I'm pretty sure they'll

figure out where we are very soon, so we need to do this fast, and then get your family out of here, because they're going to descend."

Jade went to stand behind him as he typed into the black box: *ping <mfelix@sipratech.com>* and hit Enter.

Nothing.

Ping <MFelix-HP>

The IP address came up.

"That's amazing," Jade said.

Elias turned and gave her a dubious look.

"I was never a hacker. I was a builder."

Elias shrugged, then copied the IP address and opened the *PostgreSQL* Graphical User Interface, which resembled an FTP connection interface, clicked on Connect, and left the window open. Next, he opened the *Metasploit* GUI, which looked like the command prompt—black screen, 8-bit text—and typed in the database connect for *PostgreSQL*.

Text began flashing and Jade gasped. "Oh, no," she said. "What's happening?"

"That's normal," Elias said, taking a drink of water. When it stopped, he turned to her and said, "Now comes the connection to the server. Hold on to your butts." He typed *db_nmap* and the IP address. "We're in."

Jade felt the same kind of thrill she used to feel when she and her high school friends sneaked beers out of their parents' refrigerators.

"Now we look for the exploits." He typed db_autopwn-t-p-e-s-b. "This is going to have to run for a bit."

"How long?" Jade said.

"No telling. Hopefully it'll be done before seven, because then you're going to have to find where Clementine is in the system and upload your patch."

But what if it didn't work? The question hung in the air.

"We might as well just chill on the couch," Elias said.

Jade sat next to Berko, and he put his head on her shoulder. Elias sat next to her, and she put her head on his shoulder. And soon, they were all fast asleep.

Chapter 29

September 11

JADE JERKED UPRIGHT, knocking her shoulder into Berko's head.

"Ow," he said.

"What time is it?" Jade said.

Elias jumped up and sat at the computer. "It's done," he said. "Let's see what we've got here."

Jade ran out to the foyer and peeked out the window next to the front door. A policeman.

The doorbell rang, and Fearless appeared, sleepy, one ear flipped over, *mrphing*. The upstairs hall light came on.

"Jade?" her dad called down. "Who's at the door at this hour?"

It was five thirty. "Go back to bed, Dad," Jade called. "I'll get it."

He turned the light out and went back to bed. She waited until his bedroom door shut before she opened the front door.

"Jade Veverka?" the uniformed officer asked. She vaguely recognized him as a town cop. She glanced at his name tag and remembered his name. Eric.

"Yes, sir," she said.

"Were you at Mike Dougherty's house earlier this morning, about ninety minutes ago?"

"Yes, sir," she said.

"May I come in?"

"Sure," she said.

"I've found the exploit we can use, Jade," Elias said as she and the cop came into the den. "I just need to get us in there, and then you can—"

"Sir, were you at Mike Dougherty's house earlier this morning?" Eric asked in his cop voice.

"Yes," Jade said. "He was with me."

"Sir, would you stop typing, please?"

"Just one second, Officer, I need to—"

"Stop typing now," the cop said.

"Officer," Jade said. "It is very important that—"

"I'm not talking to you," he snapped. "Sir, back away from the computer."

"I'm almost—"

"Sir. Did you assault Mike Dougherty?"

Elias moused around, trying desperately to complete what he'd started.

Eric unsnapped his holster, and at the sound, Elias slowly raised his hands behind his head. "Officer. Mike Dougherty had something of Jade's he refused to give back."

"That he bought and paid for, correct?" Eric said.

"Yes, sir," Elias said. "But we gave him money for it. It belonged to Jade."

"Would you please stand up, sir?" Eric said.

Elias's eyes flicked from Eric's face to the screen and back again and he quickly shot out his hand to the mouse and clicked it.

Eric lunged at Elias and smashed his face into the desk, a replay of what had happened at the bar in Miranda a lifetime ago.

"You're under arrest for assault, and for resisting arrest," Eric said, bringing Elias's right hand to his back and cuffing it, then cuffing his left wrist. Then the officer resnapped his holster with one hand and pulled Elias upright by his collar with the other.

"This is a misunderstanding, Officer," Berko said, following behind Jade and Elias, who was being dragged toward the front door. "Mike wanted one hundred dollars for an old Nintendo cartridge, and Elias here understandably got upset. You can understand that, right?"

"Yeah," Eric said. "But he still assaulted Mike. So I'm going to have to take him to jail."

"Listen, Jade," Elias said. "You need to finish going through the exploits. You can figure this out. You know you can. Then do your thing."

"Okay," Jade said. What if she couldn't figure it out? She liked to take her time to fully understand whatever she was working on. But she didn't have that kind of time.

The upstairs hall light came on again, and Robert, clad in sweats and a T-shirt, came running down the stairs and out the front door.

Jade followed him.

"Eric," Robert said.

"Hello, Mr. Veverka," Eric said as he opened the back door of the cop car.

"Listen, I need a favor."

"What's that?"

"I need you to let this young man finish working on my computer. It's really important. I need it fixed before he leaves. Can you let him do that? And then I'll drive him down to the court-house myself. Okay?"

Eric stood looking at Jade's dad. Eric wasn't much older than Jade.

"Mr. Veverka—"

"I'd consider it a personal favor," Robert said.

"You'll bring him over as soon as he's done?"

"Yes, Eric. You have my word."

Eric stood thinking for another moment, and Jade wanted to crawl out of her skin.

"All right."

"Could you uncuff him, please? He's no good to me unless he can use his hands, you know?"

The officer pulled out a keyring, located the one he wanted, and unlocked the cuffs on Elias's wrists.

"See you after a while," Robert said.

Elias rubbed his wrists then touched his nose, which didn't look broken, although Jade was sure it hurt.

"Thank you, Mr. Veverka," Elias said, walking up the walk toward the house.

"You bet. Just do whatever it is you need to do, all right? Then we'll see about getting you to the courthouse."

At this Robert rolled his eyes and went in the front door, followed by Elias and Jade.

"I'm going to make some eggs and bacon and coffee," Robert said over his shoulder on the way to the kitchen. "Anyone want some?"

"Please," Jade said.

Elias went back in the den and sat at the computer.

"Shit," he muttered.

"What is it?" Berko said.

"When my face went into the keyboard, it halted the process." He wearily rubbed his eyes. "Let me figure out what's going on."

"We have to wait for it to look for exploits again?" she said, aghast. "That took a long—"

"Not that far back," he said. "Just give me a minute, okay? Then it's your turn to shine."

Berko pressed his hands into his chest. "I don't think my heart can take much more of this," he said. He left the room.

"Poor guy," Jade said. "But I know how he feels."

Elias hadn't heard. He was trying to repair the damage.

Jade fidgeted for ten more minutes. It was 6:50 a.m., which meant it was 7:50 eastern time.

Elias put in a few keystrokes then stretched. "All right," he said. "It's all you now." He stood from the chair and held it out for her.

"Will you quit saying that?" she said.

Berko stood in the doorway. "Just take your time, Jade," he said. "You've got fifty-five minutes. Plenty of time."

Jade had to bite her tongue. All this "encouragement" had shoved her nerves to the very bleeding edge. She sat down and looked at the screen. She was in the system. There was the system map. She could do this. She could figure it out.

"You know what to do," Elias said.

"Okay, you know what, guys?" Jade said, her jaw rigid. "Can you wait in the kitchen? I need to concentrate."

They went out the door without another word and closed it behind them.

Jade examined the system and plunged in.

"Where are you, Clementine?" she murmured, remembering playing hide-and-seek with her sister when she was younger, and how Clem would put her hand over her eyes and stand in the middle of the room, because if she couldn't see you, then you couldn't see her.

She ran a search, even though they almost certainly renamed it. Except they hadn't.

There she was. There was Clementine, glowing on her screen. She pulled out the *Super Mario Kart* cartridge and opened it up. Inside was a two-terabyte flash drive with the AIP on it. She hoped Mike Dougherty hadn't screwed it up somehow. But she suspected he hadn't even been aware it wasn't actually *Super Mario Kart*.

As usual, a shiver of excitement and dread moved through her as she pulled it from its hiding place.

There was a knock at the front door.

Had Dad waited too long to bring Elias in to the police station? Was Eric back?

She looked at the clock. It was 7:10. He must be getting impatient for his prisoner.

But then she heard Berko scream, and a body drop to the floor.

Jade bolted out of the chair, the drive still in her hand, flung open the office door, and dashed out into the hall.

And there, in the doorway, stood Colonel Dan Stevenson.

Chapter 30

Jade gasped, smacking herself in the face with her hands as she slammed backward into her mother's china cabinet. Glass and tableware crashed behind her but it didn't register because Dan was here. He was alive.

He was alive.

And then she was in his arms, and he was saying, "It's okay. It's okay. I'm okay."

But. Her left hand was against his chest. No bandage. His face was perfect, as if it had never been beaten. His fingernails.

All ten still anchored in place.

She pushed him away and blinked at him. He smiled at her.

"What—what—" She couldn't form a coherent thought, much less a coherent sentence.

"I know, I know," Dan said, as if to a little girl who was sad her dog had run away.

Or had been shot in the chest at point-blank range.

"I don't understand," Jade said.

"Yes, you do," Dan said.

Berko slumped against the wall, staring at Dan as if he'd never seen him before. Or as if he were seeing a ghost.

"He's one of them," Elias said.

Jade whirled around at the sound of his voice. Elias stood in the kitchen doorway, his hands laced behind his head. Behind him, Connor pressed a gun into Elias's back.

"Where's my dad?" Jade said.

"They tied him up," Elias said. "A lot like they tied up Gilby, as a matter of fact."

"And where's the rest of the family?" Dan said. "I've always wanted to meet them. Especially darling Clementine, the inspiration for the new age."

Jade's mouth filled with saliva. She was going to throw up.

Never before this moment had Jade realized how powerless she was, how buffeted about by the winds of circumstance and the will of others. This was accompanied by the understanding that Dan had used her. She'd believed he cared about her, knew her, saw her. That he, above all other people in the world, understood who she was, what she was about. Now she understood he wanted to use her brain the way a john used a hooker's body—for his own gratification, his own amusement, his own ends.

He was just like everyone else who used her. Her parents used her to take care of and understand her sister. Her schools used her for awards and glory. Her friends used her for test answers. Her football team used her for recognition and extra points. That's what she was—an extra point. Not a human being with a soul.

She didn't exist. She was a tool.

And she realized too how blinded by her own ambition and desire for acclamation and approval she'd always been. Someone who lived outside herself—with only external motivation. She'd wanted Dan to love her for her. Not for what she could do for him. Not to make him king of the United States of whatever it was about to be.

But in the next instant she realized the flash drive had been knocked out of her hand when she crashed into the china cabinet. She had to retrieve it, but how could she do that without Dan and Connor noticing?

Dan stood there smiling at her, until the smile turned brittle and angry.

"You hacked into the system, didn't you? You were going to try to upload the AIP, weren't you?"

Jade didn't say anything. She couldn't remember ever having told Dan about the AIP. But she must have. Had she ever said anything about it out loud at the lab and the surveillance picked it up? But she had to focus now.

"We have to be able to use Clementine to stop the Chinese," Dan said. "Clementine will keep the power grid online."

"Martin told us all about his—your—plan," Jade said. "So you don't have to pretend anymore. You're not going to use Clementine to keep the power on. You want to use it to turn the power off."

He laid his hand on Jade's head. Then he shrugged. "Jade. You know I'm not the bad guy here. I am—we are the knights in shining armor. We're saving this country from itself."

"Don't you just love a nonspecific enemy?" Elias said. "Then anything goes. All bets are off. Kill people. Stage deaths. Terrorize employees who've done nothing to deserve it."

"Why, Dan?" Jade said. "Why?"

He shook his head. "Martin explained everything to you. I'm not going to go into it all again."

She held her hands out, entreating. "Once Clementine's on the Internet, there'll be no stopping it," she said. "There's no telling what it will do. I've told you that. You know that."

"Oh, sweetheart," he said. "We've reconfigured it so we can control it."

"You can't control it!" Jade said.

"*You* can't," Dan said. "You did your best, and we're all so proud of you. But you can let the adults take over now. We've got all the best men on it, honey. So don't you worry your pretty little head anymore."

Honey? Pretty little head?

All the best *men*?

Rage bloomed like a mushroom cloud inside her. She'd heard this kind of patronizing language her whole life. Dan had fooled her into believing he wasn't a chauvinist. He was another Sauer, another Nishant. Eager to stand on her shoulders and call himself a giant.

"I need you to give me the AIP," Dan said. "And you need to come with us. Then we'll leave your family alone. That's all you have to do."

She had to draw him away from the china cabinet, and the only thing she could think to do made her hate herself. But it had to be done. "Would you like to meet the real Clementine?"

Dan lit up, and Jade's skin crawled.

She turned to Berko, who still sat on the floor in shock at the revelation that Dan wasn't dead. "Berko, could you clean up the glass on the floor there? I don't want the dog or my sister walking on it."

Berko looked up at her with an incredulous expression.

"I know you don't feel well, but we have to protect Clementine."

She turned away from him, because she was afraid Dan would see a telling look pass between them.

"Come on, Dan," Jade said, trying to keep the venom out of her tone.

His smile lost its angry sheen and he followed her up the stairs.

"You got me," she said. "We were trying to upload the AIP. But it's too late, isn't it?"

Jade hoped Clem would stay out of sight. Because now Jade realized Dan would snatch her up and hold her hostage. If he would fake his own murder in front of her eyes, he would do anything to make sure the Clementine Program propagated.

"Here's her room," Jade said, opening the door.

Please, Berko. Find the AIP. Plug it into the computer. Hit Upload. You can do this.

"Where is she?"

"Come out, come out, Clementine," Jade sang.

She heard Berko downstairs. "I'm going to go into the den and lie down," he said. "I've been ill."

"He has," Elias said.

Jade heard the den door close.

Dan admired Clem's room, touching things, then clasping his hands behind him as he leaned in to inspect photographs and artwork on the walls.

Jade was desperate to go downstairs and make sure the AIP was loading. But she didn't dare. She had to stall Dan for long enough, and then she had to get him out of her house.

She heard Clementine giggle, but she wasn't in her room.

Dan raised his head, scenting the air like a wolf. "Where is that darling girl?"

Jade stood motionless. Dan smiled and walked out of the room and across the hall to her parents' bedroom.

She dashed out after him, and he was tapping on the door. "Clementine? Are you in there, honey? Unlock the door, sweetheart. I have some chocolate for you." Why had she ever told Dan what Clem liked?

Because she'd never guessed he was a megalomaniacal monster.

Jade heard Clementine slip off the bed, heard her mother groan, "No, Clemmy!"

Because of course her atrophied muscles no longer had the strength to restrain Clementine.

"Chocolate," Dan crooned through the door.

Clementine turned the lock and opened the door.

Dan handed her a Hershey bar and walked past her to the foot of her parents' bed. "Hello, Mrs. Veverka," he said. "I'm Colonel Dan Stevenson. I've heard so much about you! I wanted to let you know we will be taking care of you. I've talked to my contacts, and we're getting you into a stem cell study starting next week. I'll let you rest, but you're going to be feeling better soon." He turned and walked toward the door. "Come on, Jade. Let's finish the tour."

Jade looked back at her mom. The terrified and vulnerable expression on Pauline's face made Jade's chest feel like it was caving in.

"Protect your sister."

Brodeck your sizzer.

Jade nodded at her and followed Dan out and down the stairs, Clementine leading the way eating the chocolate bar.

Elias stood in the same position they'd left him in, his hands behind his head, standing at attention with Connor's gun on him.

"What's in here?" Dan said, pointing at the den.

"Storage," Jade said.

Clementine rolled her eyes. "That's Dad's office. Sheesh." She threw open the door.

Berko lay on the futon, breathing hard. Either he'd just jumped on there, or he was terrified. Probably both.

The room was dark, as was the monitor.

But sticking out of the USB port of the CPU was the AIP, the stick with a brightly colored Mario on it.

Jade was afraid by looking at it, she would draw Dan's attention to it, so she turned around and focused on the clock on the wall. It was seven forty-five.

She stood motionless, willing Dan to leave the room.

"How you doing, Berko buddy?" Dan asked. "Not feeling too well?"

Berko just stared at him.

Dan perused the photos on the wall, pointing at the one of Jade winning the science fair. "Nice," he said. After picking things up and setting them down again, he turned and walked out the door.

"All right, Jade, we've had the tour, we've had our tearful reunion, and now I need that AIP."

"I don't have it," Jade said. "My parents sold a box of my stuff last month in a garage sale. A guy named Mike Dougherty bought it, and then sold it on eBay. You can go to his house and ask him."

"You can do better than that," Dan said.

"It's true," Clementine said.

Dan whirled toward her, his face uncertain. Clementine had no ability to tell a lie, and Jade had told Dan that, so Clementine had to believe that it was true. She must have seen the transaction take place at the garage sale.

"Mario!" Clementine said, her back to everyone.

Jade's heart grew leaden inside her. Clem had spotted the colorful stick.

"It's not here?" Dan asked Jade.

"I told you." She wanted to push Dan out of the room but stood frozen. She couldn't say any more. Her mouth didn't want to work.

"What's on there?" Clem asked taking a step toward the desk.

"Clementine," Jade said sharply.

Clem's hands flew to her ears as she whirled around and grimaced.

Jade made a face at Clem.

Dan watched this exchange, suspicious, but he said nothing.

Clementine stood staring at her, but the pull of the colorful flash drive was strong. Jade set her face, and she knew Clem was trying to work out what Jade wanted. To Jade's elation, she pulled out her smartphone to use the app Jade had designed for her, the one that helped her decipher facial expressions and body language.

"What are you doing?" Dan said.

Clem went rigid at this second sharp bit of conversation.

"I—I have a—"

Dan openly relaxed his posture and forced a smile. "Can I see that?"

Clem's eyes darted from Jade to Dan and back again.

"It's okay," Jade said, trying to be relaxed too. "You can let him see it."

Clementine handed her phone to Dan.

Jade had to herd Dan and Clementine out of this room before Clementine remembered the *Super Mario* sticking out of her dad's computer.

"We're getting behind schedule," Dan said. "I need you to hand over the AIP."

"I told you, Dan," Jade said, holding her hands up. "The AIP isn't here. You've won. So just leave."

Dan regarded her. "Yeah," he said, "the problem is I don't believe you. But if you won't give me the AIP, then I'm going to take you with me, back to the Compound. And if you refuse to go, then . . ."

He moved his hand to his hip. Under his jacket, of course, was a gun. He fastened his eyes on Clementine.

Behind her, Berko gasped.

Jade stared at Dan in horror. He was going to kidnap her. Hold her hostage, make sure she didn't come up with a patch or some other fix. And once he and his group were satisfied Clementine was up and running, they'd have no more use for Jade. They'd execute her.

Her mind went into overdrive, selecting and discarding plans at lightning speed. But it wasn't fast enough, because Dan reached under his jacket.

"All right," she said. "You got me. The AIP is up in Clementine's studio." She turned to Clem and said, "Let's take Dan upstairs to your studio, show him your setup, okay?"

Forgetting all else, Clem lit up and charged for the stairs.

"Come on," Jade said.

Dan searched her face, probably wondering what, if anything, she was up to.

Jade took the stairs two at a time, dashed into the studio, and stepped on two of the surge protector switches before ripping the NOT ALL AT ONCE sign from the wall and dropping it facedown on the floor as Dan entered the room.

"Jade!" Clementine said, scandalized. "What are you—"

"Have a seat," Jade said to Dan, pointing at a chair against the opposite wall.

"The AIP," Dan said.

Jade hissed, "We're doing this my way. So you will damn well sit and listen to my sister play her music."

Dan hesitated before sitting down.

"But first," Jade said, "Clem, okay if I play something for Dan? Would that be okay?" She opened her eyes wide, willing Clementine to go along.

Clem stared at the piece of paper on the floor then back at Jade. "But—"

"Please, Clem?" Jade said, imploring.

Clementine stood blinking, then acquiesced. "Okay."

Jade sat on Clem's stool, her heart fluttering, and powered up the Lowrey, hoping against hope she could remember. Then she started picking out notes. But Clem didn't respond.

Had she forgotten? Jade tried to remember the last time they'd exchanged tonal messages. But then Clem stood straight.

"Jade!" she said, scandalized.

Jade played the notes again, more urgently.

"But I can't," Clementine said, looking at the empty place on the wall.

Yes, you can, Jade played on the keyboard.

"What are you doing?" Dan said.

Clem grew frantic. "But—"

DO IT DO IT DO IT DO IT

"No!"

Mom said. She wants to hear in her room. She can't hear unless you turn everything up. Do it.

"Jade," Dan said.

"I was just warming up for her, Dan," Jade said, standing from the keyboard.

"Mom wants to hear," Clementine said, and walked around switching on every piece of equipment, going against everything she'd ever been told, and her inflexible movements and hunched shoulders told Jade how frightened she was.

"Play your newest, Clem," Jade said. "Put on your headphones first."

Clementine put on her headphones then placed her fingers on the keyboard.

Then she brought them down in the opening notes, and a blast of sound poured from the speakers. Dan clapped his hands over his ears as showers of sparks emitted from the three faceplates and Clementine began screaming.

Then two things happened at once: the lights went out and the carpet burst into flame.

Chapter 31

"Shut her up," Dan yelled, jumping from his chair. He was trying hard to stopper his ears, so he wasn't reaching for his gun yet.

Clementine continued screaming and flailing, knocking her tiered keyboards over. Then she began hitting herself in the face.

"Shut her up, or I'll shoot her."

"You fucking idiot," Jade shouted over her sister's screams. "I can't control Clementine. No one can. Don't you get that?"

Smoke began filling the room as the old carpet lit the drapes on fire. Jade finally succeeded in restraining Clementine. Dan lunged at them and fell into the synthesizer.

"Run, Clem!" Jade screamed. "Run!" She pushed Clem as hard as she could in the direction of the door.

Clem tottered in place for a moment then dashed out the door.

Dan coughed and sputtered, attempting to wade through the carnage in the room, and Jade ran toward the door too. Just as she hit the top of the stairs, Dan threw himself against her and they careened down the stairwell. They rolled in slow motion, Jade's head striking the wall, the stair, the wall, Dan's hands scrabbling to catch hold of her hair. He grabbed her arm and it wrenched in an awkward angle and she bit her tongue.

At the bottom of the stairs, dazed, she watched Dan rise and pin a screaming Clem to the wall next to the front door.

Elias still stood at attention in the foyer, Connor's gun pointed at his back.

Smoke wafted down the stairs.

"Connor," Dan said in his commander's voice. "If Jade doesn't walk out that door in the next fifteen seconds, shoot the girl. Shoot her."

Connor's gun drooped. "Shoot her? I'm not shooting a little girl. What's wrong with you?"

"Sacrifices must be made," Dan said, released Clem, and in the same movement unholstered his own gun and aimed it at Clementine. Jade jumped to her feet and dived in front of her sister just as she felt a searing hot wasp sting in her right arm.

But she was able to shove the front screen door open and push Clementine through it.

With the attention off him, Elias elbowed Connor in the nose and wrenched his gun away from him. Then the two of them were wrestling for control of it.

Dan's gun went off a second time and Elias crumpled to the floor, still with a firm hold on Connor's pistol. Blood stained the left chest of his shirt.

Jade turned, took two steps, aimed her punting foot at Dan's elbow, and kicked as hard as she could. It gave a satisfying pop before he could shoot Elias again. He sank to the floor, bellowing.

But she'd kicked the wrong elbow.

Connor was twisting the gun in Elias's hand when the front

door slammed open and a volunteer firefighter came charging inside.

He stopped dead, confronted by Dan's gun pointed at his face.

Jade couldn't seem to move—the pain in her arm held her in place.

Then a blur passed before her and Berko was standing over Dan, stomping on his gun hand.

Dan finally let go.

Jade turned her head toward the stairs, suddenly remembering Pauline was trapped in the master bedroom upstairs.

Every thought of pain and fear gone, Jade leaped to her feet and ran for the stairs, taking them two at a time. Upstairs, smoke permeated the hall. Jade's eyes watered, her arm screaming in pain. She threw her mother's door open.

Pauline was on the floor, coughing, and Jade scooped up her mother's deteriorated frame and carried her like an infant out into the hall. She couldn't see where the stairs were, disoriented in the smoke and the building heat. Her arm was in agony as she slid her foot along the floor, feeling for the lip of the top step.

"I've got you, Mom," Jade said. Then she stepped out into thin air and pitched forward into the dark.

They fell into one of the firefighters who was nearly to the top of the staircase, and he grabbed on to the railing, which made a cracking sound under the weight of three people.

Jade was going to fall down the stairs a second time, and she didn't know if her frail mother would survive it.

But another set of arms blockaded their way and steadied everyone. It was Berko.

"Take it easy," he said, his voice calm and reassuring as he backed down slowly. The firefighter seemed to have found his feet again and the four of them moved in a group down to the main floor, where Jade collapsed as Berko took Pauline from her.

There seemed to be uniformed people everywhere, flashlight beams, stretchers, haze, and smoke. Jade watched in a fog of pain as Berko handed her mother to one of the firemen, who carried her out the front door. Jade heard Clementine screaming outside.

"Mr. Veverka's in the kitchen," Berko told another firefighter. "He's tied up. Can you help him out of here?"

Just then, Eric and another officer came dashing in. Jade tried to spot Connor and Elias, but they weren't there.

"We've got to get you all out of here," Eric said.

"Where's Elias?" Jade shouted. "Where is he?"

"I'll find him," Berko said.

Another firefighter said to Jade, "We need to clear the house." He tried to pick her up but she dwarfed him in size.

"Just help me stand up," she said.

When she was vertical, she saw stars, both with pain and the feeling of impending unconsciousness. But she stumbled out with her good arm over the firefighter's shoulders.

When she turned to face the house, the top of it was aflame, and firemen were unspooling the hose. They hooked it to the fire hydrant across the street and began spraying.

EMTs drove up in an ambulance. Jade wanted to ask everyone for ID, to make sure they weren't more of Dan's cohorts, but her voice was drowned out in the confusion and chaos.

Robert emerged from the house and Clementine ran at him like a freight train and nearly knocked him over.

The EMTs tended to her mother, an oxygen mask over her face, and Dan, who now had his hands cuffed behind him. With his dislocated elbow, that had to hurt.

She hoped so.

Another EMT made his way to Jade.

Behind him came Elias, bloody and bruised, but alive.

It was then Jade happened to wonder whether the AIP had had a chance to do its job before the power went out. Had they succeeded?

Or would the power across the country go out?

And then she passed out.

Chapter 32

September 12

BERKO, JADE, AND Elias sat in the courtyard of Ephesus Hospital, Jade and Elias in hospital-issue robes, Berko in street clothes.

"I kind of feel left out," Berko said. "I'm the only one who wasn't shot."

"You weren't trying hard enough," Elias said.

Jade laughed a little. Both she and Elias had their arms in slings, even though Elias's wound was in the upper chest. Another few inches down, and he wouldn't be here. Jade shuddered at the thought.

"You never did tell us what AIP stands for, Jade," Elias said.

"Autism Injection Protocol," she said, feeling silly about it.

"So . . . you gave the program . . . autism?" Berko said.

"Essentially, yes," Jade said. "The program removes the connections between pieces of data—jumbles it up. Then the program can no longer understand the data it is receiving, cannot interpret it, code it. So it shuts itself down, the way the real Clementine does when she doesn't understand what she's seeing, hearing, or feeling. Simple, right?"

Berko snorted. "Simple."

"Did you talk to your dad? Is Clementine okay?" Elias asked.

"She doesn't forget anything, so it's going to be a long time before she's okay," Jade said.

"That poor kid," Berko said.

"How are you doing?" Elias asked Berko.

"I'm great," he said. "In comparison to being shot, a migraine is preferable."

"Well, the power hasn't gone out," Jade said, "and it's been— what, thirty-six hours? So I'm guessing and hoping it worked. And I'm hoping the program won't find a way to overcome its autism."

"We'll see," Berko said. "The NSA and the FBI came to see me."

"Us too," Elias said, looking at Jade.

"I couldn't help but wonder if they were *really* the FBI and NSA," Berko said.

"They interrogated me for three and a half hours," Elias said. "I had to pull the 'I've been shot and I need to rest' card."

"It won't be the last time," Jade said.

"I took them out to the Compound. It's deserted," Berko said. "It was creepy. The fountain in the front of the house is still running. I showed them where we broke through the wall, and it was like walking through a museum exhibit—it was like something that happened to someone else. We went in the server room, and everything was still running."

"But the AIP should have gotten into every corner of the program," Jade said. "So it should be useless to them."

Elias shifted in his chair and groaned, his wound obviously bothering him.

"Should I call the nurse?" Berko said.

"I'm okay," Elias said, then turned to Berko. "When are you going back to Palo Alto?"

"As soon as they're done asking me questions, I assume," Berko said. "But I'm going to Atlanta first and see my mom."

"I'm going to my folks' in Reno too," Elias said.

"And then what?" Jade said.

"I need to report to Fort Severn for my commissioning, and then it's five years of service."

"So we're not going to see you for a while, then," Jade said. It had just occurred to her she was going to be separated from these men she'd spent three of the most intense months of her life with. She felt bereft at this thought.

Elias looked surprised. "Well, no," he said. "But I'll get leave, you know. We could meet somewhere, if you can travel—maybe San Diego. Or Tokyo. Or New Jersey. But it'll depend where I'm stationed."

She liked the sound of that—meeting in some exotic locale. She'd even be happy to meet Berko and Elias in New Jersey if need be.

"What about you, Jade?" Berko said. "Are you going back to Lawrence?"

"Not now," she said. "I'm going to take a break, hang around Ephesus for a while, hang out with my family. Help out on the farm, and with Clem."

Until Mom leaves us.

She didn't say it out loud, but she didn't need to. They sat in silence a moment.

"Dan's going to be tried for treason," Jade said.

"Yes, he is," Elias said.

"The Rosenbergs were the last people executed for treason, right?" Berko said.

Elias shot him a warning look.

Jade stared at the ground, her feelings at war with each other. She had loved Dan almost like a father. But he had tried to shoot her little sister. He'd completely fooled her, and used her. She feared the anger and betrayal she felt would never go away.

JADE READ THE papers online every day, *The New York Times*, *The Washington Post*, the *Wall Street Journal*, scoured them for news about the coup plot, of worldwide arrests by Interpol and federal agencies. But there was nothing. She assumed the feds didn't want to incite panic—or to give foreign enemies any bright ideas. It was as if none of it had ever happened.

Jade obsessively trolled the Internet, looking for any conspiracy rumblings. She set up a Google alert if anything came up about suspicious power outages, but nothing unusual cropped up. As she searched one afternoon, a news item about Supreme Court Justice Ruth Bader Ginsburg popped up in Jade's newsfeed about her latest controversial remark, and Jade clicked on it.

A stock photo of the Justice ran atop the item and Jade stared at it. Her skin tingled. She ran to get the one photo of Olivia she had—the framed image of her with RBG. She set it next to her monitor. RBG wore the same black jacket in both images. The same green button earrings. The same pose, shaking someone's hand.

It was the identical photo.

Identical except for Olivia.

Jade took the back off the frame and removed Olivia's photo

and held it close to her face. The edges were pixelated. The shadows were wrong. Even the proportions were slightly off.

Olivia had Photoshopped herself into the picture.

But why?

Jade got goose bumps, which caused her healing gunshot wound to sting. She turned back to her computer and brought up the White Pages in her browser and searched David and Allison Harman in Manhattan, NY.

No listing.

Looked on the NYU website at the faculty listings. No Harmans.

She found five Olivia Harmans on Facebook, but none was her. Next she ran a Google search of Olivia Harman in Baltimore. At Johns Hopkins. In Maryland.

Olivia Harman, apparently, did not exist, and never had.

One of the FBI interrogators, Theresa Espinoza, left Jade with her business card, so Jade dialed her number. When she got on the line, Jade said, "I know this is going to sound weird, but I want to talk to you about Olivia."

She explained about the photo and her search for Olivia.

Theresa sighed. "It's true," she said. "We have no federal record of a woman named Olivia Harman. We went through her room and found no identification."

"But—"

"No Harman family with an adopted Chinese daughter in New York. No student enrolled at Johns Hopkins."

"But she was there," Jade said, her head buzzing, her eyes blurring.

Suddenly she remembered it was Olivia who'd suggested they search for personnel files on themselves on the Compound server.

Jade had told Olivia about the AIP.

And Olivia had told Dan about it.

"Did SiPraTech really have that kind of power, where they could just erase someone like that? Because Elias said the gunshot that killed her came from inside the fence."

"I assume that's true."

Jade didn't know what was real anymore, whether she could trust herself or her senses or her intellect. Jade saw Olivia being shot, clinging to the fence on an endless loop in her dreams and in her memory.

"And because she didn't exist," Theresa said, "she was expendable."

Special Agent Espinoza reasoned that Olivia had been a plant by SiPraTech. She'd been embedded with Jade, Elias, and Berko to guide things, to keep watch over them, to listen in on their conversations, to spy on them. And then when she was no longer useful, they shot her to scare the others into staying in the Compound.

Jade then remembered the night they'd attempted their escape. That Martin had given them the night off. As if he'd been the one to set up the escape attempt. To set up the shooting.

"But she went along with the escape attempt," Jade said. "And they shot her. They sacrificed her."

Even though Olivia had been part of the plot, Jade believed with her whole heart that Olivia had been her friend. Nobody was that good of an actor.

Except Dan.

Chapter 33

November 1

Tomorrow the family would leave on what would surely be their last trip together, to Washington, D.C., where Jade was invited to testify before a Congressional subcommittee on domestic cyber terrorism. But this morning, Jade sat in a lawn chair behind the house, its newly painted and repaired facade betraying little of the trauma it had suffered. The oaks and maples in the yard were at their autumnal peak, brilliant red and orange, and a hint of the coming winter's chill tinged the air. That chill made her gunshot wound ache, and she expected it always would. Through the open window in Clementine's rebuilt studio, Jade heard her sister's latest composition. It had a frantic tempo, full of minor chords and sharp percussion. Her musical representation of what she'd been through. That was how Clementine processed events and information.

In her hands, Jade held the three-terabyte external hard drive that stored the original code that eventually became the Clementine Program, thinking about its journey from humble beginnings to near apocalypse.

She could re-create it. It would take time, yes, but she'd put safeguards in place, and she'd figure out how to use it properly.

In her mind's eye, she watched Olivia die. Watched Elias get shot. Watched her house go up in flames.

She stared at the hard drive. This was power. It was control. It could mean great things.

Or horrible things.

She now grasped she was too selfish, too self-interested to be entrusted with this much power. But even more troubling—there was no telling in whose hands Clementine could wind up.

She remembered the expression on her sister's face when Jade had first decoded the tones for chocolate. The look of understanding, of being understood, for the first time in her life.

Jade carried the drive into her father's workshop. She turned it over in her hands, then put it on the floor and gazed at it.

She grabbed her father's sledgehammer, swung it over her head, and slammed it into the drive with all her strength.

Chapter 34

November 3, Washington, D.C.

JADE HADN'T BEEN to Washington since spring break her senior year of college, so she was excited to be back, and nervous about testifying before Congress. Pauline, now in a wheelchair, Robert, and Clementine all accompanied her so Pauline could see the Hope Diamond at the Smithsonian one more time. She'd talked of nothing else since the trip was planned. Actually she didn't say it—Jade had designed an app for her cell phone that said it for her. Her mother had always wished she was British royalty as a child, so Jade programmed the voice to have an English accent. The one remaining body part Pauline had control of was her right thumb, so she was still able to type in what she wanted to say.

This was Clem's first trip to D.C. Her therapist was confident she had made enough progress to handle the crowds and the sight-seeing, but Jade was still tense. Elias and Berko were both in town to testify alongside Jade. They'd all planned to meet in front of the Smithsonian Castle on the National Mall at eleven to have lunch with Harry Gilby at Au Bon Pain on L'Enfant Plaza before testifying. Robert and Pauline were still back at the hotel, but Clementine insisted on coming to lunch with her new friends Berko and Elias. Jade had persuaded her to wear a patchwork skirt instead of her nightgown, but she would not be deterred from wearing her fox-ear headband. At least her hair was clean and combed.

Foreign tourists crowded the mall, milling around, taking photos.

"Where are they?" Clementine said. "I'm hungry." She stood on tiptoe, trying to find the guys.

Jade kept turning and thought she caught glimpses of Berko or Elias everywhere she looked.

"Me too," Jade said, distracted, looking at her phone. She kept trying to call one or the other, but she couldn't get a signal.

Clementine bristled with nervous energy, restless and tense being in a crowd, and she rocked foot to foot and tried to keep her hands from flapping. Jade feared a meltdown was imminent unless Berko and Elias showed up very soon. She hoped she wouldn't have to restrain a screaming Clementine and watch the crowds stare on in horror, as if Jade were torturing Clem. Some things would never change.

"Put in your earbuds," Jade said. "Listen to some music." Clem was too wound up, so Jade reached in her pocket and removed her phone, navigated to Clem's favorite Tchaikovsky piece, and hit Play. She handed the earbuds to her sister, who slipped them into her ears and closed her eyes, her head thrown back, her mouth open, as if that would help let more music into her brain. Luckily people cleared a path.

Jade turned back to a khaki uniform coming toward them, and she couldn't help herself—she broke into a run and nearly knocked Elias down. His smile lit up his whole face as he held her away by the shoulders to look her up and down. Then he hugged her, and Jade surprised herself when her eyes teared up a little.

"That's pretty girly of you," Elias said, pulling out a handkerchief for her.

"Shut up," she said, wiping her eyes. He looked so handsome in his uniform.

"Have you seen Berko yet?" he asked.

"No," Jade said. "He's late."

She turned around to bring Clementine into the circle. She wasn't there.

Panic rose up in Jade's chest as she swiveled in a circle, trying to catch a glimpse of her sister.

"What's wrong?" Elias asked.

"Clementine," Jade said. "She was just right here." She looked frantically around, then pulled out her phone and dialed Clem's number, even though her sister never answered her phone.

"Which way did she go?" Elias asked, going into full search and rescue mode.

She couldn't have gotten far. Unless. Someone had taken her.

But Jade would have heard her scream. Wouldn't she? Or had she been too wrapped up in her tearful reunion to notice?

Clementine's phone rang endlessly in Jade's ear.

"She's wearing her fox-ear headband," Jade said.

Then she spotted her, far down Jefferson Drive, running and pointing.

"There she is," Jade said, and started running after her. Clem must have spotted Berko.

Mom and Dad were going to kill her.

Running in heels was difficult, and Jade's suit jacket was already wet at the armpits. She kept running into knots of people. Why did groups of six have to walk side by side?

"Excuse me," she said, trying to push through and keep her eye on her disappearing sister. "Clementine!" she shouted, but Clem probably still had her earbuds in, so she couldn't hear anyway. She was headed for 7th Street, and if she was chasing someone, there was no way she would pay any attention to the DON'T WALK sign, even if people were stopped at the crosswalk. Elias shot past Jade.

"Is that her?" he shouted as he went by.

"Yes," Jade said, terrified he would grab her and she'd lose it and the whole day would be ruined. Jade was even more afraid Clementine would get hit by a car. What had she seen? A cardinal? A multicolored scarf? What was it? It must have been completely compelling for her to run off alone like this.

"Clementine!" Jade screamed, and people turned to stare.

Elias got to her just before she stepped off the curb and spun her in Jade's direction so she could see her sister. Smart thinking. Clem's eyes were wide and distracted. "The hair," she said breathlessly. "The hair."

"The hair?" Jade said.

Clementine pointed across the street. "The hair!"

Jade's gaze followed the pointing finger.

"What is it?" Elias said, bent over and panting.

Walking away from them across 7th was a girl with bright blue hair, a similar shade to what Olivia's had been, and Jade's heart dropped. Clem thought she'd seen Olivia.

How would Jade explain it to her? An abstract concept like death was hard enough for a neurotypical, but for Clementine . . .

The blue-haired girl stopped. She turned to the left and reached into her purse, her profile vivid in the sunlight.

Elias gasped. "Jade," he whispered.

"I see her," she said.

The girl was Asian, and her face was remarkably familiar.

Elias hit the Walk button on the pole repeatedly. "Come on," he said to it. "Come on, come on."

"The hair!" Clementine said triumphantly.

Olivia's voice in Jade's mind, what she'd said just before she was shot: *It's going to be okay. Trust me. It's going to be fine. No matter what happens. You'll see.*

The street light changed to yellow and Elias grabbed both Veverkas' hands and pulled them out into the crosswalk. Horns honked.

They ran, threading through cars, heedless of the danger.

It couldn't be.

No matter what happens.

They made it to the other side, and Jade looked for the blue head of hair, right, left, straight ahead, but the girl had disappeared into the crowd.

Olivia was gone.

Acknowledgments

MORE THAN EVER, I'm grateful to the following people:

My amazing agent, Michelle Johnson of Inklings Literary Agency, who's a constant encouragement.

Chloe Moffett, my phenomenal Witness Impulse editor, for her discernment, uncommon sense, and instinct.

Sherri Brackney, for lending me her horse, Kodak, for this novel.

Members of the World's Greatest Critique Group, Because Magic, for the World's Greatest Brainstorming Session that resulted in this book: Lynn Bisesi, Deirdre Byerly, Claire Fishback, Marc Graham, Nicole Greene, Mike Haspil, Laura Main, and Chris Scena.

Henry Bradford, for the original artificial intelligence concept.

Kim Rasmussen, for allowing me to co-opt her family name for our heroine, Jade.

Michael Gallup, for the refrigerator repairman.

Zak Wool, for his peerless nerd reference expertise.

Rob Stormes, for his idiosyncratic computer science acumen.

Chloe Hawker, for her editing skills, wit and wisdom as my cohost on The Lively Grind Café, and robust and unapologetic nerdiness.

Layla Hawker, for allowing me to share her experiences and struggles with autism.

And as always, my rock, my roll, my knight in tarnished armor, Andy Hawker, my perfect partner in life, crime, and backyard brainstorming.

Want more suspense from LS Hawker?
Keep reading for an excerpt from her debut thriller,
the story of a young woman on the run for her
future . . .
from the nightmares of her past:

THE DROWNING GAME

Available now wherever ebooks are sold!

An Excerpt from

THE DROWNING GAME

SIRENS AND THE scent of strange men drove Sarx and Tesla into a frenzy of barking and pacing as they tried to keep the intruders off our property without the aid of a fence. Two police cars, a fire truck, and an ambulance were parked on the other side of the dirt road. The huddled cops and firemen kept looking at the house.

Dad's iPhone rang and went on ringing. I couldn't make myself answer it. I knew it was the cops outside calling to get me to open the front door, but asking me to allow a group of strangers inside seemed like asking a pig to fly a jet. I had no training or experience to guide me. I longed to get the AK-47 out of the basement gun safe, even though it would be me against a half-dozen trained law men.

"Petty Moshen." An electric megaphone amplified the man's voice outside.

The dogs howled at the sound of it, intensifying further the tremor that possessed my entire body. I hadn't shaken like this since the night Dad left me out on the prairie in a whiteout blizzard to hone my sense of direction.

"Petty, call off the dogs."

I couldn't do it.

"I'm going to dial up your father's cell phone again, and I want you to answer it."

Closing my eyes, I concentrated, imagining those words coming out of my dad's mouth, in his voice. The iPhone vibrated. I pretended it was my dad, picked it up, hit the answer button and pressed it to my ear.

"This is Sheriff Bloch," said the man on the other end of the phone. "We have to come in and talk to you about your dad."

I cleared my throat again. "I need to do something first," I said, and thumbed the end button. I headed down to the basement.

Downstairs, I got on the treadmill, cranked up the speed to ten miles an hour and ran for five minutes, flat-out, balls to the wall. This is what Detective Deirdre Walsh, my favorite character on TV's *Offender NYC*, always did when emotions overwhelmed her. No one besides me and my dad had ever come into our house before, so I needed to steady myself.

I jumped off and took the stairs two at a time, breathing hard, sweating, my legs burning, but steadier. I popped a stick of peppermint gum in my mouth. Then I walked straight to the front door the way Detective Walsh would—fearlessly, in charge, all business. I flung the door open and shouted, "Sarx! Tesla! Off! Come!"

They both immediately glanced over their shoulders and came loping toward me. I noticed another vehicle had joined the gauntlet on the other side of the road, a brand-new tricked-out red

Dodge Ram 4x4 pickup truck. Randy King, wearing a buff-colored Stetson, plaid shirt, Lee's, and cowboy boots, leaned against it. All I could see of his face was a black walrus mustache. He was the man my dad had instructed me to call if anything ever happened to him. I'd seen Randy only a couple of times but never actually talked to him until today.

The dogs sat in front of me, panting, worried, whimpering. I reached down and scratched their ears, thankful that Dad had trained them like he had. I straightened and led them to the one-car garage attached to the left side of the house. They sat again as I raised the door and signaled them inside. They did not like this one bit—they whined and jittered—but they obeyed my command to stay. I lowered the door and turned to face the invasion.

As if I'd disabled an invisible force field, all the men came forward at once: the paramedics and firemen carrying their gear boxes, the cops' hands hovering over their sidearms. I couldn't look any of them in the eye, but I felt them staring at me as if I were an exotic zoo animal or a serial killer.

The man who had to be the sheriff walked right up to me, and I stepped back palming the blade I keep clipped to my bra at all times. I knew it was unwise to reach into my hoodie, even just to touch the Baby Glock in my shoulder holster.

"Petty?" he said.

"Yes sir," I said, keeping my eyes on the clump of yellow, poisonous prairie ragwort at my feet.

"I'm Sheriff Bloch. Would you show us in, please?"

"Yes sir," I said, turning and walking up the front steps. I pushed open the screen and went in, standing aside to let in the phalanx of strange men. My breathing got shallow and the shaking started up. My heart beat so hard I could feel it in my face, and the bump on my left shoulder—scar tissue from a childhood injury—itched like crazy. It always did when I was nervous.

The EMTs came in after the sheriff.

"Where is he?" one of them asked. I pointed behind me to the right, up the stairs. They trooped up there carrying their cases. The house felt too tight, as if there wasn't enough air for all these people.

Sheriff Bloch and a deputy walked into the living room. Both of them turned, looking around the room, empty except for the grandfather clock in the corner. The old thing had quit working many years before, so it was always three-seventeen in this house.

"Are you moving out?" the deputy asked.

"No," I said, and then realized why he'd asked. All of our furniture is crowded in the center of each room, away from the windows.

Deputy and sheriff glanced at each other. The deputy walked to one of the front windows and peered out through the bars.

"Is that bulletproof glass?" he asked me.

"Yes sir."

They glanced at each other again.

"Have anyplace we can sit?" Sheriff Bloch said.

I walked into our TV room, the house's original dining room, and they followed. I sat on the couch, which gave off dust and a minor-chord spring squeak. I pulled my feet up and hugged my knees.

"This is Deputy Hencke."

The deputy held out his hand toward me. I didn't take it, and after a beat he let it drop.

"I'm very sorry for your loss," he said. He had a blond crew cut and the dark blue uniform.

He went to sit on Dad's recliner, and it happened in slow motion, like watching a knife sink into my stomach with no way to stop it.

"No!" I shouted.

Nobody but Dad had ever sat in that chair. It was one thing to let these people inside the house. It was another to allow them to do whatever they wanted.

He looked around and then at me, his face a mask of confusion. "What? I'm—I was just going to sit—"

"Get a chair out of the kitchen," Sheriff Bloch said.

The deputy pulled one of the aqua vinyl chairs into the TV room. His hands shook as he tried to write on his little report pad. He must have been as rattled by my outburst as I was.

"Spell your last name for me?"

"M-O-S-H-E-N," I said.

"Born here?"

"No," I said. "We're from Detroit originally."

His face scrunched and he glanced up.

"How'd you end up here? You got family in the area?"

I shook my head. I didn't tell him Dad had moved us to Saw Pole, Kansas, because he said he'd always wanted to be a farmer. In Saw Pole, he farmed a sticker patch and raised horse flies but not much else.

"How old are you?"

"Twenty-one."

He lowered his pencil. "Did you go to school in Niobe? I don't ever remember seeing you."

"Dad homeschooled me," I said.

"What time did you discover the—your dad?" The deputy's scalp grew pinker. He needed to grow his hair out some to hide his tell a little better.

"The dogs started barking about two—"

"Two a.m. or p.m.?"

"p.m.," I said. "At approximately two-fifteen p.m. our dogs began barking at the back door. I responded and found no evidence of attempted B and E at either entry point to the domicile. I retrieved my Winchester rifle from the basement gun safe with the intention of walking the perimeter of the property, but the dogs refused to follow. I came to the conclusion that the disturbance was inside the house, and I continued my investigation on the second floor."

Deputy Hencke's pencil was frozen in the air, a frown on his face. "Why are you talking like that?"

"Like what?"

"Usually I ask questions and people answer them."

"I'm telling you what happened."

"Could you do it in regular English?"

I didn't know what to say, so I didn't say anything.

"Look," he said. "Just answer the questions."

"Okay."

"All right. So where was your dad?"

"After breakfast this morning he said he didn't feel good so he went up to his bedroom to lie down," I said.

All day I'd expected Dad to call out for something to eat, but he never did. So I didn't check on him because it was nice not having to cook him lunch or dinner or fetch him beers. I'd kept craning my neck all day to get a view of the stairs, kept waiting for Dad to sneak up on me, catch me watching forbidden TV shows. I turned the volume down so I'd hear if he came down the creaky old stairs.

"So the dogs' barking is what finally made you go up to his bedroom, huh?"

I nodded.

"Those dogs wanted to tear us all to pieces," the deputy said, swiping his hand back and forth across the top of his crew cut.

I'd always wanted a little lapdog, one I could cuddle, but Dad favored the big breeds. Sarx was a German shepherd and Tesla a rottweiler.

The deputy bent his head to his pad. "What do you think they were barking about?"

"They smelled it," I said.

He looked up. "Smelled what?"

"Death. Next I knocked on the decedent's— I mean, Dad's— bedroom door to request permission to enter."

"So you went in his room," the deputy said, his pencil hovering above the paper.

"Once I determined he was unable to answer, I went in his room. He was lying on his stomach, on top of the covers, facing away from me, and—he had shorts on . . . you know how hot it's been, and he doesn't like to turn on the window air conditioner until after Memorial Day—and I looked at his legs and I thought, 'He's got some kind of rash. I better bring him the calamine lotion,' but then I remembered learning about libidity on TV, and—"

"Lividity," he said.

"What?"

"It's lividity, not libidity, when the blood settles to the lowest part of the body."

"Guess I've never seen it written down."

"So what did you do then?"

"It was then that I . . ."

I couldn't finish the sentence. Up until now, the shock of finding Dad's body and the terror of letting people in the house had blotted out everything else. But now, the reality that Dad was dead came crashing down on me, making my eyes sting. I recognized the feeling from a long time ago. I was going to cry, and I couldn't decide whether I was sad that Dad was gone or elated that I was finally going to be free. Free to live the normal life I'd always dreamed of.

But I couldn't cry, not in front of these strangers, couldn't show weakness. Weakness was dangerous. I thought of Deirdre Walsh again and remembered what she always did when she was in danger of crying. I cleared my throat.

"It was then that I determined that he was deceased. I estimated the time of death, based on the stage of rigor, to be around ten a.m. this morning, so I did not attempt to resuscitate him," I said, remembering Dad's cool, waxy dead skin under my hand. "Subsequently I retrieved his cell phone off his nightstand and called Mr. King."

"Randy King?"

I nodded.

"Why didn't you call 911?"

"Because Dad told me to call Mr. King if something ever happened to him."

The deputy stared at me like I'd admitted to murder. Then he looked away and stood.

"I think the coroner is almost done, but he'll want to talk to you."

While I waited, I huddled on the couch, thinking about how my life was going to change. I'd have to buy groceries and pay bills and taxes and do all the things Dad had never taught me how to do.

The coroner appeared in the doorway. "Miss Moshen?" He was a large zero-shaped man in a cardigan.

"Yes?"

He sat on the kitchen chair the deputy had vacated.

"I need to ask you a couple of questions," he said.

"Okay," I said. I was wary. The deputy had been slight and small, and even though he'd had a sidearm, I could have taken him if I'd needed to. I didn't know about the coroner, he was so heavy and large.

"Can you tell me what happened?"

I began to repeat my account, but the coroner interrupted me. "You're not testifying at trial," he said. "Just tell me what happened."

I tried to do as he asked, but I wasn't sure how to say it so he wouldn't be annoyed.

"Did your dad complain of chest pains, jaw pain? Did his left arm hurt?"

I shook my head. "Just said he didn't feel good. Like he had the flu."

"Did your dad have high cholesterol? High blood pressure?"

"I don't know."

"When was the last time he saw a doctor?" the coroner asked.

"He didn't believe in doctors."

"Your dad was only fifty-one, so I'll have to schedule an autopsy, even though it was probably a heart attack. We'll run a toxicology panel, which'll take about four weeks because we have to send it to the lab in Topeka."

The blood drained from my face. "Toxicology?" I said. "Why?"

"It's standard procedure," he said.

"I'm pretty sure my dad wouldn't want an autopsy."

"Don't worry," he said. "You can bury him before the panel comes back."

"No, I mean Dad wouldn't want someone cutting him up like that."

"It's state law."

"Please," I said.

His eyes narrowed as they focused on me. Then he stood.

"After the autopsy, where would you like the remains sent?"

"Holt Mortuary in Niobe," a voice from the living room said.

I rose from the couch to see who'd said it. Randy King stood with his back to the wall, his Stetson low over his eyes.

The coroner glanced at me for confirmation.

"I'm the executor of Mr. Moshen's will," Randy said. He raised his head and I saw his eyes, light blue with tiny pupils that seemed to bore clear through to the back of my head.

I shrugged at the coroner.

"Would you like to say goodbye to your father before we transport him to the morgue?" he said.

I nodded and followed him to the stairs, where he stood aside. "After you," he said.

"No," I said. "You first."

Dad had taught me never to go in a door first and never to let anyone walk behind me. The coroner frowned but mounted the stairs.

Upstairs, Dad's room was the first one on the left. The coroner stood outside the door. He reached out to touch my arm and I took a step backward. He dropped his hand to his side.

"Miss Moshen," he said in a hushed voice. "Your father looks different from when he was alive. It might be a bit of a shock. No one would blame you if you didn't—"

I walked into Dad's room, taking with me everything I knew from all the cop shows I'd watched. But I was not prepared at all for what I saw.

Since he'd died on his stomach, the EMTs had turned Dad onto his back. He was in full rigor mortis, so his upper lip was mashed into his gums and curled into a sneer, exposing his khaki-colored teeth. His hands were spread in front of his face, palms out. Dad's eyes stared up and to the left and his entire face was grape-pop purple.

What struck me when I first saw him—after I inhaled my gum—was that he appeared to be warding off a demon. I should have waited until the mortician was done with him, because I knew I'd never get that image out of my mind.

I walked out of Dad's room on unsteady feet, determined not to cry in front of these strangers. The deputy and the sheriff stood outside my bedroom, examining the door to it. Both of them looked confused.

"Petty," Sheriff Bloch said.

I stopped in the hall, feeling even more violated with them so close to my personal items and underwear.

"Yes?"

"Is this your bedroom?"

I nodded.

Sheriff and deputy made eye contact. The coroner paused at

the top of the stairs to listen in. This was what my dad had always talked about—the judgment of busybody outsiders, their belief that somehow they needed to have a say in the lives of people they'd never even met and knew nothing about.

The three men seemed to expect me to say something, but I was tired of talking. Since I'd never done much of it, I'd had no idea how exhausting it was.

The deputy said, "Why are there six dead bolts on the outside of your door?"

It was none of his business, but I had nothing to be ashamed of. "So Dad could lock me in, of course."

About the Author

LS HAWKER grew up in suburban Denver, indulging her worrisome obsession with true-crime books, and writing stories about anthropomorphic fruit and juvenile delinquents. She wrote her first novel at fourteen.

Armed with a BS in journalism from the University of Kansas, she had a radio show called *People Are So Stupid*, edited a trade magazine, and worked as a traveling Kmart portrait photographer, but never lost her passion for fiction writing.

She's got a hilarious, supportive husband, two brilliant daughters, and a massive music collection. She lives in Colorado but considers Kansas her spiritual homeland. She is the author of *The Drowning Game*, a *USA Today* bestseller, and *Body and Bone*. Visit her website at LSHawker.com.

Discover great authors, exclusive offers, and more at hc.com.